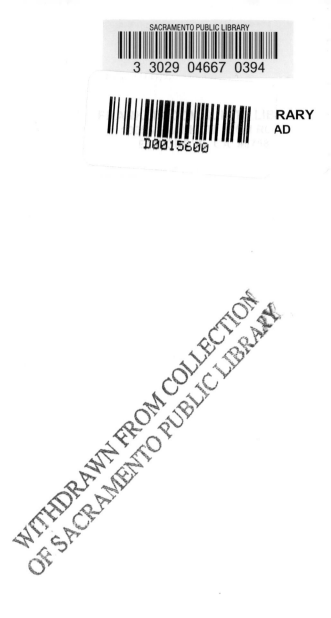

# LAY THAT TRUMPET
# IN OUR HANDS

*Bantam Books*

New York   Toronto   London   Sydney   Auckland

# LAY THAT TRUMPET
# IN OUR HANDS

Susan Carol McCarthy

LAY THAT TRUMPET IN OUR HANDS

A Bantam Book / February 2002

Book design by Laurie Jewell

Library of Congress Cataloging-in-Publication Data

McCarthy, Susan Carol.
    Lay that trumpet in our hands / Susan Carol McCarthy.
        p. cm.
    ISBN 0-553-80169-4
    1. Girls—Fiction. 2. Florida—Fiction. 3. Race relations—Fiction.
4. African Americans—Fiction. 5. Ku Klux Klan (1915–)—Fiction. I. Title.
PS3613.C35 L39 2002
813'.6—dc21                                              2001043155

*Published simultaneously in the United States and Canada*

Bantam Books are published by Bantam Books, a division of Random
House, Inc. Its trademark, consisting of the words "Bantam Books"
and the portrayal of a rooster, is Registered in U.S. Patent and
Trademark Office and in other countries. Marca Registrada.
Bantam Books, 1540 Broadway, New York, New York 10036.

PRINTED IN THE UNITED STATES OF AMERICA
BVG    10   9   8   7   6   5   4   3   2   1

*For Dad, Mother and Gam.*
*And for all the others whose*
*time in the fire was Florida*
*in the early '50s.*

Most of the Southern Belle states chose their widest, wildest rivers and seduced them into hardworking husbandry. In Big Delta marriages that still prosper, Mississippi claimed her namesake, Alabama her Mobile, and Georgia her Savannah. But Florida—skinny, flat-chested baby sister to the Belles—had slimmer prospects. Rejecting old Suwannee, Florida chose the Orange Blossom Trail, not a river at all but a slick 600-mile highway that knew how to dance.

The Orange Blossom Trail, also called Route 441, snake-charmed poor Florida, from her redheaded Georgia border through the skinny, sink-holed waist of the state to the wild abandon of her southern tip. While romancing her with dreamy visions of life in paradise, the Trail openly auctioned Florida's best beaches to the highest Yankee bidders. Later on, in a scandalous orgy of profit-taking, her lesser parts were tendered, cheaply, placing liberal Northerners, Orthodox Jews and devout Catholics cheek-by-jowl amongst the grandchildren of Confederate aristocrats, raging Crackers, and dirt-poor blacks who sought work wherever they could. "It's the social equivalent of a Molotov cocktail," my father liked to say.

In the spring of 1951, that cocktail combusted, blowing the roof off our state for nine nightmarish months. What happened is historical fact, and, now that the State Attorney has unsealed the Grand Jury documents, public record:

Florida's Klansmen, who for twenty years had confined their activities to assault and battery of adulterers and the occasional cross-burning, turned murderous. In March of 1951 they grabbed, stabbed and shot nineteen-year-old Negro citrus picker Marvin Cully. Then, in a high-speed chase down the Trail to the Orlando airport, they attempted to abduct N.A.A.C.P. Attorney Thurgood Marshall (future Supreme Court Justice Marshall). Later, with little attention and no intervention from law enforcement, Klansmen blew the hell out of the Carver Village Housing Project for Negroes with two 100-pound bundles of dynamite, set off blasts at the Coral Gables Jewish Center, the Hebrew School, and several Catholic churches. The horror seemed endless until finally the brutal double murder, by dynamite, on Christmas night got the attention of President Harry Truman, vacationing in Key West.

To this day, my family is in disagreement as to precisely when the nightmare began. For me, it was the morning Daddy and Luther discovered Marvin, beaten, shot and dying in the Klan's stomping grounds off Round Lake Road. My brother Ren disagrees. He points to the small cluster of scars that begin just a hair outside his left eye and trail horizontally across his temple to the top of his ear. Ren claims it started when the men in white robes took the unprecedented step of shooting at two white children. Mother and Daddy shake their heads. In their minds, the real beginning was much earlier when, as brash young newlyweds on a Florida honeymoon, they let a fast-talking agent entice them into twenty-seven acres of "prime grove land in the charming town of Mayflower."

It was afterwards that our family, the only Northerners left by then, and our circle of secret friends contrived the showdown between Mr. Hoover's F.B.I. and the central Florida K.K.K. *When* it all began and *why* remains debatable. So much lies buried with Marvin and the others and with their white-robed killers. In the end, all we have, all we can take refuge in, is *how*, for each of us, one thing led to quite another.

## Chapter 1

L uther's on the back porch knocking on the door. Inside my cocoon of bedcovers, first thoughts, like moths, flutter. Temperature's dropped and the men have come to work the smudge pots. I see them in my mind, dark, bundled bodies shuffling, soft calls anticipating the all-night battle against a freeze, gloved hands passing shiny thermoses filled with fresh, hot coffee, maybe something stronger. No, no, the dusky wings whisper: winter's gone, the trees long into bloom, new fruit already the size of sweet peas. I wake with a start. *What is Luther doing here, now?*

There it is again, his distinctive *tappety-tap-TAP*. Across the hall, Mother and Daddy's voices arc in surprise, recognition, then concern. Daddy's feet hit the floor. I hear him yank on pants, belt buckle jangling, jerk open their door, and stride to the back. In my room Buddy's tags jingle at the window, nose pressed against the screen, tail gently slapping wood. I slip down beside him as, suddenly, the porch light slants across the tangerine tree outside my window. A breeze carries the scent of blossoms and the sound of voices into my room.

"Good Lord, Luther, what is it?" Daddy asks.

"It's Marvin, Mist'Warren. He ain't come home. Armetta's about worried herself to *death*. The boy went out 'round eight, telling his mamma he'd be back 'fore midnight. Ah been looking for him since one. Run into Jimmy Lee just now, swears he saw Klanners cruising the Trail where Marvin's s'posed to be."

"The Klan? Where on the Trail?"

"Joe's Jook, up to Wellwood. Marvin's sweet on one of them girls up there."

"Marvin had any run-ins with the Klan?"

"Nawser, but the girl say he left 'round 'leven."

"What do you think?"

"Ah'm hoping we could check on Mistuh Myer's Valencia grove this morning, drive slow-like past Round Lake, take a look."

"Come on in. I need to get my shoes on and some coffee."

Opening my door, I see Mother, a blur of dark curls and blue robe, flash through the hall and into the dining room. Buddy and I trail her into the kitchen.

Luther's at the table, chair nearest the door, staring down into the frayed innards of his field cap. Daddy's at the stove fumbling with the coffeepot. Mother moves to help him. Touching her elbow in thanks, he turns to retrieve his work boots from the porch.

"Sorry to bother you, MizLizbeth," Luther says to Mother's back. "Hey, Roo," he says to me, abbreviating his usual greeting. Everything about him, normally cola-colored, is gray-cast: his eyes glow darkly in ashy nests of wrinkles; a frost of unshaved stubble smudges his chin; his clothes, usually pressed and proper, hang loose and rumpled. Buddy pads over to him, tail wig-wagging, and rests his muzzle on Luther's knee.

"Luther and I need to take a drive, honey," Daddy says low-voiced to Mother. "Marvin's missing and it's cruise night on the Trail."

"But, Marvin's *not* . . ." Her eyes zigzag between the two men.

"Thought we'd check on Myer's Valencias, swing by Round Lake," Daddy says calmly, talking code in front of me.

"Can I go?" I ask.

"ReesaRoo, we don't know what's out there." Daddy lifts a booted foot onto the side bench, tying leather laces. "Besides, aren't you supposed to be watching for the DeSoto? She's due in today and your mother says her room's not ready." *Thrust and parry, Daddy's a master at it.*

"Your mamma comin' in today?" Luther asks, his smile showing a glint of the 24-karat canine Marvin calls his "golden dog."

"Yep, we get her for Easter this year," Daddy replies, tying the other boot.

"She *some*thin', Miz Doto is. And Ah *love* that car!"

"Fits her perfectly, doesn't it?" Daddy says, shrugging into his jacket.

My grandmother's DeLuxe, drive-without-shifting, custom DeSoto coupe is the source of our family's nickname for her. Once, when I was two or three, I answered my parents' request to "watch for the DeSoto" with an eager "Here comes Doto!" and the name stuck.

"Coffee's ready, sugar's on the table." Mother lays spoons and two steaming mugs in front of them. "Get you anything else?"

Luther's eyes thank Mother for her kindness, then dart to Daddy's.

"I think we'd best get going, honey," Daddy answers, not sitting, swigging coffee deeply.

Luther stands, visibly relieved, and ducks out the door, tossing "See y'all later" over his shoulder.

Daddy throws his good arm around Mother and pulls her to the barrel of his chest. "Warren, take Buddy with you," I hear her urge in a whisper.

"Don't worry, Lizbeth," he replies with a kiss. "Bye, Roo, don't forget the hospital corners on Doto's bed. Here, boy!" As the shepherd jingles after him, I see Mother check the time on the kitchen clock.

"*Where* on Round Lake?" I want to know.

"Reesa," she sighs, clearly unsure how much she wants to tell, "there's been talk about a lemon grove, one of Mr. Casselton's, but . . ."

*Mr. Casselton.* In our county, where local boosters declare citrus is king, Emmett Casselton, owner of the sprawling Casbah Groves, considers himself the area's crown prince. In our house, where the only thing worse than an "arrogant son of a bitch" is an "ignorant damn Cracker," Emmett Casselton is both.

"You mean the Klan's taken Marvin to the Casbah?" My voice, my whole throat quivers on the phrase favored by local biddies, black and white, to reel in wayward children . . . "You better be good," they warn, "or the Klan'll take you to the Casbah!" I never understood it, never connected it to Emmett Casselton's vast acreage—until now.

"I don't know, Reesa. I doubt it. I *do* know, however," Mother says, retreating behind her Poker Face, "in the time it'll take me to fix breakfast, you can finish your grandmother's bed. Go on now. I'll call you when it's ready." Gentle hands turn me toward the door.

The window at the top of the stairwell glows oddly orange; daybreak's flaming the treetops of the back grove. *Marvin, where are you?*

Both my younger brothers lay sound asleep in Mitchell's room. I switch on the light in Ren's room opposite, its windows facing west and the driveway. *Daddy and Luther should just about be there by now.*

Ren's mattress is bare, except for the tidy stack of Doto's pink sheets. During the nine months she's elsewhere, our grandmother's sheets, two sets of them, sit folded in the upstairs linen closet. The sheets are from downtown Chicago's Carter-Ferris-Mott store. "I can't sleep on *any*thing else," I heard Doto tell Mrs. Ruth Ferris at last year's Florida Party at the big Ferris house south of town. From there, she launched into "My aunt Ethel was a Carter, of the Cape Cod Carters; I'm sure we're related to your father-in-law's partner." *If he's in that lemon grove, Buddy will find him.*

Southerners set great store by their ancestry, but it's a rare Rebel who can go toe-to-toe with my Yankee grandmother and win. Doto dotes on her lineage the way other old ladies delight in dahlias or Staffordshire teacups. Given half a chance, she blatantly brags she named Daddy, her firstborn, for "Richard Warren of the *Mayflower*"; her daughter Eleanor for "the wife of William the Conqueror" and Uncle Harry for "the Revolutionary War hero General Light-Horse Harry Lee, of the New York Lees, not those people in Virginia."

*Shouldn't they be back by now?*

Stuffing and fluffing Doto's pillows, I hear, *finally*, the roar of the truck engine, Buddy's barking and the urgent blast of Daddy's horn. I run to the open window and yell, "Daddy, what's wrong?"

He jumps out onto the driveway and shouts, "Roo, get your mother. We need blankets, towels—quick!"

Hurtling down the steps two, three at a time, I nearly crash into her, arms full of linens from the downstairs closet. Together, we race out of the house to the truck.

Luther's on his knees in the back. Daddy grabs towels and blankets, yells "Stand back now!" and springs to the side-board, bending low. A raggedy moan rises from the shadows of the truck bed. Mother steps forward to peer over the side and, with a sharp gasp, spreads her arms like wings and folds them backwards, trapping me behind her. I wiggle away and dash to the tailgate. Jumping up on the back bumper, I see with a shock the blood-covered body in the back.

Marvin Cully, who I've known all my life, who taught me to pick tangelos without ripping the fruit cap, who showed me the secret of steering a go-cart, who started the game of rhyming my name, lies drenched in blood in the bed of my father's truck. His head and eyes are covered with something, a familiar fabric, one of Ren's striped T-shirts, turned into a terrible blood-soaked turban. Bright red, dark brown, dried black blood is everywhere: congealing in cuts on his jaw and neck, seeping through rips in his shirt and pantlegs, oozing out of scrapes on the tops of his bare feet. "Marvin! You all *right?*" I cry as the sickening sweet smell heaves my stomach into my throat. His lips, bleeding in a bright red trickle onto his chin, don't move, can't answer.

"G'wan now, Roo!" Luther yells in a garbled plea, replacing a stained picking sack with a soft towel under Marvin's head.

"Lizbeth!" Daddy barks, settling blankets over Marvin's chest.

Mother's hands, like claws, yank me down, turn me around, clutch me to her chest. "No, Roo, no!" she cries, walking stiffly backward toward the house. Her heart, like mine, drums in my ear.

"Lizbeth, call Doc Johnny! Tell him we have a bad case of Klan fever, *really* bad! We'll be at his back door in ten minutes. Okay?"

"Okay," Mother says, steering us onto the walk. "Go!"

"Damn them," Daddy swears. "Damn those damn Crackers to hell!"

The truck engine growls and jerks into reverse down the driveway. As the front porch door slams behind us, two figures float in the bright sunlight now filling the stairwell. "Mother?" the boys call, sleepily scratching themselves.

"Ren, take Mitchell into the kitchen," she commands, waving them off to the back. She reaches for the phone to dial Doc Johnny and as she does so, lets me go. At my side, a dark, damp nose sniffs its concern; I feel myself sinking, sobbing into the furry softness of Buddy's neck.

*Chapter 2*

Our house is old, "turn of the century," my parents say. "New England saltbox in a Miss Scarlett petticoat," Doto always calls it, meaning the wide screened porches that flounce around the ground floor with the kitchen, like a bustle, in the back. When my parents bought it from old Mr. Swann, the house had two big bedrooms upstairs but, after Mitchell was born, they converted the broad side porch into a downstairs bedroom for themselves, with a smaller one in the back for me.

After Mr. Swann sold it to them, he just walked out, leaving his linens, china, dining room table, his piano in the living room—everything but his clothes—behind. Said he wouldn't need them where he was going. As it turned out, Daddy says, that piano was a lifesaver. When Daddy caught the polio, the summer I was born, playing the piano helped him regain the use of his right hand and most of his right arm. It also kept him from going nuts, he says. Still does.

Daddy glances at me when I enter the living room, but keeps on playing, nodding his okay to join him on the bench. He's dressed for the funeral in white shirt and dark tie; his suit coat hangs off the mantel, like a strange, coal-colored Christmas stocking.

Strangeness has descended on our house like a winter fog bank, blurring the lines between the last few days: *Marvin's dead, gone forever,* the words singsong in my head trying to convince my heart they're true; Doto here, finding everything in an uproar; Doc Johnny unable, or unwilling, to state the cause of death; Constable Watts shrugging it off as a jook-joint fight, stopping just short of calling Daddy a liar about Round Lake Road. "Besides," the string-bean Cracker laughed, tall and rangy in his constable uniform, "everybody knows the Opalakee Klan don't kill niggers like they *use* to." Daddy came home fuming. "In the old days," he told us, meaning before the polio, "lawman or not, I'd have pretzeled that peckerwood." Before I was born, they say, my father had a torrential temper, huge as a hurricane, fast and physical. But the polio, he says, taught him patience. The man I know is more circumspect, with a temper that veers toward geological. When Daddy's upset, he turns to stone, granite-faced, flinty-eyed. Now, he sits rock-like at the piano, a one-man Mount Rushmore, fingering his thoughts.

The song "I am a poor wayfaring stranger" is one of the saddest in the Mayflower Baptist hymnal. We'll sing it on Palm Sunday, the week before we sing the happiest song, "Up from the grave He arose, with a mighty triumph o'er His foes."

"Daddy," I ask him, "is it true, what Doto says about Richard Warren being called the Stranger?"

"Yes, honey. On the *Mayflower,* the Pilgrims were the Saints and they called the people like Richard Warren, whose company was paying for the voyage, the Strangers."

"When we studied them last fall, Mrs. Beacham said she never heard of such a thing."

"True story, Roo," Daddy says, fingertips teasing out the chorus.

"Doto says she's afraid she jinxed you by naming you after him."

"Maybe so, Roo. Sometimes I know exactly how he felt."

"Will the funeral last long?"

"Several hours, I guess. There's the service and the burial, then the gathering at Luther and Armetta's. Afterwards, there's a meeting with Reverend Stone and some elders."

"What about?"

"Options, Rooster."

"You mean about finding out who killed Marvin?"

"The Klan killed Marvin, Roo. The question is why. And what's to be done about it."

"But you've always said the Klan was nothing to be afraid of, just a bunch of good ol' boys playing boogey-man."

Daddy lifts his hands off the keyboard and drops them in a ball in his lap. His back, ramrod straight when he plays, curls forward, shoulders falling. The right one, his "polio shoulder," dips lower than the left. His chin juts forward in a craggy outcrop.

"Like Doto says, we are strangers in a strange land. The Klan's been around here for years—stupid stuff mostly, burning crosses, pestering couples parking in the dark, picking on Negroes they thought were getting uppity, whatever that means. But this week, they crossed the line."

"But May Carol's Daddy's in the Klan. May Carol says it's nothing but a card club, an excuse to play poker. And, Armetta works for them in their house!"

"Lord, Roo, it's a complicated mess," he says, straightening up again, chest expanding, blue eyes blazing. "I wish we'd known more about it before we bought all this property and—"

"Warren?"

Mother's voice, the scent of her shiny, shampooed hair and the unzipped back of her black dress hush him. Daddy stands to help her. She turns with a murmured thanks, lifting a handful of dark curls off her neck. Normally playful and softly pretty, Mother's face looks stiff and drawn today, like she's steeling herself to get through these hours.

"Roo, make sure you finish up the breakfast dishes before Doto does," she says. Then, leaning forward, with a glance upstairs and a flash of dimple, she whispers, "If she starts putting things away, it could easily turn into a 'let's clean out the cupboards' project."

"Okay," I say, grateful for the reminder.

Doto is the queen of clean. Since arriving on Thursday, she's been "spot cleaning," a corner here, a closet there, all in the name of "helping your mother out." Mother's handled this with distracted grace, thankful for the help. Daddy's accused Doto of marking her territory, like a dog does its yard.

"We should be going, don't you think?" Mother says, checking her wristwatch.

"Yep," he says as he grabs his coat and strides to the stairwell. "We're leaving, Doto. Bye, Ren, Mitchell," he calls in the direction of the boys' upstairs whining. "I'm sure those kids have the cleanest ears in town by now," he tells us. A wide, roguish grin gleams suddenly, whitely against his tanned face.

"You look like a pirate," Doto told him the other day, stepping regally out of her new DeSoto.

"At your service, m'lady," Daddy had laughed, extending his hand, bending in a low Errol Flynn-like bow.

They make a handsome couple, I think, as my parents cross the front porch and turn to call, "Bye, Reesa. Be good."

Ears scrubbed, breakfast dishes stowed, porches swept, my brothers and I gather at the kitchen table with our grandmother, who's investigating her wallet for "cash on hand."

"Now, about lunch," Doto says. "I'm thinking clam chowder might hit the spot. What do you all think?" We all know that the only place for miles around that serves such a thing is the Lakeview Inn in Mount Laura, which means huge hot fudge sundaes for everyone.

"Sure! You bet!" we say, delivering the response she's after.

"Let's take a little drive then, shall we?"

We pile into the big DeSoto, the boys sinking into the white leather back seat, inhaling greedily the smell of new car.

Doto fits her DeSoto like candy in a wrapper. This one, a special order, is Mediterranean blue, which looks like turquoise to me, white interior, and chrome everywhere. Doto's glasses are cat-eyed in a shape almost identical to the DeSoto's taillights; her hair, permed and combed in twin side waves, reminds me of the car's back fins. Between us, in the front, is her brown leather map box, containing the Triple A's most up-to-date routing from her home outside Chicago to Mayflower, Florida; Mayflower to Bozeman, Montana (Uncle Harry's home); Bozeman to Baltimore (where Aunt Eleanor lives) and back again to La Grange, Illinois.

The DeSoto's engine purrs like a happy cat as Doto backs

carefully out of our driveway and noses north to the crossroad off Old Dixie Highway, then onto the Orange Blossom Trail. Unlike the larger towns of Opalakee south of us and Mount Laura to the north, Mayflower is little more than a place where the Trail picks up a couple side streets, Old Dixie on the east side and Citrus on the west. Dead center, where most places have a courthouse or a city hall, stands the Mayflower Citrus processing plant, Emmett Casselton's giant co-op, turning most of the local fruit into trainloads of frozen Jiffy Girl juice concentrate.

Across the street, "like a wart on old Emmett's nose," Daddy says, is our family's small, fancy-fruit packinghouse. "Independent Grower—Packer—Shipper" it says on tall billboards facing the traffic both ways. Passing by in the DeSoto, we see the signs Mother and Daddy put out on their way to Marvin's funeral. "Closed for the Day" they say, blocking both entrances to the gravel parking lot. Beside the packinghouse is our Trail-side grove, which runs to Mr. Fred Turnbull's Standard Oil station, then his grove, then the office of "Buy a Patch of Paradise!!! J.J. Jenkins, Real Estate & Insurance." At the north end of town is Tomasinis', the small store run by our friends Sal and Sophia Tomasini, the only other Northerners in Mayflower, and the source of meat, milk, bread and other staples for the residents of The Quarters. Voight's, at the south end, is where most white people shop.

Just beyond Tomasinis' is the entrance to The Quarters, the steeple of St. John's African Methodist Episcopal Church and the funeral assembly of old, smudge-colored cars and trucks. Our parents' Chevy Styleline wagon is the only white-owned vehicle there.

Doto shakes her head as we pass by. "That poor young man. Such an abominable waste!"

We all fall silent, thinking our own thoughts of Marvin, his long easy stride, his wide-as-the-world grin, his love of a rhyme and a joke. He and his father have picked fruit for us forever, and since that awful morning two days ago, I've used my best memories of him to try to push away that picture of his body in Daddy's truck. Marvin was the one who turned my real name, Marie Louise, and my nickname, Reesa, into "Reesa-Roo-How-Do-You-Do," "Rooter-Tooter-Where's-Yo'-Scooter" and, my favorite, "Rootin'-Tootin'-How's-Yo'-Shotgun-Shootin'." Marvin was always good about letting me in on things that everybody else seemed to know already, like the fact that Luther wasn't his real daddy. Marvin's real daddy died or ran off when he was little, but "that's all right," he told me, because "Luther's *twice* the man mah real daddy was." It was Marvin and Luther who gave us our German shepherd Buddy, because "nobody oughta live in the middle of an orange grove without a good dog." When we first got Buddy, he sometimes vanished back to Luther and Armetta's house in The Quarters. Marvin would tie a rope around Buddy's neck and walk him home to us. "Hey-Root-Hog-Lost-A-Dog?" he'd call from our back porch.

Only Marvin could tell me when it was officially spring. "It ain't oh-fishal 'til the granddaddy bird calls it's time to '*Whip-Poor-Will!*' and the big bull 'gator bellows back, '*You leave ol' Will alone fo' Ah come over there, give yuh what fo'!*'"

"Who's Will and what did he do?" I'd ask each year, mock suspicious.

"I don't know, but *whatever* it was, his wife was in on it, too," he'd say, looking at me sideways.

"Now, how do you know that?"

" 'Cause, Roo, the other birds cry '*Whip-Will's-Widow!*' "

"Marvin, I never heard the birds say that!"

"Oh, *lots* of folks hear, but only a *few* listen," he'd reply, dropping his chin, narrowing his eyes at me.

The sky is bright, bird's-egg blue, cloudless; the sun March-warm, not yet summery hot. The DeSoto glides past the pure geometry of the groves. So my grandmother won't see or say anything about my tears, I turn away, tapping out the rhythm of the green rows flying past the window, haunted by the awful singsonging inside my head: *Marvin's dead, gone forever.*

North into Lake County, we reach the historic New England-style mansion that's the Lakeview Inn. The Inn sits between two stands of navel trees still in full bloom, on a slight ridge above pretty Lake Laura. As we pull into the driveway, the smell of orange blossoms and fried food fills the car. The azaleas, blazing pink against the wide white porch, look like they'd smell good, too, but I know they have no scent at all.

"Your grandfather and I used to winter across the lake from here," Doto tells four-year-old Mitchell, reaching out to rub his buzz-haired head. "The first time I brought your father here, he was a babe in arms."

Mitchell squints up at her, knitting his pale brows at the idea of a baby Daddy in Doto's arms. We call him our human fireplug because he's about that high and wide, and bursting with me-too energy. Spitting image of your uncle Harry, Doto says. Eight-year-old Ren, on the other hand, is lean and lanky, with Mother's curls and easygoing disposition except, Doto says, for the streak of the daredevil that's pure Daddy.

The Inn's hostess, who's older than Doto and remembers her, greets us loudly, exclaiming over how big we've grown, and settles us in a booth with a view.

Outside, the lawn runs down to the lake. People stroll on white crushed-shell pathways admiring more pink azaleas, late red camellias, lavender clusters on the lolly-popped chinaberry trees and the sweet, sun-colored jessamine trained over a trellis. Beyond the lake, orderly rows of blossoming trees march up and over the rolling hills. This is the Florida the snowbirds fall for.

The menus, the size of newspapers, dwarf us. We know what we want so we slap them shut right away and order as soon as our waitress appears. Doto sips her iced tea and Ren and I carefully suck our Coke straws. Mitchell's another story. Since our baby brother is not yet accustomed to Doto's strong opinions on table manners, the appropriate use of a straw and napkin, she quietly lectures him. Just after the waitress delivers our food—clam chowder for Doto, fried clams and French fries for us—a loud burst of male laughter from the booth next door startles us.

"The hell of it is, they grabbed the wrong nigger!" roars one of the men.

Doto's soup spoon freezes midair; her eyes slit at the man's language.

"They cruised the juke joint and saw him, young buck leanin' up against this white Caddy with New York plates. Uppity-ass burr-head smart-talked Jimmy Sims at his garage. They got the bastard, shut him up right quick and headed for a little stompin' party at Round Lake."

The man telling the story stops for a noisy swig of his drink.

"Reed Garnet, y'all know him? Got there little late and that half-dead nigger looks up at him and whimpers, 'Mr. Reed, Mr. Reed, it's *me*, Marvin!'"

Again the table laughs, this time at the storyteller's high-voice impersonation of the Negro dialect. Doto glares at us around the table, hazel eyes beading the unmistakable message *don't make a sound.*

"Well, Reed, he was hoppin' mad, called those boys a bunch of morons, told them this boy's mamma works in his house and now what were they gonna do? J. D. Bowman, y'all know that crazy Opalakee boy, just got back from Korea? Well, J.D. he just laughed, pulled out his pistol and shot that nigger boy in the head. 'Problem solved,' he told ol' Reed."

At this, the table's other occupants guffaw, slapping the tabletop in high humor. The speaker snickers, "I saw ol' Reed at the Wellwood Cafe, said I hoped he wudn't too broke up about it. It's good t' kill a nigger every once in a while, keeps the rest of 'em in line."

More murmurs and loud laughter follow.

"Way *I* look at it . . . one less nigger makes the world a cleaner place. Mary Sue, honey, it's my turn to buy these ol' boys their pie and coffee."

We sit in our booth, silent, lips tight, chests rising and falling in long, slow breaths. Tears collect inside my eyelids; I fight them off by pinching the back of my hand so hard the pain takes my mind off crying. The waitress brings the check to the men next door, hidden by the flowered curtain between our booth and theirs. The speaker pays; coins rattle as she makes change from her apron.

Three men slide and rise out of their booth, backs to us, hitching up their pants. The one closest to us, the storyteller, has on matching green-gray shirt and pants. As he ambles out of the dining room, he lifts his hat—the wide flat brim of a Lake County Sheriff's Deputy—onto his head. The men disappear out of the dining room, their boots clomping across the hardwood floor like dry thunder rolling off the horizon.

Doto sucks air deeply, bends forward, cat eyes glinting behind her glasses. She hisses: "Not a word until we're in the car."

"Awful quiet crew today," the redheaded waitress tells us with a smile. A curly wire pin on her uniform spells out "Mary Sue." Pink apron pockets bulge with order tickets and change. "Y'all save room for dessert?"

Ren and I cut our eyes at Mitchell, who's salivating for his hot fudge sundae.

"Just the check, please," Doto says with a frozen smile.

*Chapter 3*

---

Our family huddles around the kitchen table as Doto re-tells the story we heard in the restaurant. Her lips curl in distaste at the words she must use to tell it exactly. Beside her, Daddy's jaw mirrors hers in its hardening. Mother's eyes, red-rimmed from the funeral, stay on his; the single dimple in her left cheek missing in a mask of sadness. Beside me, Ren twists a buried fist in the pocket of his baseball glove. Doto is livid.

"To hear that idiot talk about Marvin like the boy was an animal, a dog to be put out of its misery, I swear I could have killed him with my bare hands."

The image of my 110-pound grandmother throttling that 200-pound Deputy flickers through my mind. The eyes behind her cat glasses are shooting sparks.

"I want you to call that Opalakee Constable and get him over here. This has got to be an important clue in his case."

"The Constable has no case, Doto," Daddy tells her in a flat voice that puzzles me.

"Well, this ought to give him one," she retorts.

"The Constable is a card-carrying Klan member. His standard line with anything involving a colored is 'We'll look into it' and he never does."

"But, Daddy," I say, "Marvin's *dead!*"

"Can't you call the Sheriff, or one of the County Commissioners?" Doto demands.

"The Sheriff, the Commissioner, the Opalakee Chief of Police, they're all Klan members. Even goddamn Governor Fuller Warren is one of them!"

"Governor *Warren*," Doto snorts. "That's one Warren that is no *possible* relation of ours!"

Shoving herself up and out of her chair, she paces the yellow linoleum. "The Klan *owns* this state like Capone owned Chicago," she rails, turning like a teacher, finger raised to make her point. "He owned the city, the county, the state, but . . ." Her eyes lock onto Daddy's. "You remember how they got rid of *him*."

Daddy studies his mother and I can see the wheels begin to turn. He leans forward, elbows on the table, chin on top of his folded hands, staring at the squiggly pattern in the blue Formica.

"The F.B.I.," he says. "I don't know how Mr. Hoover feels about the Klan, but I know he's no fan of cold-blooded killing. We could try to contact him . . . but how?" The veins in his temple jump. "We couldn't possibly call him," he says. "We'd never get through. Besides . . ."

"Maybelle . . ." Mother says it quietly.

"Would likely listen in and blab all over town," Daddy nods, completing her thought.

Our family has the unfortunate fate of sharing a party line with our two-doors-up neighbor Miss Maybelle Mason, who's also the town postmistress and perpetual old biddy. Miss Maybelle listens in on other people's phone calls as a form of entertainment. At the post office, where everybody has a box, she takes it personal if anyone dares receive a letter without a proper return address. It's rumored she opens such letters to verify their claim to space in her postal slots.

"That old bird lets out writing a letter as well. If the F.B.I. wrote us back, we'd never hear the end of it. But . . . Buuut . . ." Daddy says. "We *could* send a registered letter from downtown Orlando and use your address in LaGrange for the return."

"Of course." Doto lights up in support of the plan. "Blanche would forward it here inside my weekly packet."

"It could *work*," I say, seeing it all inside my head.

"It will work!" Doto declares.

"Blanche," Mother adds softly, "is our trump card."

"That's the plan then," Daddy says. He leaves the kitchen and goes into the small office off the living room. We hear the snap of paper rolling into his typewriter and the clack of the keys punching out the story of Marvin's murder for Mr. J. Edgar Hoover of the Federal Bureau of Investigation.

Doto walks to the refrigerator, patting her hair waves. "Lizbeth," she says, opening the Frigidaire, "I believe I owe these children some ice cream. Got any fudge sauce?"

*Chapter 4*

---

I did not go to school the Thursday Marvin died, or the day after that. The funeral was on Saturday; and Sunday went by me in a blur.

"Please," I begged my parents this morning, "don't make me go! I don't want to, not today, not *ever* again."

The idea of returning to a place where most people's lives have flowed right along uninterrupted by blood-wet bodies and bald-faced lying and bad people doing awful things; the thought of playing Red-Rover-Red-Rover-Can-Reesa-Come-Over as if Marvin's alive and laughing as he should be, and his poor old parents aren't sitting broken-hearted in their house—"I can't," I cried, "I just *can't!*"

Doto, ever the diplomat, replied, "I don't blame you. I couldn't ride in that smelly old school bus either. How about we drive down in the DeSoto? Maybe you'll feel differently when we get there."

My grandmother is the reason I'm here this morning, trying to pretend like I belong. I sit in the same desk, surrounded by the same children who were here before. Up front, Mrs. Beacham carries on in her same old brown suit and ugly lace-up shoes. But no one, none of it, feels the same.

Sunlight floods through the wall of windows, brightly white. I sit, deliberately opening my eyes to the whiteness, then closing them to ghostly black; seeing day full of life, then, behind flickering eyelids, trying to imagine death.

The idea that life is as fragile and full of holes as a lace curtain terrifies me. The other kids in this room have no idea. Well, maybe one of them does.

I see her two rows over, three seats ahead of me, but we've avoided each other's eyes all morning. May Carol Garnet knows about Marvin. She has to because Armetta works in her house. Beyond housekeeping, Armetta mothers May Carol in ways Miz Lucy Garnet never could. I can tell from here, by her unstarched dress, her plain, unplaited ponytail, that Armetta, May Carol's other mother, has not yet returned to work at the Garnet house.

May Carol and I know each other. We've spent time at each other's houses, made cookies with Armetta, laughed with Luther, endured Marvin's big-brother-like teasing our whole lives. But we are not friends.

Maybe it's her "Southern-ness" that gets in the way. The tendency to sort everything and everyone according to appearances. But maybe, just maybe, it's my sense of "other-ness," an in-the-blood inability to be a joiner. Like Doto says, our family runs long on being in, but not of, the places we call home.

Outside, a row of orange trees lines the school playground. Six days ago today, I saw Marvin for the last time, standing by the trees that edge our backyard.

"Looky here, Rootin'-Tootin'," he'd called to me, "here go

Mistuh Bee payin' his respects to Miss Angel Blossom. You know the story, don't yuh? 'Bout how Mistuh Bee got his stripes, and his wings, too?"

"Tell it to me, Marvin," I remember asking.

"Well, it goes like this," he said, sitting on an orange crate. "After God got done creatin' the world and everythin' in it, He was mighty proud of the way things turned out. 'Course, His angels was mighty curious 'bout what God done. So, God told 'em, 'Y'all g'wan down there, angels, take a look-see.' Now, angels, like humans, come in all different measures and band together with others they size. So, the band of littlest, tiniest, tee-ninchy angels flew down together and landed in a orange grove 'bout like this one, made it smell like heaven on earth. When those angels looked down on God's new-made ground, *what* did they see? The first big ol' fire ant, red as the devil, beatin' up the first big ol' black bee with a cat-o'-nine-tails, saying '*Ah's* your Massa now, bee, get to work!' Well, that whippin' is what gave Mistuh Bee the stripes on his back. And what made the leader of the tee-ninchy angels fly down and cry, 'You ol' devil ant, get back underground where you belong 'fore Ah tell the Massa of the Universe what you done!' Now, that fire ant high-tailed it into his hole right *quick*! Then, the angel no bigger than a blossom turned to poor Mistuh Bee and noticed God had forgotten to give him wings. 'Here, Mistuh Bee,' that angel say, 'you take mah wings, Ah'll grow some more. You take these wings and you fly 'way up high in them trees, make your home where they *ain't* never no evil ants.' That's how Mistuh Bee got his stripes, and his wings, in a single day. And that's why, ever since, when the groves grow blossoms that smell like heaven, Mistuh Bee flies back, pays his respects to the Angel Blossoms that set him free."

"Marie Louise!" Mrs. Beacham's voice in my ear, her big brown shoes on the floor beside my feet, make me jump.

"Shall I ask the school nurse to schedule a hearing check?" Her face is like a walrus, fleshy folds wobbling off her chin.

"Pardon me?"

"Here's your worksheet: Transportation Systems of the Ancient Egyptians. There are others that we covered in your absence. Meet me at my desk, please. May Carol Garnet, you may as well come, too."

While the rest of the class works at their desks, we stand together in front of Mrs. Beacham. I notice with a shock May Carol's fingernails. Usually shiny and shell pink, the polish is chipped, nails bitten to the quick. Her hair, normally braided, slips limply out of her ponytail. She's a small thing, pink and pretty (unlike me who's a medium everything— medium brown hair, middle-of-the-road size, looks I know are "fair to middlin' "). I'm surprised to hear May Carol's missed as much school as I have; and to see that her eyes, like mine, are sunken and dark-circled.

I'd like to ask what she's upset about—Marvin's death or Armetta's absence?—and tell her things I'm *sure* she doesn't know—about her daddy being there that night and all. But of course that's not possible. She's the daughter of a Klansman and I'm to keep my mouth closed.

# Chapter 5

I t's an ironclad tradition. On Palm Sunday, the congregation of Mayflower Baptist, the only white church in town, has dinner-on-the-grounds.

Under the ruthless direction of Miss Maybelle Mason, the old snapping turtle who runs the post office, Ren and the boys from the Royal Ambassadors bivouac the long tables under the big live oaks beside the sanctuary. While Miss Maybelle fumes over straight lines and wide-enough walkways, Miz Naideen West, the preacher's pinch-faced wife, fusses over the white sheets she calls tablecloths (which are the exact same ones she calls drapes during the Children's Christmas Pageant). On top of the sheets, she spreads long palm fronds for decoration. After church, the women will cover them with their specialties.

Everyone knows who cooks what best, and for weeks now, when the church ladies pass each other at the post office or in Mr. Voight's grocery store, they fawn and nod with exaggerated politeness. "You *are* makin' your fried chicken, your baked beans, your carrot Jell-O salad, aren't you?" they chirp like birds to one another.

When they see Mother, these women have one thing on their minds. "Lizbeth, you are bringin' that *scrumptious* fruit cocktail cake of yours!" It's always the first dessert to disappear.

Unlike most people around here, we weren't born Southern Baptist. Doto and her family are self-described Lukewarm Methodists and Mother's from a long line of Congregationalists, which is practically Episcopalian. When my parents arrived in Mayflower, they were newlyweds, barely past twenty, and kept to themselves. The following year, though, it was obvious that Mother was expecting me and, even more so, that Daddy got the polio. After Doto and Doc Johnny (and Luther, of course), Miss Maybelle Mason, eyes like a hawk, was first on the scene. Of course, she organized the church ladies in nothing flat and the casseroles arrived, like clockwork, for months. As Mother recovered, and Daddy improved, they were honorbound to repay the brigade for their diligence. The price was membership in Mayflower Baptist Church.

Of course, the major prerequisite is baptism. But it's an often-told, true story that Daddy caught the polio in the very lake where the baptisms take place, and refused to enter it again or allow Mother to, either. Citing some sort of "Biblical precedence," the minister agreed, and my parents' waterless entry into the congregation gave new meaning to the term "dry Baptists."

It was afterwards that Miss Maybelle, who always has her ears open, heard Daddy playing the piano and revealed his talent to the community. Long story short, Daddy got roped into leading the Mayflower Baptist choir, a job which he vows is infinitely preferable to being a Deacon.

Although we attend every Sunday, my parents take "the long view" on a number of church tenets, the most notable being the ban on alcohol. Daddy, a quick Bible study, never minds pointing out that the Apostle Paul encouraged Timothy to "drink a little wine for thy stomach." "Surely," Daddy says, "*Paul* enjoyed a glass of the grape and *so* can I."

On Mother's part, she just bakes her fruit cocktail cake exactly as her mother does, flooding the coconut and pecan mix on top of the cake batter with a generous cup of rum, then covering all with brown sugar and dots of butter.

None of this means my family's not *spiritual*. (Though what happened to Marvin has put me at odds with God these days.) To their credit, our parents have spent considerable time discussing the difference between Faith—the abiding belief in a Divine Creator that's as plain a part of a hundred-year-old oak tree, or a fiery red sunset, as the nose on your face—and Religion—which is the rigamarole that makes *some* folks figure they've got a leg up on everybody else.

Usually, my favorite part of Palm Sunday is the young people's Bible Drill, the hotly contested game of who-can-find-it-fastest, played in the lag time between the end of church and the blessing that begins dinner-on-the-grounds. Usually I love the competition, and to tell you the truth, usually I do quite well.

But this year, because of Marvin and all, I didn't feel like competing. In fact, I'd made up my mind *not* to participate until Doto told me about the prize—four tickets to the glass-bottom boat ride at Silver Springs—and suggested, if I won, I might give them as a thinking-of-you gift to Luther and Armetta.

It was Marvin, after *all*, who turned me into a first-class Bible Driller, by sharing his secret.

"Think of the Bible as a rainbow, Roo," he told me. "See the books in colors. The beginning ones are red: Genesis and all the begets and begats and the Moses books through Judges, *scarlet* red. After that comes the name and story books starting with Ruth and going through the poem books to the juicy Songs of King Solomon. They navel orange. After that, you got the four major prophets, Isaiah, Jeremiah, Ezekiel and Daniel, plus a whole batch of minor prophets, twelve actually, Hosea through Malachi. They daylily yellow, and *that's* the end of the Old Testament.

"Up next, they's the Jesus stories with the four Gospels and the Acts, they your green section with the words 'spoken by our Lord and Savior' in red letters—green and red like Christmas, y'see. Then, they's the Apostle Paul's letters to *all* the different churches all over the ancient *world* starting with the Romans through the Hebrews. They blue, Mediterranean Sea blue. At the hind end of things, you got the other letters from James, Peter, John and Jude; they's violet. No need to give the Revelations a color, *everybody* knows where they is." Marvin was a patient and inventive teacher.

Today, in his honor, when our Sunday school teacher Miz Agnes Langford calls "Time for Bible Drill!" I join the others elbowing their way into formation in front of the food tables. I prefer, and take, the end.

"Attention!" Miz Agnes commands and we straighten up like good Christian soldiers, Bibles at our thighs, pinned in the curve of our right palms.

"Draw swords!" comes next, which means Bible front and center, face-down on left palm, right hand on top, thumb at the ready.

After that, Miz Agnes calls book, chapter and verse: "Ezekiel 34:12."

*Yellow*, I think, *middle of the book*, and take a breath.

She calls it again: "Ezekiel 34:12," then gives the command: "Charge!"

I breathe out, thumb the Bible open to the middle, check book name and chapter, top right corner, check verse numbers bottom left, and step forward.

"Reesa?" she says.

"Ezekiel 34:12," I say, then read, *"As a shepherd seeketh out his flock in the day that he is among his sheep that are scattered; so will I seek out My sheep, and will deliver them out of all places where they have been scattered in the cloudy and dark day."*

Miz Agnes *always* picks out comfort verses.

"That's right, Reesa, and what a comfort. Attention!"

I step back into the line and we start again. The person who finds the most verses first wins.

One Sunday, only once, she let me call the verse. To amuse the others, I picked a recent discovery from the orange section, Song of Solomon 7:2: "Thy navel is like a round goblet that wanteth not liquor: thy belly is like a heap of wheat set about with lilies."

Miz Agnes was not comforted and spoke to my parents afterwards. Later, Daddy laughed and asked if I was trying so hard to shock Miz Langford, why didn't I go with the one about *I am a wall and my breasts are like towers?*

"Be bold," Daddy told me, "or what's the point?"

Today's Palm Sunday Bible Drill comes down to a tie breaker—me versus Billy Roy Sparks, who's two years older and can say the books of the Bible backwards. I'm not worried. Truth is, I usually beat him.

The others stand back, while Billy Roy and I square off for the final selection. The adults are hungry, their interest roused by whiffs of rapidly arriving country ham, fried chicken and cinnamon sweet potato "sue-flay." Miz Naideen and several other ladies stand sentry, using long palm fronds to wave the flock of greedy flies and wandering fingers away from the food platters.

Miz Agnes shushes the crowd, holding up two plump hands, palms forward, for quiet. She turns to face us, raises a dramatic, sausage-shaped finger and calls "Attention!"

Billy Roy and I straighten in front of the crowd.

"Draw swords!" she cries.

*Ready.*

"John 12:12 and 13," comes the call.

*Green section, red letters.*

"John 12:12 and 13. Charge!"

I thumb and scan and step out in a flash, but Billy Roy is there, one plaid-shirted, Vitalis-shellacked hair ahead of me.

"Billy Roy?"

"John 12:12 and 13," he says, and reads, *"On the next day, much people that were come to the feast, when they heard that Jesus was coming to Jerusalem, took branches of palm trees, and went forth to meet him, and cried, 'Hosanna: Blessed is the King of Israel that cometh in the name of the Lord!'"*

As everyone applauds, I'm not mad at Billy Roy. I'm really not. But I could kick myself for not seeing *that* one coming, it being *Palm Sunday* and all.

"You have to think ahead," Daddy says. I should've known.

Dinners eaten, dishes gathered, the ladies of the church having duly noted which pots and pans were picked clean and which weren't, whose had gone first and whose hadn't, Mother and Doto wave me over.

"Reesa, please go round up the boys and see if Daddy's ready to go," Mother says, her fruit cocktail cake with rum long gone. Not even crumbs are left.

The boys are bent over a hot game of Acorns, jacks played with sticks and nuts scavenged from the feet of the big oaks. I holler at them to finish up and find Mother.

Daddy's with the men gathered in the deep shade beside the sanctuary. As I walk up, one, a tall, paunchy citrus man named Ralph MacElvoy, is saying:

"Luther and Marvin've picked my tangerines for years. Those boys're damn fine pickers, 'scuse me, Reverend. Fast, too. How's ol' Luther takin' it?" he asks, nodding in Daddy's direction.

"Hard as any *man* would who lost his only son," Daddy says, his careful choice of words glinting in Ralph MacElvoy's direction. My father can't abide the Southern custom of calling a grown man a *boy*.

Mr. MacElvoy gives Daddy an odd, sharp look. His eyes narrow slightly, then slide hastily away from my father's steely gaze. Daddy's not a large man, but he has the presence of somebody much bigger.

"I think this business up in Lake County's made the Opalakee Klanners a little trigger happy," Aldo Brass, one of the church deacons, says in his slow, thick Alabama drawl.

I learned all about this Lake County *business* when I got my pre-Easter perm at Miz Lillian's Beauty Parlor. Not that Miz Lillian told me directly, but it was all the other ladies talked about. The story started a year or so ago, when a white couple was driving home after dark and their car broke down on a back country road. Another car with four young Negroes stopped to help and offered them a ride to the gas station. The man didn't want to leave the car, so the woman went for help.

"Though what white woman in her right mind would get in a car with four Negroes, I want to know!" Miss Iris, Miz Lillian's assistant, said, eyes wide in the large mirror that runs the length of the shop.

"And what *husband* would let her!" Miz Lillian wondered, raising a perfectly penciled eyebrow.

The woman didn't come back, but the next morning, her husband found her talking to the man at the gas station. The woman and the man told her husband she'd been kidnapped. The day after that, she said those Negroes had *bothered* her.

Southern ladies use the word "bother" to mean anything from an inappropriate glance to rape, which is, apparently, *a fate worse than death*. The more serious the infraction, the further they drop their chins and their voice tones. From the steep descents surrounding me, the woman obviously claimed *the worst*.

All the white men in Groveland got riled up about that and Sheriff Willis McCall deputized the whole bunch into a posse. The posse searched the county for the men who the papers called "the Groveland Four." One man was shot "trying to escape," but three others were caught and stood trial together.

An all-white jury declared them guilty, sentencing two to The Chair and the other one, who was only fifteen, to Life in prison. When the N-double A-C-P got wind of it, their New York attorney, Mr. Thurgood Marshall, said the trial was unfair and filed an appeal. The Florida Supreme Court said the trial was fine, but Mr. Thurgood Marshall took the story all the way to the *U.S.* Supreme Court. The U.S. Supreme Court said it wasn't fair *at all*, on account of the jury being all white men and the local newspaper getting everybody all riled up about it. Miz Lillian read us the part in *Time* magazine where Justice Robert Jackson said, "This is one of the best examples of one of the worst menaces to American justice I've ever seen." So, now there's to be a new trial for the two men on Death Row.

"And don't you bet Sheriff Willis McCall is fit to be tied about that!" Miz Lillian's long, red-tipped fingers expertly flip the elastic cords off the pink and green curlers on my head.

"Isn't he some muckety-muck with the Klan in Lake County?" Miss Iris asked, wrist-deep in Miz Sooky Turnbull's henna rinse.

"Nuthin' I heard about him'd surprise me a bit," Miz Lillian replied.

"I know some folks don't think much of the Klan," Miz Sooky, our across-the-street neighbor, called from the sink, "but as a *woman*, I have to say I sleep better knowin' the Klan's around to keep the Nigras from goin' *wild*."

In the mirror, my face flushed furious at Miz Sooky's ignorance. Miz Sooky's not a bad person. She really isn't. She's always doing nice neighborly things like bringing over fresh-baked banana bread or sharing home-grown tomatoes. But, like a lot of people around here, she's got a gigantic, gaping *hole* in her head when it comes to Negroes. Fact is, never *once* in my life have I seen Miz Sooky that she hasn't worked in some reference to what she calls their "dark danger to Southern womanhood."

Miz Lillian, who's as smart as a whip, pursed her red lips at me in the mirror and together we shook our heads. Miss Iris made a face at Miz Sooky's lumpy old sack-dressed body, reclined headless at the sink, her square-cut hands like turnips, spotted and gnarled from gardening without her gloves on. *As if any man, besides old Mr. Fred, would want to bother your frumpy old bones,* I thought.

"Sooky?" Miz Lillian said, changing the subject firmly, "You bringin' your sweet corn salad to dinner-on-the-grounds this Sunday?"

Deacon Brass leans against the big oak tree like a scrawny stork, jacked up one-legged, perched on his heel. After a long, slow drag on his Pall Mall, he lifts his chin, blows smoke and drawls, to no one in particular, "Re-trial or not, those two boys are gonna *fry.*"

*And what about that murdering J. D. Bowman? Will he fry, too?* Or, I want to scream at him, at all of them, *does Justice wear a hood on top of a mask?*

Daddy, seeing my face, intercedes. Smooth as molasses, he asks, "Your mother ready, Roo?"

I nod, mute, feeling the familiar catch in my throat, the pinch in my chest that comes from not being able to speak my mind.

"Gentlemen," Daddy says, throwing an arm around me that's half warning, half comfort, and nods our goodbye to the men in the shade.

*Chapter 6*

---

At four-thirty, Ren and I race to the brick-front post office at the end of our street. *This is it,* we've decided, one week to the day since Doto's friend Blanche forwarded the notice that Mr. J. Edgar Hoover had received Daddy's letter. This is the day we'll receive his reply.

Together, we duck through the heavy, half-glass door, hoping to avoid our postmistress' evil eye. Hands on the counter, Miss Maybelle Mason unpleats her neck, squinting into the afternoon sun, an old turtle sniffing for trouble.

"Marie Louise!" she snaps, stopping us in our tracks. "You two want to explain why you're not in school today?"

"Easter vacation, ma'am, all week," I say, wondering why she'd hit us with such an obvious question. The front porch of the post office is also our school bus stop.

Each school day, Miss Maybelle watches us and the Samson boys like a hawk, making sure we don't sit down on either of the two benches out front which she informs us are "U.S. Government property!" I'm sure she keeps track of school vacations closer than we do.

"How old are you now?" she demands, giving me the once-over.

"Twelve, going on thirteen in July," I say, resenting her greenish-yellow gaze.

"Good. My niece from Virginia is comin' to town next month and she's bringin' her daughter who's about your age. I'm callin' your mother to have you two play together while my niece and I visit."

Miss Maybelle stops, not having asked me if I'm interested or anything, but clearly expecting a reply. As if, in addition to the P.O., she's the boss of the *world.*

"I'll tell Mother you'll be calling her, ma'am," I say lamely, hating how she makes my blood boil.

"Don't forget! Now, what kind of trouble you two gettin' into with no school all week?"

"No trouble, Miss Maybelle, just playing at the packing-house or down at Dry Sink." Ren's scratching the back of his left leg with his right foot.

"Dry Sink! There's no place around here called Dry Sink. What are you talkin' about?" she demands. Nothing sets her off like an inaccurate address.

"You know it, ma'am," I say. "That big, dry sinkhole in the back grove behind our house."

Miss Maybelle's age-spot-speckled face creases briefly into her snapping-turtle smile. "*That* what you call it? When I was a girl, it was Little Lake Annie, the local swimming hole."

"Dry Sink? A swimming hole?" we ask, truly amazed.

"Certainly was. We had a rope off the big old oak tree on the side, used to spend hours swinging off it into the lake," she cackles.

Ren and I look at each other, dumbstruck.

"You kids today have no idea what *real* fun is!" Miss Maybelle huffs. "Go on, now. Marie Louise, tell your mother she'll be hearing from me."

Ren and I beat a path around the corner to P.O. Box 122, second section, third row from the top. Moving fast, to escape Miss Maybelle and recover the conviction that "This is the Day!" Ren misdials the combination the first time and has to do it again. Finally, the little glassed door springs open. There it is—the large manila envelope from La Grange, Illinois, and a handful of small ones. I grab them all and, after cat-walking carefully past the front counter, we fly the half-mile back to the house.

Doto's where we left her, enthroned on the screened front porch with the large leather journals she calls her "bookwork." In the blue one, she records her "monthly updates" from the trustee who administers her father's estate. In the red book, she tracks her "income and outgo."

We burst through the screen door and our grandmother looks up, cat eyes twinkling. We thrust the envelope into her hands, grabbing our sides and gasping from the run.

Slowly, she takes her silver letter opener and slits open the top. Mother, having heard the door slam, appears expectant on the porch, reading glasses in hand. As Doto removes the stack of smaller envelopes from their enclosure, we eye each one for an official-looking clue. Quickly, she spreads them fan-wise like a bridge hand, scanning the return addresses in the upper left corners. Her face falls in the message *it's not here.*

"Look again," we insist, as she deals the stack, one by one, face up on her ledger book.

*Not there.* Even though last week's packet gave notice that our registered letter had been duly delivered to F.B.I. head-quarters, even though he's had a whole seven days to respond, Mr. J. Edgar Hoover has not yet found time to reply.

"Damn," Ren says glumly. As the three females sur-rounding him look at him sharply, he levels his eyes, obvi-ously feeling justified.

"Double-wide Hoover dam," Doto tosses the compliment to what she calls his *mettle*.

"Triple-toed beaver dam," he tosses back.

"Daddy's in the car barn." Mother sighs, veiling her dis-appointment. Ren and I run to deliver the news.

E aster Sunday, Miss Maybelle nabs me in the vestibule. "Marie Louise, I hope you haven't forgotten our social plans?" she says, squeezing a face-crease in my direction. "My grandniece Maryvale will be here the second Saturday in May and I'm sure she can't wait to play dolls with Miss Reesa McMahon!"

"Dolls!" I grouse to Mother once we're seated in the church pew. "You think Maryvale is some little bitty old biddy like Miz Maybelle?"

"I doubt it, Roo. I'm sure the Good Lord broke the mold after He made Maybelle," Mother murmurs. "Now, sit up straight, here comes Daddy and the choir."

*Chapter 7*

Easter night, Mother and I are peeling eggs when all of a sudden Buddy, asleep by the door, shoots to his feet and winds up his tail. At Luther's *tappety-tap-TAP*, Mother calls, "Come in!"

"Evenin', MizLizbeth. Howdy-Doo-Roo," Luther calls back. His over-bright smile's a poor mask for the dark grief lines crisscrossing his face. "Y'all have a nice Easter?"

"Okay, how about you?" Mother asks gently.

"Good as could be, all things considered," Luther says, dropping his eyes quickly to pat Buddy. My throat tightens at his sideways reference to Marvin, and following his lead, I swallow *hard*. After a moment, Luther looks up again. "How'd the program go?"

Under Daddy's direction, the choir performed an Easter cantata.

"Came off well," Mother says and leaves it at that.

The Easter service had been agony for me. I'd gone unprepared for the effects of the familiar story—the bright young man, so kind and gentle, so gifted at storytelling, the murderous mob, the uncaring officials, the terrible sorrow of his family and friends. Of course, Jesus' story turned out considerably better than Marvin's. The rousing finale, *Up from the grave He arose with a mighty triumph o'er His foes,* left me sobbing. Miz Sooky Turnbull, sitting in the pew behind us, reached up and patted me encouragingly, heartened, I'm sure, by the hope that I'd somehow blundered my way into salvation. It wasn't that at all, of course. Jesus rose, *a victor o'er the dark domain.* Marvin's dead, *gone forever.*

"How about yours?" Mother asks him.

Few white people realize that besides being the best citrus pruner in the county, Luther's choir director at St. John's A.M.E. And nobody, outside our family and his choir members, knows that the choirs of both churches often perform similar programs, courtesy of sheet music passed between the two directors.

"It was fine," Luther says, his eyes appreciating Mother's kindness.

I watch the two of them, marveling at the way they tiptoe around each other's pain, like the way your tongue probes yet protects a toothache.

"Armetta do her solo?" Mother inquires.

"Ah wish you could've heard her." Luther's smile is real this time. "Not even Paul Robeson hisself coulda sung 'bout the balm of Gilead any better. The whole church-house was lifted up, lifted right up."

"Wish we could've been there. Please tell Armetta I'm thinking of her," Mother says, laying a soft hand briefly on his forearm. "Reesa, show Luther in to Daddy, please."

Luther trails me into the living room where Daddy sits at the piano working on his new piece.

"Evenin', Mist'Warren. What we got here?" Luther takes his reading glasses out of his shirt pocket and puts them on his nose. "Rhap-so-*dee* in Blue," he reads. "How's it go?"

"You know this, don't you?" Daddy asks. "I used to. Forgot all about it 'til Doto showed up with the sheet music."

"Can Ah hear it?" Luther asks with the briefest flash of his old self. Daddy sees what's coming. Settling in on the sofa, so do I.

"Play it for me, Mist'Warren," he chides Daddy gently.

Musically, Daddy and Luther are different as night and day. While Daddy works hard mastering his pieces, Luther has the ability to hear a song once and play it back, perfectly at first, then even better, embroidered with whatever he hears inside his head. In the comfortable, comforting game they've played for years, the rules are simple: Daddy plays first for Luther, then Luther returns the favor.

When Daddy lays his hands on the keyboard, everything about him elongates. His head rises above an upright back. His legs extend flatly to the floor, right foot on the pedal, left toes gently tapping. His fingers stretch out on the keys, wrists flat.

"Rhapsody in Blue" is my new favorite song. When Daddy plays it, I imagine I'm in a place far away from here, where people are nothing but nice to each other. I see it clearly inside my head:

A beautiful ballroom, the handsome, tuxedoed gentleman and the charming Miss Rhapsody—a vision in sky-blue chiffon, swirling about her, around them as they dip and float across the polished marble floor. The sound of sophisticated music, the perfume of jasmine and orange blossoms fill the air, and her hair, with sweetness.

"That's a *fine* song. You played it right elegant!" Luther tells Daddy at its end.

"Thank you, sir." Daddy nods, ceremoniously yielding the piano bench to his old friend.

Luther sits. His long, loose-jointed body curls over the keyboard, palms pressed together briefly as if in prayer. Lightly, he lays one finger, then another, on the keys, tickling out the La-Da-Dee-Da of the opening. Then, fanning his fingers like a faith healer, he plays. Once the basic line is laid, he begins his embroidery, threading twice as many notes as Daddy did. Elbows, arms and his entire right leg pumping, angular yet effortless, like an ibis taking flight. Mother appears in the doorway. Doto, Ren and Mitchell crowd the upper stairwell.

Luther's version of the song is local—less Rhapsody, more Blue. His lady lays sobbing-hearted on her bed, waiting for the one who has not come. Memories of their last perfect dance together fall like leaves onto the crumpled heap that was her party dress, now abandoned on the floor. At one point, she gets up, suddenly alert, certain he's come. But, *no*, she realizes. *No*body's there. Sinking back into bed, sadder than before, she knows he's *not* coming, not tonight, not *ever* again.

*Oh, Marvin . . . Remember when I said I wasn't looking forward to teenage dances because I didn't know how; and you said, "Don't worry, li'l Rooster. Ah'll teach yuh t' Car'lina Shag with the best of 'em!" Who's going to teach me now?*

When Luther finishes, my entire family applauds him wildly. He looks up, dazed and distracted by a sorrow so thick it's seeped out his fingertips. He nods, thanking us all. "No, Luther, thank *you*," Doto calls from the top of the stairs. "That was wonderful."

"You's most kind, Miz Doto," he says softly.

Doto says goodnight and herds the boys back into their bedroom. Mother returns to the kitchen and I remain, temporarily forgotten, on the sofa.

In a voice worn and tired, Luther says quietly to Daddy, "Mist'Warren, Ah come for your help."

After their first year in Mayflower, my parents say, they asked Luther to stop addressing them with the customary *Mistuh* and *Miz* attached to their names. "We're friends," they told him, "our first names will *do*." But Luther wouldn't have it.

"Ah 'preciates what you saying, and Ah'm proud to call you friends 'cause you's quality folk; but you's in the South and got to get use to they ways. If Ah was to call you jus' Warren and Lizbeth, the white folks 'round here bound to think *you's* crazy, and they'd laugh at you and leave you alone. Worse'n that, they'd take a notion that *Ah's* getting uppity and that don't bring nothing but trouble, Ah *mean!*"

Eventually my parents surrendered to Luther's logic, yet, in his way, Luther rebelled against it, pruning the customary *Mistuh* down to *Mist'* for Daddy, grafting *Miz* and *Lizbeth* into a single word.

What is it, Luther?" Daddy asks, sitting in the chair nearest the piano bench, leaning forward.

"Armetta's plum grief-struck over losing our Marvin. Since it was the Klan that kilt him, and Mistuh Reed Garnet's a member, Armetta swears she can't never set foot in they house again. Miz Lucy Garnet's been up to our house with they little girl crying, *please* come back, saying Mistuh

Reed had nothin' to do with it, it was the Lake County devils that kilt our boy. Armetta won't take a listen—though she loves that li'l May Carol like her own, such a sweet child. But, Mist'Warren, Armetta's use to working, she *needs* to work, take her mind off funeralizing. Ah'm wondering if you might have something for her to do. Not in the house. We know MizLizbeth likes to tend her own. But, maybe at the packinghouse, cleaning up, clearing out. Just enough to get by 'til she finds herself a new fam'ly to work for."

Daddy sits silently, thinking.

*Yes!* I think. *You must say yes!*

"We don't usually hire help this time of year, except for Robert, who sweeps up a couple times a week. But . . . it has been several seasons since the showroom had a thorough cleaning. We could keep Armetta busy for a week or so, maybe two. That help?"

Luther's and my shoulders sag in relief. "Bless you, Mist'Warren. Thank you. Can she start tomorrow?"

"Eight o'clock, before it gets too hot."

Luther looks down at the keyboard, then back at Daddy.

"They's something else . . ."

Daddy's nod tells him to continue.

"Ah had a visit from Mistuh Harry T. Moore. You know who he is?"

"Leads the N-double A-C-P over in Brevard County, doesn't he?" Daddy says. "Helped the Negro teachers get a bigger paycheck?"

*N.A.A.C.P.? Marvin used to joke that those letters meant Negroes Annoyed by the Abuse of Colored People.*

"That's him, 'cept he's the State leader now. Mr. Moore heard 'bout Marvin and come to see me and Armetta, asking what the authorities been doing 'bout it. Ah told him Constable Watts says he's 'looking into it,' which is 'bout like a diamondback wonderin' where that rattlin' noise come from."

"Exactly."

"So Mistuh Harry T. Moore say he talk to Mistuh Thurgood Marshall 'bout what happened. You know him? Head lawyer for the national N-double A-C-P in New York City?"

"Know *of* him."

"Mistuh Moore say since we was together when we found Marvin, Mistuh Marshall be wanting to talk to you, Mist' Warren. Mistuh Moore say Ah need to ask if you'd be willing to talk to them."

"Of course, Luther. I'd welcome the opportunity to speak with either of those gentlemen."

"Mistuh Moore say Mistuh Marshall been a good friend of the coloreds in Florida. He say Mistuh Marshall has big friends in Washington, D.C., might be able to get the local authorities to pay more attention to this."

"Tell Mr. Moore I'll be happy to help, any way I can."

"The hang of it is," Luther says, his voice all of a sudden choked, and his eyes glimmer, "Jerry Tee heard some of those ol' Crackers talkin' at the gas station. They say the Klan wasn't even after Marvin. They just confused him with somebody else in a white Cadillac with New York plates."

Luther's head drops, his shoulders fold in on it as he begins to sob. Daddy's eyes are watery as he puts his arm around Luther's bent-over back. I feel hot tears rising, their wetness racing down my cheeks.

"I heard that, too," Daddy tells Luther softly.

Luther tugs a large plaid handkerchief out of his pants pocket and wipes his eyes and his nose.

"Mist'Warren, the Klan done kilt-dead our boy for nothin'."

Daddy takes a shuddery breath. "I know, Luther, and I can't even begin to tell you how bad I feel about it."

"Thank you," Luther says, blowing his nose and wiping his eyes again. "Ah couldn't tell Armetta 'bout that, and Ah warned Jerry Tee he better be muffle-jawed in her direction; her heart's done broke enough already. Ah 'pologize for spoiling your evening. It's just been a rope . . ."

*God! How did You let this happen?*

"No apologies, Luther. Armetta's isn't the only heart that's hurting around here," Daddy says sadly, catching my eye across the room.

"Folks in The Quarters are scared outta they wits; most of 'em grabbin' they chil'ren off the street at the least li'l noise or the motor-by of a white man's truck. The chil'ren are having night terrors, too. Hardly a night goes by that Ah don't hear a couple of 'em, up and down the way, waking up screaming in they beds."

"Luther, these people must be stopped. There *has* to be a way."

"Ah wish they was, Mist'Warren. Ah sincerely wish they was."

*But who?* my heart cries. *How?*

# Chapter 8

I'm running through the dark grove to keep up with the others. Just ahead of me, a woman hoists a boy roughly to her hip. I watch him bury wide, frightened eyes into her bony shoulder. Just behind me, the voice of one man urges on another, in words I don't understand. On both sides, trees like fountains tunnel the row; their leaves too long and too thin to be citrus, with round red fruit I think may be pomegranates.

The way is steeply uphill. I'd like to stop and catch my breath, but I'm afraid of getting trampled by the heavy feet hammering the hard ground behind me. Chest heaving, back wet with sweat, *finally* I reach the tree break.

A crowd surrounds the hill's rocky crest. Without stopping, I squirm my way into them, past rough elbows and dark, cutting eyes, desperate to reach the center. I know this scene by heart. I've flipped past it a million times, green section, middle of the book, above small block letters that spell GOLGOTHA. *Except*—and the shock of this hits me like a fist—on the towering, rough-hewn cross, red neon lights flash JESUS SAVES. At the base of the cross, a circle of angry men are kicking and hitting the man on the ground; horrible movements made spastic by the pulsing red lights. "*Some*body! *Help* him!" I scream, outraged at the strangers craning their necks to see. "Marvin!" I cry, pushing, kicking, clawing through the crowd, "Marvin, it's *me*, Reesa!"

"Reesa, wake up! You're all right, honey, wake up!"

In the small constellation of our family, Daddy may be the sun, but Mother is our moon. Hers is the face that lights the night's shadows.

"You were dreaming. What happened?" Mother asks, the sound of her voice and scent of her hair proof that the nightmare is over.

"I was trying . . ." I sob into the softness of her shoulder. "Trying so hard to save Marvin. But they wouldn't . . . I couldn't get to him."

"Nobody could, honey. I'm sorry."

"Jesus couldn't save him. And neither could I," I tell her darkly.

"It was a dream, Reesa. Nothing but a bad dream," she says, smoothing my hair. "Poor thing, you're all right now. Lay down. I'll stay here for a while and rub your back. Go to sleep now, honey. Good night, sweet girl." Under Mother's soothing lunar light, I drift back into shallow sleep.

T he mid-morning light paints the white walls of my bedroom silvery. Outside, a breeze threads the needles of the pine tree by the car barn. A lone bird calls loudly from the top of it.

*That bird sure wants somebody's attention,* I think. *Whip-Poor-Will,* he cries again and my eyes fly open. Somewhere, off in the direction of Lake Opalakee, another sound seems to answer him, low, rolling like thunder but more alive, the bellowing of the lake's notoriously big bull 'gator.

*It's officially spring,* I remember. *Oh, Marvin, I heard it! I listened and I heard. Can you hear it, too, wherever you are?*

The house is uncommonly still. This late, Mother and Daddy are long gone to the packinghouse. The boys are off, too, on a field trip with Doto to the plane show at Orlando's airport.

In the kitchen I see Mother's left a place mat, napkin and bowl in front of the Shredded Wheat. I eat my breakfast in the sunny kitchen, listening again for the whippoorwill, wondering who taught Marvin all the things that he taught me. *Maybe I'll ask Armetta,* I think as I head out the door. She'll be at the packinghouse today. *Maybe not,* I reason, remembering Luther's visit. Apparently, unless they bring it up directly, care for a grieving person is best done sideways.

Outside, under a bright bowl of spring blue, the world seems soaked with color. Green grass laps like a river around Mother's island of rosebushes. Pink, coral and scarlet blooms cast a net of fragrance over bright orange butterflies that dip and bob as if tied by an invisible tether.

Across the street, a pair of redbirds hop along the pitched roofline of the Turnbulls' old house, the crested male singing bravely to his mate. That house is rented to the Carmichaels: Miz Evelyn Carmichael sings alto in Daddy's choir and, a lot of folks say, is a dead ringer for Ava Gardner. But her husband, poor pale-faced Mr. Frank Carmichael, they say, doesn't look a thing like Frank Sinatra. Their teenaged son Robert works for us part-time at the packinghouse. He calls my parents Mr. and Miz Mac, and me Macarooni. Robert wears white, rolled-sleeve T-shirts, like Marlon Brando on the movie posters for *Streetcar Named Desire*. He has a motorcycle which he's forever riding or working on in the Carmichaels' garage.

Next door, in front of the Turnbulls' new house, modern concrete block with shiny terrazzo, a pair of scrub jays complain bitterly to Miz Sooky Turnbull and I don't blame them. Miz Sooky stands with her back to me surveying the all-white Easter garden that's been the talk of the town for weeks. White azalea bushes, in full flower, flank the sides of a giant magnolia tree serving up milky blooms the size of soup bowls. In front, a stand of pearly Easter lilies trumpet behind the row of white-starred bushes Miz Sooky calls cape jasmine. Mother calls them gardenias.

On Easter Sunday, Mother and I were standing in a circle of ladies outside the church when Miz Esther Hall raved, "Sooky, your Easter garden is to die for! Whatever made you think of an all-white display?"

"You'll probably laugh," Miz Sooky trilled, "but I was at the station, taking Fred his lunch, when a carload of Nigras pulled in for gas. It was hot, so they piled out of the car thirsty, but, of course, none of them had enough money for Coke-Cola so they headed for the water fountain. Fred pointed out the sign, and of course, you never know if they can read, so he told them 'Whites Only, No Coloreds!' Well, that's when it came to me . . . a white-only garden without a *stitch* of color!"

As the rest of them tittered on about how lovely the whole thing looked and smelled, Mother and I left in search of Daddy. Truth is, I was mad at Miss Sooky, at all of them, for shoveling out their comments like a bunch of garbage on Marvin's grave.

In her new henna rinse and green gardening smock, Miz Sooky looks like an overgrown stamen in the heart of a fat white swamp flower, its scent impossibly concocted. To me, the whole white garden thing's unnatural and that's what the squawking blue jays are trying to tell her.

Fortunately, she doesn't see me. I stick to my side of the street until I'm past her—I do not want to talk to her, I do not trust what I might say—then sprint into the Turnbull orange grove. There's a dirt road running across it that we call "Fred's shortcut" because it connects the Turnbull house on Old Dixie Highway to the Turnbull station next to our business on the Trail. I've used it forever to walk between home and the packinghouse.

Like most of the groves around here, the Turnbulls' navel trees are trailing late bloom from treetop to grove floor, like a bride's veil. Gratefully, I slip away from Miz Sooky into the close, sweetly scented passageway.

"Ah heard our preacher waxing on poetical 'bout 'the lilies of the field,' " Marvin said once. "Personally, Ah hain't never seen no field full of lilies but Ah shore do love a grove in Blossom Time. Ol' King Solomon hisself wudn't 'rayed such as these!"

The leaves on the trees are full and richly green, lighter and finer than they'll be later, in the high heat of summer. Soon, I think, sniffing blossoms, the last of the bright white petals will fall, taking their heavenly scent with them. The little green vases inside will swell in Green Time, from pea-sized globes to full-size fruit, golden and juicy at Orange Time. That won't happen until November. And it wouldn't happen at all, I remember, if Mistuh Bee and Miss Angel Blossom didn't do their part.

At the end of Fred's shortcut, the scent of orange blossoms gives way to the reek of high octane and hot asphalt at Turnbull's Standard Oil. Just inside the work bay, next to the Coke cooler, I see the cold-water fountain and notice, for the first time in my life, the sign Miz Sooky talked about. It hangs, fat black letters on white cardboard, a good head higher than me, at adult eye level.

Is it new? I wonder. The curling edges of the cardboard, a diagonal smear of old grease give me my answer. Without stopping, as I always have before, I wave politely to old Mr. Fred, who nods above his newspaper, feet up on his desk, in front of the electric fan. Seeing that sign, realizing it's been there forever, I feel suddenly embarrassed. Like I've been an ignorant player in an awful game. *Shame on you*, I tell myself, resolving never to drink from that fountain again. And I feel it, the bee sting of shame on me.

At the highway, I quicken my pace. In the fall and winter, when our navel trees are heavy with fruit, the big billboards invite the snowbirds to "Pick An Orange Free!" and "Send Some Florida Sunshine To The Folks Back Home!" Earlier this month, Daddy and Robert changed the panels to pull in the warm weather folks with "Ice-cold Orange Juice, Fresh-squeezed," "All-You-Can-Drink For A Dime! (Limit 3)." Nobody in their right mind has any business drinking more than three glasses of orange juice. If the bulk of it doesn't make you sick, the acid will.

Across from me, the tall gray tanks and buildings of Mayflower Citrus climb like turrets of some medieval castle, quiet this time of year, after winter's roar of fruit juice processing. At its highest peak, like an eagle's nest, is the room with windows all around and a clear view of every operation: the private office of Mr. Emmett Casselton. You can't see him from here, but everyone knows he's there—pulling all the strings in town. Emmett Casselton is head of Mayflower Citrus, king of Casbah Groves, and, no doubt, chief of the Klan that murdered Marvin.

My thoughts, like arrows, fly at Casselton's wide-open windows: *A truckload of shame on you, too.*

# Chapter 9

T here you are!" Mother dimples as I enter our showroom. She sits on her stool behind the register, paperwork piled neatly in front of her. "Find your breakfast?"

"Yes, ma'am. Thank you."

"Armetta brought you something today," she tells me in a voice that says *mind your manners*.

I follow her gaze to the back of the showroom where Armetta Cully, Luther's wife, my friend Marvin's grieving mother, stands at the top of our stepladder. White cloth and spray bottle in hand, she's tackling the high glass shelves of the marmalade section, dressed in the white uniform and thick-soled shoes she used to wear at May Carol's house in Opalakee. It's the first time I've seen her, since Marvin and all, and I approach her, fearful of saying the wrong thing.

"Hey, Armetta," I call softly, shyness suddenly clogging my throat.

"ReesaRoo," she croons, setting aside her cloth and climbing quickly down. "Gotta getta a look at *you*!"

I can't help but smile, reminded that "Ol' Gonna-Gotta-Getta" was one of Marvin's pet names for her.

"Girl! You weren't no bigger than a minute when you was born . . . you a pretty half-hour now!" Armetta exclaims, a grin brightening her face, tiny gold tendrils curling around her teeth.

Maybe it's her smiling eyes, so like Marvin's but not exactly, her teasing tone, or the gentleness with which she places her palm under my chin and lifts it to look at me; all of a sudden, an ocean of sorrow slams over me, stealing my breath away. Worse yet, the four terrible words that have bashed against my brain, beat like wild birds caged inside my chest, fly out my mouth. "Oh, Armetta," I cry, before I can stop myself, "Marvin's *dead, gone* forever!"

All at once, I fall and am pulled sobbing into the wide, warm circle of her arms. Armetta's twice the size of Mother. In the soft talcum-scented saddle between her breasts, I feel, rather than hear, the beat of her great heart.

Behind us, crunching gravel, car doors open and slam, signaling the arrival of a carload of customers.

Armetta walks me quickly into the cool quiet of my parents' office, hidden in the crook of the L-shaped showroom.

"Oh, child," she says, stroking my hair, softly weeping. "Mah boy, he loved you like a sister."

"He was my best friend," I sob. "He was the best friend in the whole world and, and . . ." I try to stop crying but I can't. "*Everything* seems all upside down without him."

Armetta holds me, anchors me, as my head spins with the

awful truth that the world I knew, bright and warm and fun, has spun and quaked and fallen *away* to reveal something infinitely less simple, more dangerous and complicated than I ever imagined.

She holds me close, then, after a time, she pushes me just far enough away to see my face. Sternly, she says, "Reesa, lemme tell you somethin'. When Ah was 'bout your age, Ah lost someone, too. My old grandmamma told me somethin' Ah've never forgot. God is the potter, she said, and we clay in his hands, soft and weak which don't do at all. It's our time in the fire, don't y'see, that gives us strength and shows His purpose. Without that, we couldn't hold water. Y'understand?"

I bite my lip, unsure. God and I aren't exactly on speaking terms these days.

"God has His plans, honey, for all of us—you, Marvin, me, your mamma and daddy, everybody. And, He gotta prepare us. Time in the fire don't burn us, y'see, it helps us be ready for whatever's ahead."

"But Marvin's gone for*ever*," I wail in protest.

"His work was done, Reesa. His time come."

"But why couldn't he just die natural? Why'd it have to be so *aw*ful?" I want to know as the terrible memory of him groaning, bleeding in the truck bed flashes through my mind.

"Oh, child, there's no explainin' the meanness in this world." Armetta shakes her head, wipes wetness off her cheek, then cradles my hands in her palms. "But there's goodness here, too. You can't never lose sight of that, hold on to it. It's the goodness that gets us through."

"Do you . . . really *believe* we'll see Marvin again . . . up there, I mean?"

"Ah do, child, Ah *do*," she says gently. Her eyes seem lit from within, her great face shines with faith. "In the meantime . . ." she says, dropping her chin like Marvin used to, "Ah brought you some snicker doodles, and, since those boys done traipsed off to O'landah, Ah 'spect you get the whole plate to your own self."

"Snicker doodles?"

"Your mamma put 'em over there," she says and points to the desk in front of the showroom window, "next to your puzzle."

"Thank you, Armetta," I say, hugging her, "for . . . well, everything."

"Have some cookies, girl. Ah gotta get myself back to work," she says, but holds me real tight a moment longer before she goes.

I sink into Mother's desk chair. The crunchy sweetness of a snicker doodle can't cover the taste of bitter grief in my mouth. Staring through the shelves of the shell-lamp section, I hear Mother making change for a customer.

Beyond her, in the driveway, a second car wheels in and parks beside the people just leaving. I recognize, with surprise, the big blue Pontiac that is May Carol's mother's car.

Miz Lucy Garnet, blonde hair, pink shirtwaist and big black sunglasses, steps out of her car alone. As she greets my mother, I wonder where May Carol could be.

"Hey, Lizbeth. How you doin' today?" Miz Lucy calls, tucking her glasses with a snap into a small white purse.

"Trying to stay cool," Mother says. "How about you? Looks like it's heating up pretty good out there."

"Yeah, probably, I had the air conditioner on." Miz Lucy sounds distracted as she scans the showroom, spotting Armetta at work on the honeys and marmalades. "Listen, Lizbeth, would it be okay with you if I have a li'l conversation with Armetta? Won't take a minute."

Mother, apparently not wanting to speak for her, turns toward the stepladder and calls, "Armetta?"

Through the office window, I can tell Armetta's noticed Miz Lucy but elected to keep on cleaning.

Miz Lucy strides, high heels clacking across the concrete floor, around the rack of postcards, past the three big show-cases of small souvenirs, to the great wall of glass jars in the back. "Armetta, could we talk a minute?" Miz Lucy calls up the ladder.

"Ah got lots to do here, Miz Lucy."

"Armetta, *please?*"

Armetta carefully, quite deliberately sets aside her spray bottle. She lumbers down and off the ladder, keeping the white cloth in her hand. Miz Lucy cups her elbow and pointing to the shell-lamp section, just in front of me, says, "How 'bout over there?"

The two women move to a spot in front of the open window. May Carol's mother is a fragile, pretty woman, a Southern Belle who married well. Next to her, Armetta stands at least a head taller, her arms thick and powerful next to Miz Lucy's frail white ones.

"Armetta," Miz Lucy says urgently, in a voice so low that both Armetta and I incline our heads to hear. "I'm about to go out of my *mind*. May Carol can't sleep, won't eat, won't hardly do a thing 'cause of missin' you. Durin' the day, that girl's like a haunt, wanderin' from room to room. Every night, she just cries and cries. What can I *say*, what can I *do* to get you to come back to us?"

"Miz Lucy, you know this has nothin' to do with you and that chil'."

"Yes, Armetta, and you have to know that Reed had nothin' to do with Marvin's death."

"No, ma'am, Ah can't know that. Ah'm not saying Mistuh Reed pulled the trigger, or nothin' like that. But Ah know it was the Klan that kilt mah Marvin and that Mistuh Reed's a member."

"But, Armetta, there's three different Klan dens around here. Reed's is just a card club, bunch of overgrown boys playin' poker."

Armetta looks off into the sunshiny distance outside and breathes deeply. The broad planes of her face are still when she turns back to Miz Lucy.

"Miz Lucy, Ah can't. Ah just can't feature comin' back to your house, cleanin', cookin', puttin' clothes in the closet, seein' that white robe hangin' in there."

"Armetta, I could make him keep his robe at his mother's house. I could bring him to you and he'd *swear* on the family Bible that he had nothin' to do with this. Reed said he would if it'd help you feel comfortable comin' back to us."

"Ah'm sorry, Miz Lucy—"

But Miz Lucy cuts her off, whispering like a cry, "Armetta! Don't you see I'm *beggin'* you *here*!"

Armetta takes another long, slow breath. "Miz Lucy, Ah'm just as sorry as Ah can be. Ah'm sorry for you and Ah'm sorry for li'l Miss May Carol and Ah'm sorry that mah Marvin lies rottin' in his grave at age nineteen with cuts on his body and a bullet hole in his head. Ah could never, *ever*, again work in the house of a Klan member."

Miz Lucy Garnet, whose blue eyes are full of wobbly tears, takes a step backward. She fumbles with her white purse, finds and pulls out her big black sunglasses. Putting them on, there inside the showroom, she says, light-voiced, "So, you goin' to be workin' permanent for Warren and Lizbeth now?"

"This is jus' temporary, cleanin' mostly, gettin' things ready for the summer season," Armetta answers.

"Then what?"

"Ah hope to find me another family to work for."

"In Opalakee?"

"Yes, or here or Wellwood, it don't matter. Ah'll find somethin', some place."

"I'm sure you will, Armetta. And I'm sorry we couldn't straighten this out."

"Marvin's killin' is somethin' that won't stand straightenin', Miz Lucy."

"Goodbye, Armetta." Miz Lucy says it quietly. She turns to go, but stops midway and turns back. Removing her glasses, she's obviously remembered something.

"May Carol asked me to say 'hey' for her," she says, biting her pink lip.

"You tell that chil' she's a angel, tell her Ah said she'll always be a precious li'l angel to me."

"I, uh . . ." Miz Lucy looks up at the ceiling, bosom rising, as if she's collecting herself from the very air. "I, uh . . . don't suppose I could get a copy of your snicker doodle recipe for her? May Carol, uh . . . she asked me to ask."

"You know it's outta my head, all my recipes are; but . . ." Armetta's face softens. "Ah'll try. If Ah can figure out the measures, Ah'll write 'em down and send 'em to you."

"Thank you, Armetta. We'll watch for it."

Miz Lucy Garnet turns on her white patent-leather heel and strides quickly out of the showroom. Passing Mother, she waves vaguely in her direction. "Lizbeth," she nods and keeps on walking out into the sun shining on the Pontiac, high heels crunching the gravel driveway.

Armetta shakes her head and treads slowly back to the

marmalade wall, climbs steps, picks up her spray bottle and resumes her work.

"Time in the fire," she'd told me. *Seems to me some people get more than their share.*

"You all right?" Mother calls to her.

"Ah'll be fine, MizLizbeth. 'Ventually Ah'll be jus' fine."

*Chapter 10*

Somewhere, someone must have put grieving to music. There must be a song that, when you hear it, helps your heart heal its aching hole. I don't know that person, and I don't know that song. But, I do know, mine has lyrics—*Marvin's dead, gone forever*—and that my brother Ren's is a simple series of beats—*Bhhh-dmmm (pause) pfff;* sometimes harder, *BHH-DMM,* sometimes softer, *Buhhhh-dummmm,* with a varying pause, and a final *pfff.*

Ren's grief song is the sound of a solitary person throwing a baseball that hits the ground, bounces against the car barn wall, arcs through the air and into a lonely glove. The rhythm, sometimes fast, sometimes slow, changes with the distance between the ball and the wall, which alters the arc and the glove pocket's answer.

I can see my brother outside my bedroom window, a lean little figure facing a big, blank wall, on the bright opening day of Major League play. For baseball fans across the country, this is a personal holiday. But for Ren and Marvin, it was a holy day in the sacred celebration of Heaven on Earth.

Marvin gave me nicknames, Bible Drill secrets, Mistuh Bee stories. But his gift to Ren was baseball.

Two years ago, on my brother's sixth birthday, Marvin gave Ren his first glove and the great love of his life. He had Daddy's permission, of course, because Daddy can't play—the polio withered the muscles required for an overhand throw. So it was Marvin who taught Ren to catch a ball, fire a pitch, hit a curve, follow a game on the radio and love the Brooklyn Dodgers.

Marvin wasn't alone, of course. Old Sal Tomasini, the Italian grocer who grew up in Brooklyn, was in on it, too. The same year Ren got his glove, the Dodgers won the 1949 National League pennant, Marvin's hero Jackie Robinson was picked Most Valuable Player, and Sal and Marvin christened Ren their lucky charm.

Above Sal's small store, which caters to the folks from The Quarters, is the cheerful, cluttered apartment where he and Sophia live. Rising above that is the twenty-five-foot radio antenna that connects Sal and the fans who gather behind his store on game days to the Brooklyn Dodger Radio Network.

No doubt, they're all there now, sitting on the benches under the scrub pines, watching the game in their minds with the help of the Dodger's honey-toned storyteller, The Rhubarb, Red Barber.

Old Sal was here earlier, offering Ren a ride. But Ren refused.

"We can'ta open widout you!" Sal had said in his thick Milano-by-way-of-Brooklyn accent. "You are our lucky charm! Besides," he'd pleaded, "It's Preacher Roe pitching; you don't wanna miss *him*."

Ren said nothing, and everything, with a shake of his head. Chin on his chest, face unreadable under the bill of his blue cap, he'd mumbled, "Sorry," and turned away, walking resolutely down the drive to face the car barn wall.

Sal's eyes, behind his thick glasses, grew pained; their sadness magnified by the high-power lenses. His white mustache drooped over lips pursed in disappointment.

"Sorry, Sal," I'd told him, by way of comfort.

He'd thanked me with a wave of his small hand, adjusted his own ancient Brooklyn cap and driven away.

*Bhhh-dmmm (pause) pfff.* The lonesome sound of Ren's solitary play is a world away from the complex chatter of catch with Marvin.

For the past two summers, the driveway where Ren stands now, facing the wrong way, was his and Marvin's playing field. In front of an imagined crowd (Ebbets, of course), the two of them, fifteen feet apart, re-enacted baseball's greatest plays, playing multiple positions as their personal heroes. Marvin was most often Jackie, the great Jack Roosevelt Robinson, white baseball's first black player. Ren was sometimes Preacher Roe, the Dodgers' league-leading pitcher, sometimes himself as a grown-up pitcher, Ren "Rocket Man" McMahon. ("When Rocket Man's on the mound, nobody orbits the bases!" he'd crow.)

"But can The Rocket do it again?" Marvin would taunt, his throw finding Ren's glove with a firm *Thwap!* Ren would squint, hard, and hurl the ball back—*Thwap!*—and the imaginary game would begin, with Marvin, imitating Red Barber, calling the play-by-play:

"Rocket Man's held the flock scoreless, folks, through

eight innin's. Bottom of the ninth, one away, with Reese on first. Snider steps in to face McMahon.

"Rocket Man checks Reese, an' delivers. Duke swings— *Thwap!*—It's a blue darter over the shortstop's outstretched glove. The left fielder picks it up an' rifles it to second— *Thwap!*—No, suh! *Too* late!

"Listen to those fans as Jackie Robinson approaches home plate. Jackie leads the league in runs scored, an' bases stolen. PeeWee's on second, Snider's at first. Here's The Rocket's windup, an' the pitch—*Thwap!*—It's a bullet back to the box. Rocket Man snags it, turns and fires it to second, doublin' off a surprised PeeWee Reese!—*Thwap!*—Oh-ho, doctor! Rocket Man McMahon has single-handedly *won* the game!"

"Waa-hooo!" Ren would holler, tossing his glove high in the air, tipping his cap to the imaginary crowd.

*What's he thinking now?* I wonder as the sound of Ren's vigil echoes in my room. *BHH-DMM (pause) pfff.* He's not much of a talker, even on good days. Mother says he gets that from her side of the family. Oh, he can go on forever about baseball and his precious Brooklyn Dodgers. But when it comes to something personal, like "You missing Marvin, too?," forget it.

I asked Marvin once, "What's the big deal about baseball, anyway?"

He and Ren were taking a break, sitting in the shade beside the house.

"Well, Ah'll tell you, Roo," Marvin replied, rubbing his chin. "Ah heard Red Barber say 'baseball's like life.' His life, maybe. Not mine. Ah'd say baseball's a bit of Heaven on Earth and Ah can prove it, too. Wanna see?"

"Sure," I said, sitting down beside him.

Marvin drew a diamond in the dirt. "Looky here. If this is

heaven, y'got to have the Father, Son, and Holy Ghost, right? Well, the pitcher's like God, standin' highest on the mound, playin' catch with The Son behind home plate. Backin' God up is the Holy Ghost, the shortstop who's all over the place. With me so far?" Of course I was. "Okay! Now, behind these three, there's two bands of angels, three each: Cherubim on the bases, Seraphim in the field. Heaven on Earth!" He laughed. "But, Roo, wouldn't be Heaven without a pearly gate and that's right here," he said, stabbing home plate. "And behind the gate is St. Peter hisself, dressed in a suit. Also called the umpire," he said, as if I didn't know.

"Now, jus' like Heaven, a batter comes knockin' at the pearly gate, askin' God and St. Peter, 'Can Ah come in?' 'We'll give you three tries,' the two of them say. God loves threes, don't y' see—three around the mound, three bases, three outfield, three outs. So the batter tries his hardest, and his teammates try, too. But here's the best part, Roo: Once you get in, you jus' as good as anybody else. In Heaven, they don't count the color of your skin, or the cut of your clothes, or whether your shoes are shined or not. In Heaven, a black man can out-hit, out-run, out-field a white man and live to tell about it. A black man, black as Jackie Robinson, can be picked Most Valuable Player, over hundreds of white men. That ain't like life, Roo. That's Heaven on Earth!" Marvin had grinned, and sat back satisfied he'd proved his point. Looking at me sideways, he'd flashed me his V-for-Victory sign which, for Marvin, meant *I know what I'm talkin' 'bout here,* or simply, *gotcha!*

Wait 'til next year!" Marvin promised Ren last October, after the Dodgers lost their pennant to the "Whiz Kids" from Philadelphia.

Baseball's next year begins today: Jackie Robinson's a Cherubim on second base, Preacher Roe's passing judgment on the mound, the fans are assembled in Ebbets Field and under the pines behind Tomasinis' store. But Ren's outside facing a big, blank wall. And Marvin?

*Marvin's dead, Buhhhh-dummmm, gone forever, pfff.*

## Chapter 11

The month of April falls with the last of the orange blossoms into May. Armetta's gone to work for Mr. and Miz Charles Clark in Wellwood. Miz Clark is the former Patsy Lee Berry, youngest daughter of the Wellwood Berrys, who are fine folks with no apparent Klan connections. Mr. Clark is from New Orleans and as nice as can be. The Clarks' first child, Parlee Berry Clark, has just arrived and her parents need Armetta's steadying hand.

Ren and I continue our daily dashes to the post office but, to tell you the truth, I'm starting to think Mr. J. Edgar Hoover couldn't care less about a cold-blooded murder in the middle of an orange grove.

On a night in early May, Mother, Doto, Ren and I sit around the kitchen table attempting Pinochle. Under Mother's patient tutelage, we've worked our way up from Go Fish and Old Maid through Crazy Eights, Rummy, Hearts, and Canasta, to Pinochle, her prerequisite for instruction in Bridge.

Daddy, with a sleepy Mitchell slung over his good shoulder, ribs Mother, "You know, you're probably this town's only serious card-playing Baptist."

"Don't forget Lillian!" she mock-protests.

"Twice a year does not a card shark make," Daddy calls on his way upstairs. "Besides, you taught her everything she knows."

Mother grins, cuts and deals.

All of a sudden, Buddy, our live alarm system, scrambles up and runs to the back door. Nose to the crack, his tail ticktocks welcome while, at the same time, a small warning growl rolls around his mouth.

Luther's knock follows and, opening the door, I see the source of his mixed reception. Behind him, just outside the circle of porchlight, stand two white shirtfronts split by dark ties, men dressed for business.

"Evenin', Roo. Y'all finished supper?" Luther asks quietly.

"Yessir, we have."

"Ah brought a couple people to see your daddy."

"Please come in," I say, pulling the screen door wide.

Mother and Doto look up and hastily collapse their card hands.

"Evening, MizLizbeth. Ah'd like you to meet Mistuh Thurgood Marshall and Mistuh Harry T. Moore."

"Gentlemen, welcome," Mother says, rising from her chair and extending her hand. "Please meet my mother-in-law, Mrs. Dorothy McMahon."

"How do you do?" Doto stands, offering her hand in that queenly way she uses whenever she meets anybody.

"And this," Mother continues, "is Marie Louise."

Although they seem to be about the same age, the two strangers are quite different. Mr. Marshall's a great golden bear of a man. His hand swallows mine in a firm, hearty shake. Mr. Moore hangs back, slim, dark, dignified. He meets me with his eyes before offering his grip.

"Also known as Roo, I hear," Mr. Moore says. His smile is warm and kindly. N-double A-C-P, I remember, from Daddy and Luther's talk.

"Pleased to meet you," I say.

"And our son, Warren, Jr., who we call Ren," Mother says. Ren does Daddy proud, shaking hands firmly, level-eyed.

"It's a pleasure meeting all of you," Mr. Marshall says, openly surveying the kitchen. Unlike Luther and Mr. Moore, his hair is straight and brown. He sports a handsome, close-clipped mustache and a taffy-colored tweed jacket, an unusual fabric for Florida, but of course he's the lawyer from New York.

"You're a long way from home, Mr. Marshall," Doto says.

"I've had business at the Lake County courthouse all week," Mr. Marshall explains in a voice that seems to rumble around the room. "Spent today with Harry registering voters. Heading home tonight."

"Looky here!" Luther says, grinning gold. He pulls a small white card out of his shirt pocket. "Says *here* Ah'm a duly registered Democrat in the County of Orange, State of Florida. Come next spring, Ah get to vote in the primary elections. After that, Ah'll help pick the President of the United States."

"Haven't you voted before, Luther?" Ren asks.

"Nope," Luther says.

Mr. Moore explains smoothly, "Orange County's been a little slow in giving us the vote, but thanks to Mr. Marshall here, we're back in the registration business."

"Good Lord, that amendment passed, what? Twenty years ago?" Doto asks Mr. Marshall.

"Thirty, actually!" Mr. Marshall's laugh is hollow. "But," he tells Doto, "I doubt you need me to tell you the pace down here is a bit behind the rest of the country."

Doto shakes her head in weary agreement.

"How's the voter registration coming?" Mother asks Mr. Moore.

"Pretty good, so far." A shy grin widens his narrow, thoughtful face.

"Harry's being modest," Mr. Marshall booms. "Before he got involved, less than four, four and a half percent of the Negroes in this state were registered. Now, we're up to nearly thirty percent, which is *twice* the rate of any other Southern state!"

"Good for you!" Mother says. "I'm sure it hasn't been easy."

Mr. Moore nods, offers a honey-toned thank-you, then adds gently, "Ma'am, I need to get Mr. Marshall to the airport in about two hours. Luther said your husband might have a word with us?"

"Of course. He's upstairs putting our youngest—"

Before she can finish, Ren and I are up and in motion. "We'll get him right away," we say and race out the door.

"Would you like some iced tea, coffee?" Mother asks as we tear through the dining room and up the living room stairs.

"Daddy!" we tell him on the landing. "Luther's here . . . Mr. Harry T. Moore, Mr. Thurgood Marshall . . . to see you."

"Here? *Now?*" he asks.

"Isn't this great?" I ask, heart pounding. *At last, somebody's going to do something about Marvin's murder!*

"Yes," Daddy says. Suddenly, he's all business. "You two stay up here while the adults talk," he tells us curtly and heads down the stairs.

Ren and I gape at his back, at each other, in surprise. It's not like him to exclude us from living room conversation. *Aren't we witnesses to the conversation at the Lakeview Inn?* I sulk. Together, my brother and I sink into the dark of the upstairs landing, lean against Doto's bedroom door, and listen to the introductions downstairs.

"Mr. McMahon," Mr. Marshall begins.

"Please, call me Warren," Daddy says warmly. He sounds glad they're finally here.

"Warren, we're compiling a file on what happened to Marvin Cully. I'd like to hear your story and that of your mother."

"Hold on. Let me get my notes."

I hear Daddy's steps into his office, the slide of a file drawer opening and closing, and his quick return to the living room.

"What I have here are four documents: The first is the notes I made on Thursday, March eleventh, the day Luther and I found Marvin on Round Lake Road. Except for poor Marvin, the scene looked pretty much like there'd been a party . . . beer cans, cigarette butts, a couple of broken branches on the orange trees, lots of wheel tracks nearby."

I hear the sound of rustling papers as the sheets change hands.

"How'd you know to go to this place?" Mr. Moore asks.

"Everybody knows where the Opalakee Klan takes people," Luther says.

"If we hadn't found him there, we'd have checked the

Ocoee Klan's stomping grounds off Winter Garden Road,"
Daddy adds.

"Harry, can you research these properties, find out who
owns them?" Mr. Marshall asks.

"Oh, I can tell you that," our father says. "Emmett Casselton's a big citrus man around here and long-time Klan
member."

*Talk about how the Klan's been taking people to the Casbah for
years!* I urge Daddy in my head, but he's not listening.

"Good. What else do you have?" Mr. Marshall asks.
Though we can't see him, his presence rolls up the stairwell.
This is a man who, one way or another, makes things happen,
gets things done.

"These are Doc Johnny's notes on Marvin's condition
when we brought him in. I've called the coroner a couple
times for his report. I'm not even sure there *is* a report."

As he reads the notes, Mr. Marshall makes little clicking
sounds with his tongue against the roof of his mouth. I'd
asked to see the notes—after Daddy finally finagled them out
of Doc Johnny's nurse—but Mother said no. "She's seen too
much already," she told Daddy. *As if reading about it would be
any worse than the real thing,* I'd told Ren.

"Here's a transcript of the conversation my mother and the
children heard at the Lakeview Inn on Saturday, March thirteenth. My mother and I sat down afterwards. She dictated, I
typed. As you can see, I'm not the world's best typist."

Again, there's the sound of paper shuffling and a silence.

"Did you get a look at this Deputy, ma'am?" Mr. Marshall asks.

"Unfortunately, only from the back," Doto answers. "He
was a burly man, about your size, with big brown freckles all
over the back of his neck and hands. Big-boned, too. I'd guess
Irish descent."

"And the waitress. Can you remember her name?"

"No," Doto says, "I'm sorry."

"Mary Sue!" I cry out, and six pairs of eyes seek me mid-stairwell. Leaning over the banister, I explain, "She had a curly pin on her uniform that said 'Mary Sue' plain as day. And that's what the Deputy called her when he asked for the check."

"You're very observant, young lady." Mr. Marshall nods, making a note. "Anything else?"

"The other two men wore grove boots, like Daddy's. One was tall and real skinny, stooped like Ichabod Crane; the other was older, with dark hair like Mother and a big bald spot on the back."

"That's right, Reesa," Doto says. "I'd forgotten."

"Any other details?" Mr. Marshall asks.

Ren's voice at my elbow startles me. "The deputy's gun had a fancy handle."

Mr. Marshall's eyes shift alertly up to Ren. "What do you mean, *fancy*?"

"It was white, like the inside of a shell," Ren tells him.

"Like a pearl?"

"Yes, like that, and marked, carved maybe?" Ren says.

"Donnelly," Mr. Marshall says grimly. "Deputy Earl the Pearl Donnelly. It figures."

"Ren, Roo, you've been a big help. Thanks." Daddy's look sends us back into the dark recess of the landing.

"Warren, do you know these people Donnelly mentioned?" Mr. Marshall asks Daddy.

"I know Reed Garnet; but I'm sure Armetta can tell you more than I can."

"Yes, we've spoken with her."

"J. D. Bowman's another story. I know his father. The old man's a loudmouthed bigot, worked for Emmett Casselton for years. Has a grove of his own, but since most of the local pickers won't work for him, Bowman hires migrant labor instead. I don't really know J.D., but he has the reputation of being a wild hare, a real chip off the old block. I don't doubt for a minute that what my mother heard is exactly what happened. This last is a copy of a registered letter I sent J. Edgar Hoover mid-March."

"Heard anything back?"

"Not a word."

"Doesn't surprise me. The Director's had his hands full, and he's not exactly color blind," Mr. Marshall says, and I think his voice sounds careful. "Plus, this situation's a little tricky. Here in Florida, murder is a state crime. If local lawmen choose not to act, the feds have to be creative because they lack the authority to get involved. If you would, Warren, I'd like a copy of all this."

"I typed everything with carbons, in triplicate. Take whatever you'd like."

"Warren, how would you compare the Orange County Klan to the group I'm dealing with in Lake County?" Mr. Marshall asks.

"Well, the first difference is the sheriff," Daddy says without hesitation. "Willis McCall is a racist son of a bitch— 'scuse me, ladies—and his deputies are pond scum."

"I have to agree with your assessment." Mr. Marshall's tone is weary.

"Not that our sheriff's much better," Daddy continues, "but he's a lot less arrogant. The second thing is there are three different Klans here in Orange County. I don't know much about the one in Orlando except they seem to have the good sense to leave the folks in Eatonville alone. There's another Klan in Ocoee-Winter Garden and that crowd's a lot like the Crackers in Lake County. You know about the signs, don't you?"

"What signs?" Mr. Marshall asks.

"You mean the ones in Ocoee?" Luther says.

"What signs, Luther?" Mr. Marshall asks.

"Driving in and outta town, they's signs on both sides sayin' '*Nigger—If you can read this: Don't let the sun set on your head in Ocoee.*' "

"Harry, make a note," Mr. Marshall says with a rumbly sigh.

"The Opalakee Klan's a little different," Daddy says. "The names I know read like the town's social register. Most of the oldest families are involved. Their grandfathers brought The Klan with them from Georgia and the Carolinas. The fathers are pretty sedate, but the sons . . . Well, before the war, they mostly pulled college-boy pranks on young couples parked in cars and old coloreds whose fear amused them. Obviously, they're men now . . . veterans, with experience in killing."

Despite the fact that six adults sit in it, our living room is silent.

Ren and I exchange looks. What's happening down there? Finally, Mr. Marshall clears his throat. "Warren, Luther said you'd be a big help and you certainly have been. I can't make any promises. The problem is the state's jurisdiction and the lack of hard evidence. If the coroner removed the bullet, if the bullet happened to match J. D. Bowman's gun . . . Well, we'll see what we can do."

"Marvin was a good friend, not just to me and Lizbeth, but to our children. We'll do whatever we can to help."

People are standing, shaking hands.

We hear Mr. Moore quietly singling out Mother. "Thank

you for the coffee, ma'am, and for opening your home to our little meeting." Daddy, meanwhile, is insisting that Luther and Mr. Marshall, turning toward the kitchen, leave by way of the front door. Doto opens it for them and bids Mr. Marshall a warm "Good night and safe journey."

As our parents and Doto head back to the kitchen, Daddy tosses up the stairwell, "You two go to bed!"

"Now, we're *getting* somewhere," I tell my brother, punching his shoulder in celebration. I feel light-headed with tonight's progress.

But Ren is less confident, his face pinched in disappointment. "Not exactly Dick Tracy and Sam Catchem, are they?" he pouts, wanting more from Mr. Marshall than "We'll see what we can do."

"No, they're *not*," I tell him, "but since nobody else seems to give a good damn 'bout Marvin, they're all we've got!"

# Chapter 12

At quarter 'til one on the steamy hot Saturday before Mother's Day, I amble over to Miss Maybelle's to meet her grandniece Maryvale. Miss Maybelle's on her lunch hour from the post office and I've been told to be prompt. Expecting the worst, I'm relieved to see that the girl swinging her bare legs on Miss Maybelle's front porch is dressed like me in shorts, T-shirt and sandals. And there's not a doll in sight.

"Hey, there," I call as I open the wood-and-wire front gate.

"Hay's for horses; try grass, it's cheaper!" the girl calls back. Her face is full of freckles and her brown eyes crinkle beneath red-brown bangs when she grins. "You Reesa?" she asks.

"That's me. You Maryvale?"

"Puh-lease call me Vaylie. I've been Maryvaled to death this week!"

I figure the pretty woman opening the screen door is Vaylie's mother. Miss Maybelle's in full steam behind her, jangling keys to the post office in hand.

"You two met already? Good." Miss Maybelle takes charge as usual, brisk in her postmistress' uniform. "Marie Louise, this is Maryvale's mother, Miz Laverne Carrollton."

Miss Maybelle acts surprised that I know enough to step forward, shake hands, and say "Pleased to meet you, having a nice trip?"

Miz Laverne's more redheaded than her daughter and her teeth are bright white against the reddest red lipstick I've ever seen. Her skin is pearl-colored with tiny lavender veins showing through. Although she wears makeup like a movie star, I see dark purple circles under her eyes. There's a small bruise like a violet-colored butterfly on the ivory inside her wrist.

Miss Maybelle checks her watch and spouts orders. "Laverne's keeping me company at the post office while I sort the afternoon mail. Marie Louise, you must return Maryvale at precisely five o'clock. I went over this with your mother in case you forget."

"Yes, ma'am," I say nicely, hating her.

As we trail them down the walk, I marvel at Miz Laverne's ability to walk so smoothly in spiky heels next to Miss Maybelle's MacArthur-like march. At the street, they turn right toward the post office and Vaylie and I peel left, toward home.

"That woman's a witch," Vaylie says. "She always like that?"

"Pretty much." I grin. "Our school bus picks us up every day in front of the post office. No matter what the weather, boiling hot, freezing cold or pouring rain, she never lets us wait inside. 'I'm runnin' a branch of the United States Post Office, *not* a nursery school! This building is for official *business* only. You hooligans stay off those benches, too. They're official government property!' You'd think the fate of the entire nation rests on those benches staying empty."

Vaylie's laughing at my version of Miss Maybelle's ornery old attitude. "She wanted us to stay over a few days, but our Atlanta cousins warned us that an afternoon was 'bout all we could stand."

"Where you headed next?"

"Over to Winter Park to stay with a school friend of Mamma's. We're *on tour*, Mamma says, but mostly we're takin' a break from Daddy."

"Is your father sick?" I ask.

"Sort of. I mean, he's all right most of the time. But sometimes he gets to feelin' melancholy and then he drinks and turns mean as a snake. Usually only lasts a couple weeks, but when Mamma sees his melancholy comin', she tells Whit and Claudette to take over and we go on tour."

"Who are they?"

"Whit and Claudette? They're our colored maid and butler, been takin' care of Daddy since he was a boy. Claudette says melancholy runs in Daddy's family, but Whit says it was *The War* that did him in. Whatever the reason, Mamma and I leave town 'til they get Daddy back on track. Where you takin' me?" Vaylie asks as I turn down the grove road.

"Dry Sink. It's this old, dry sinkhole where my brother Ren and the Samson boys are waiting to have a rattler race."

"What's that?" Vaylie asks, breaking into a run beside me.

"Ren and Roy and Dwayne have been out in the palmetto scrub all week with their fork sticks looking for rattlesnakes.

Caught some and trapped 'em in burlap bags. First, we all climb up the tree, then we lower the bags and let 'em free. The rattlers race for cover into the brush outside the sinkhole. You won't believe how fast they go!"

In the clearing, where, on one side of the hole, our grove stops and, on the other side, the Samson palmetto scrub begins, Vaylie declares she's never seen a sinkhole before. "Where'd it come from?" she pants.

We wave to the boys, who are already up in the giant oak, and run around Dry Sink to join them.

"Daddy says this whole state's just a thin layer of limestone floating on a million underground rivers. Every once in a while, either a river rises or the ground sinks, then you wind up with a big hole like this one," I explain.

"Swell!" Vaylie hoists herself easily onto the lower branches of the tree, yelling "Hey" to the boys above us.

"This is Vaylie," I tell them. "Don't drop those snakes 'til we get up there!"

Ren, Roy and Dwayne are champing at the bit to get started. "What took you so long?" Ren grumps.

"Got here as soon as we could!" I blaze back at him. "Get this show on the road!"

Vaylie and I scramble above them, cushioning our seats with the Spanish moss that hangs like lace around us. Vaylie wrinkles her nose. "This stuff stinks."

"That's not the moss; it's *rattler* taint!" I say, watching her eyes balloon open.

Each of the boys holds a squirming burlap bag with two ropes attached. Side by side, the three of them lock their legs on the tree limb and "skin the cat." Now upside down, like a trio of acrobatic puppeteers, they use the ropes to lower the bags into position, behind the starting line drawn in the dirt.

"Now, Roo, *now*!" Ren hollers.

"On your mark," I yell. "Get set! *Go!*" The boys yank on one of their ropes to release the slip knot on the other. Instantly the snakes are free, their terrible beauty churning the pale gray dust. From our tree, we watch and hoot and yell as the fat brown diamondbacks coil and uncurl, tail bells rattling, split tongues flicking, angry, hooded eyes surveying each other and the barren sinkhole for cover.

"Won't they kill each other first?" Vaylie gasps, mesmerized by the drama below.

"No, watch! They want to run for cover, but the big one—see him?—the race won't start 'til *he* says so."

The biggest one, diamond head high above the others, twirls himself into position, twisting a giant coil across the necks of the other two, then, darting and dancing, presses their heads down into the dirt.

Dominance established, Ren's snake, the smallest, is first to quit the dance. It stretches out flat—at least four feet—and wriggles its way toward Dry Sink's side and the stand of palmetto. The other two join him and the race begins. Screaming, we cheer them and howl as Roy's snake, the big one, pulls ahead and vanishes into the scrub, with Ren's and Dwayne's just behind.

All of a sudden, the boys punch each other in victory and defeat, a big clap of thunder yanks our attention to the sky. While we were looking elsewhere, a dark mound of clouds has boiled itself into a surly black storm bank. Out of nowhere, lightning flashes on top of us, sparking a mad scramble out of the tree. A high branch in a giant live oak is no place to be in a Florida thunderstorm. Gasping at the splat of raindrops the size of soup spoons, flinching at the roar of the thunder, the boys veer left through the scrub toward

Samsons'. Vaylie and I run right, through the grove toward home.

In the kitchen, Doto looks up from her letter-writing. "When I heard the thunder, I knew you'd be home soon. You must be Maryvale," she says, regally extending her hand.

"*Vaylie*, please, ma'am. Vaylie Carrollton."

"I've driven through the town of Carrollton in Virginia. Any relation?"

"Yes, ma'am, my daddy's family's lived there forever, raisin' horses and growin' tobacco."

"You may call me Doto."

"Dodo? Like the Dodo bird?" Vaylie is puzzled but polite.

I laugh. "No, Doto, like DeSoto, the kind of car she drives."

"Pleased to meet ya," Vaylie says, stretching her freckles in a smile.

"Likewise, I'm sure," Doto nods. "If you girls want a snack, there are Oreos in the jar and milk in the Frigidaire," she says, turning her attention back to her letter.

"Mind if we sit out the storm in the attic?" I ask.

"Be my guest," Doto waves.

The roof of our house is heavy-gauge tin, and the third-floor attic, accessible only through Doto's room, is the best possible place to enjoy a good storm. The slant of the rain, the wind, the thunder and lightning create what I call the tin-tin symphony. Vaylie and I spread out a quilt on the wood plank floor and, like the Sorcerer's Apprentice in *Fantasia*, conduct the elements with our cookies dipped in milk. After a while, when the storm dies down to a slow drone, Vaylie's attention turns to the attic.

"This all y'all's stuff?" she asks, picking her way around an old trunk.

"Nope, most of it was Mr. Swann's. He used to own this house. Mother keeps threatening she's going to throw it all out."

"Who's this?" Vaylie's holding up a picture of a serious-looking lady in a big black hat.

"No idea."

"Kinda ugly, isn't she?" she says, setting down the dusty gold frame.

"Sort of, but like Mother says, 'pretty's only skin-deep.' "

"Yeh, and my mamma says, 'Sometimes pretty's all you got.' " Vaylie says, smearing her hands on her shorts.

"I think your mother's *very* pretty," I say.

"Well, *of course* she is. She was Miss Richmond at age eighteen, went on to become Miss Virginia, 1937. She was the prettiest girl in our state, that's why Daddy married her." Vaylie's picking through an old button box.

"My father married Mother because she was a Bridge Champion," I tell her proudly.

"What's that?" Vaylie frowns, holding a pair of silver buttons up to her ears.

"Well, it's someone who's really good at the card game called Bridge. He met her at a country club tournament. It was a member-guest event, and she was the guest of another member. Daddy says Mother beat the socks off everybody there, in spite of the fact that her partner was a dummy. He says that after she demolished his hand, he had to ask for hers."

"Your daddy proposed to your mother because she *beat* him at cards?" Vaylie asks, not believing me.

"That's what he says, and because right before she wins, she flashes him her Judy Garland grin."

"Your mother looks like Judy Garland?" Vaylie's impressed.

"Well, yes, *we* think so."

"Whoa, what's this?" Vaylie asks, standing tiptoe to pull a fat hatbox off the top of an old armoire.

"Hat, maybe?" I wonder, moving closer to see.

The box top's pattern is barely visible under its thick coat of dust. Vaylie lifts it and the eyes of a handsome young man in military uniform smile back at us. "Neat," Vaylie says, lifting the photo to reveal a flag folded in a triangle, and a stack of yellow papers.

"Let's turn on the light," I say, stepping around an abandoned rocker to reach the switch.

The top newspaper clipping is somebody's death announcement.

*Lieutenant Richard Randall Swann, U.S. Army, Slain in Second Battle at River Marne*, the black headline reads. We check the date. September 28, 1918.

"This stuff's ancient," Vaylie says, sorting quickly through the rest of the stack.

"He must have been old Mr. Swann's son. Looks a lot like Tyrone Power, don't you think?"

Vaylie doesn't answer. Instead, she gasps. "My Gawd, Reesa, look here!"

The party scene cut from the yellowed newspaper is of a cluster of ladies behind a lace-draped table topped with a big silver punch bowl, a party cake and a tall vase of flowers. Below it, the line of print says *Miss Maybelle Mason to Wed Local Hero*. Dead center, a pretty young woman smiles broadly for the camera. The date is September 15, 1918. Vaylie reads me the story:

Mrs. Blanche Ogden Swann entertained at her home on Old Dixie Highway Saturday night in honor of Miss Maybelle Mason, who will wed the highly decorated

Lieutenant Richard Randall Swann on Sunday, October
15th. The affair was a variety shower and the bride received many beautiful and useful gifts. After a delicious
supper was served, the ladies entertained themselves
with games. A mock wedding was the source of much
merriment. Guests included: Mrs. Caroline Mason,
Misses Bertine Turner . . .

". . . and a whole bunch of other names." Vaylie hands me the
article.

"Oh, Vaylie," I say, comparing dates, "he died ten days after the party, two weeks before the wedding!"

"How *aw*ful for Great-Aunt Maybelle!" Vaylie exclaims,
looking back at the smiling bride-to-be. "Poor thing, how'd
she ever get over it?"

"Maybe she didn't, Vaylie. Some things, well, *some* things
you never get over."

"I know," she says darkly. "Like people being mean to
each other who ought not to."

"And getting killed," I add, "for no reason at all."

"Girls!" Doto calls from the bottom of the stairs. "It's
four forty-five. Doesn't Vaylie have to be at Maybelle's by five
o'clock?"

"Oh, Lord," Vaylie says, holding up the hatbox, "think
we should take this stuff to her?"

"I don't know. It might . . . well . . . mightn't it bring up
a batch of memories best left alone?"

"You're probably right." Vaylie sighs, replacing the lid
very carefully, returning the box to the top of the armoire. "It
explains a lot, though, don't it?"

Outside, the road has switched from the dry, baked asphalt
of a few hours ago to a shiny wet ribbon reflecting us. Rain-

washed leaves glitter in the sun. Walking back, we talk quietly about our secret discovery under the dust in the attic. Vaylie promises to quiz her grandfather, Miss Maybelle's brother, for more information; both of us swear to be pen pals for *life*.

In the driveway, Vaylie's mother leans against her big blue Cadillac. Purse and keys in hand, it's clear she's ready to go. Miss Maybelle checks her watch as we enter the gate.

"Not bad, Reesa. Your mother have to remind you?" she queries, her metal-rimmed glasses glaring in the sun.

"Doto did, actually." Vaylie grins widely. "But we had the *best* time together! Thank you for *thinking* of it, Aunt Maybelle!" she says and, with a great rush of feeling, flings her arms around our wrinkled old postmistress.

Miss Maybelle freezes inside Vaylie's embrace, then pats her, stiff-handed, on the back, wanting to be let go.

"You're welcome, Maryvale," she says formally, smoothing the front of her post office uniform, almost as if wiping off Vaylie's warmth.

"I'll write you the very first second I can," my new friend vows as she hugs me goodbye.

With the best of intentions—to somehow comfort an ancient heartache—Vaylie's left Miss Maybelle plainly unsettled, a step off her usual statue-like control. As the two of us stand awkwardly by the road, watching the blue Cadillac disappear, I want to tell Miss Maybelle, *Vaylie didn't mean to make you uncomfortable, she's never lost anyone so she doesn't understand.*

Grief, I think, signs you up in a separate, invisible club, members selected at death's awful randomness. "Gone forever" is our password, lingering sorrow our secret handshake. If you haven't lost someone important to you, you can't begin to know the rules. Truth is, you don't even know the club exists.

As my own grieving heart recognizes another, my life-long view of Miss Maybelle as the angry old snapping turtle shifts. Opening the gate for her, calling a soft yet proper "good evening, ma'am," I resolve to treat her more kindly from now on.

All of a sudden, Doto's three big suitcases appear from under her bed, lined up, mouths open, across her window seat. I'm sorry to see her go, but she's promised Uncle Harry she'll leave this week, crossing the country to Montana before the Memorial Day traffic hamstrings the highways.

"I'll be back for Christmas, though," she promises Ren and me, "and, of course, I'll call right away if we hear anything from Mr. Hoover."

A few days later, Vaylie's letter arrives, addressed in a fat loopy script that could only be hers. It's postmarked Carrollton, Virginia and bears, in the top left corner, where the return address belongs, the heart-shaped greeting: *Hello, Great-Aunt Maybelle!!!*

Miss Maybelle, who's placed the envelope under her counter rather than in our box, points out the infraction sternly. "The U.S. Postal System frowns on *any* implication that one of its workers is taking familial advantage," she lectures me.

"I'll write Vaylie right away and explain," I promise.

"That won't be necessary, as I've already informed her mother!" Miss Maybelle snaps back.

"I'm sorry, Miss Maybelle," I say, attempting the appropriate remorse on Vaylie's behalf. Miss Maybelle eyes me sharply, grading my sincerity. Apparently, I pass.

"*You* didn't do anything," she says with that wave that means *get on about your business.*

"Thank you, ma'am," I grin, then call, stopping her in mid-turn, "and, Miss Maybelle?" She scowls, impatient. "Thank you for introducing me to my new pen pal. I've never had one before."

"You're welcome, Reesa," she says, creasing her face briefly, not so business-like, in my direction.

Inside the offending envelope, Vaylie writes:

*Dear Reesa,*

*Whit and Claudette tracked us down in Winter Park, said c'mon home, so here we are! Boy, was Daddy glad to see us! He surprised Mamma with a new dinner ring, a big emerald the size of a snake eye! The real thing, not the marble—I've seen a rattler race and know the difference. Mamma was as happy as could be until I opened my present—a new Rod Laver tennis racket.*

*"The child's already got more freckles than a field hand, why would you give her something that keeps her out in the sun, instead of away from it?"*

*"'Cause it's what she wanted," Daddy said, and after that, they had a big ugly fight that I refused to listen to and left the room.*

*I did talk to Mamma about coming back to Florida next time Daddy has a "spell," but she said if it happens this summer, we're heading north out of the heat and if it's not 'til fall, she'll have to take me someplace educational since I'd be missing school. Boston maybe, or Washington, D.C.*

*Oh, Reesa, didn't we have the* BEST *time together? I just*

*hate that we live so far apart. Please write me just the* SECOND
*you get this.*

Love, VAYLIE

*P.S. Do you think I have too many freckles?*
*P.P.S. What kinds of things do your parents fight about?*

# Chapter 13

To tell you the truth, before Marvin's murder, and the visit to our home by Mr. Harry T. Moore and Mr. Thurgood Marshall, I didn't read the newspaper much, had no idea *who* they were. But now that we're familiar, I notice their names often. The paper doesn't think much of Mr. Moore's efforts in Negro voter registration. It thinks even less of Mr. Marshall ("Mr. Civil Rights," they always call him) for forcing the retrial of Walter Lee Irvin and Samuel Shepherd, the two young Negroes accused of raping a Groveland white woman last year.

Since we met them, both Mr. Moore and Mr. Marshall have stopped by our packing-house almost regular. When you compare the paper's descriptions of them as the "strident insurgent" and "pugnacious parliamentarian" to the well-mannered gentlemen we've come to know, you have to wonder if the reporters ever actually talked to them.

Sometimes they drop in together, sometimes separate, to exchange papers with Daddy, enjoy a cool drink and use our bathroom in the back.

"You've *no* idea how rare access to a clean rest room is to a man of my color in this part of the country," Mr. Marshall says.

Mr. Harry T. Moore, the former schoolteacher, never fails to ask Ren and me about our homework. One day, he helped Ren master long division. Another time, when I was writing a report on Ancient Rome, he proved quite knowledgeable about the Caesars, Julius and Augustus.

"Although," he told me, "I much prefer the Greeks to the Romans."

"Why's that?" I asked, curious.

Mr. Harry's eyes lit up like twin headlamps. "Rome was a republic where only the rich had rights. But Greece! Greece gave us democracy—one man, one vote—the fairest form of government on earth! Greece gave us Plato, Socrates and Aristotle. Do you know Aristotle, Reesa?"

I'd never seen Mr. Harry so spirited. "Not really," I answered.

"Aristotle was brilliant!" he declared. "Aristotle said democracy rises out of one very important notion—that those who are equal in *any* respect are equal in *all* respects. 'Democracy,' Aristotle said, 'is best attained when all persons alike share in the government to the utmost.'" Mr. Harry stopped and raised his eyebrows in that teacher way that means *Are you getting this?*

"And that's why registering Negro voters is so important?"

"You betcha, girl!" he beamed, and told Daddy I'd earned "an A for the day!"

Fortunately for Ren and me, this school year's wound down to its inevitable end, the Friday before Memorial Day weekend.

"It's wrong to live in a state that's half water and not *enjoy* it!" Mother exclaims, cajoling her wary, unwilling family out the door. Nobody wanted to come on this Memorial Day Picnic, but here we are.

To Mother, a "picnic by the shore" on Memorial Day is an ironclad tradition, cast in her Midwestern childhood. To Daddy, Memorial Day, or any military holiday for that matter, is a painful reminder that his private war with polio left him unfit for the important battles against Hitler, Mussolini, and Hirohito. Daddy prefers a private observance, away from the marching bands, strutting veterans and cheering crowds lining Main Street Opalakee today.

The quiet cypress-rimmed cove off the St. John's River seems no different from the last time we came, last year. But none of us are quite the same. Mitchell, for instance, can swim. He and Buddy plunge in eagerly after Ren, whose passion for baseball has been re-channeled into a daily scrutiny of the Brooklyns' box scores. Last summer, Ren and Marvin hit no less than a hundred fly balls a day.

Mother and Daddy, having set up camp, sit in the shade of our beach umbrella. Daddy scans one of the three newspapers he's taken to reading regularly, clipping stories with his small fruit knife. These days, he's constantly compiling files for Mr. Harry, answering lists of questions from Mr. Marshall. I don't know what the questions are, but I do know that every answer must be three times verified by separate, unwavering sources. What will become of the answers puzzles me, too; but their careful completion has become my father's second occupation.

Beside him, Mother, festive in her blue polka-dot sundress, plays solitaire, shuffling and sorting, shifting and stacking. Now that Doto's left us for Montana, and the awful events of the spring have given way to summer, she's hoping, Mother says, for "some sort of normal."

A ways from my parents, I stretch out on my beach towel watching the water. The surface of the cove shines like metal, with dark emerald sparkles between the knees of the cypress trees. These days, I find myself watching *everything*, with the clear hope of not being caught unaware. Ever since Marvin's murder, I've come to despise surprises:

There in the cypress shadows, for example, a small, smooth log turns. Is it really wood? Or the slow, oily coil of a deadly water moccasin?

Beyond the splashing boys, two dark bumps surface among the sheltered water hyacinths. Another log? Or the dangerous, double-lidded eyes of an alligator?

Except for the turbulence trailing the boys, the water is a mirror, reflecting a bright blue sky, cottony clouds and the green lacework bowing the heads of the kneeling cypress. On its surface, the cove's as peaceful as a prayer. *But nothing is truly as it seems*, I know. Not me, not Mayflower, not the whole entire world. And especially not old Miss Maybelle two doors down the road.

I pull out Vaylie's letter and read, again, the sorry sequel to the already sad tale:

*Dear Reesa,*
    *I just got back from a big family dinner at my*
*Granddaddy's. It was fun, cousins galore, but nothing like a*

*rattler race which, by the way, nobody believes I really saw!
After dessert, I got the chance to ask Granddaddy the real scoop
on Great-Aunt Maybelle.*

*Oh, Reesa, it's even sadder than we imagined. The battle her
fiancé was killed in was the very last one of the war. Even
though he was supposed to come home before it, he <u>volunteered</u> to
stay! Granddaddy says the news hit Great-Aunt Maybelle so
hard she wouldn't leave her room for months, not even for
Christmas dinner. When she finally did come out, she told the
family she didn't want to talk about her fiancé or what
happened—ever again! And as far as Granddaddy knows, she
never has.*

*Granddaddy told me the young man was Mr. and Mrs.
Swann's only son and that his mother was so upset that she
died the next spring of a shattered heart. Isn't this just the
<u>saddest</u> thing you ever heard?*

*I asked him if that's the reason why Great-Aunt Maybelle
is so mean to everybody and all he'd say is "Everybody's got
their reasons, Vaylie, whether you know 'em or not."*

*Are you excited that summer's here? Write SOON!!!*

*Love, VAYLIE*

*P.S. If what Granddaddy says is true, that we all have our
reasons, I've been trying to figure what mine are. Do you know
yours?*

I've brought pen and paper with me to reply:

*Dear Vaylie,*

*If your grandfather's right, if everyone has their reasons,
then somebody stole my share.*

*These days, the reasons behind just about everything baffle
me. Like what really happened to Miss Maybelle and why?*

*Or, how can a bunch of men murder my friend Marvin and the whole of Mayflower act as if it never happened?*

*Marvin's mother Armetta says, "Time in the fire prepares us for what's ahead." But that doesn't make sense to me. Did God kill Miss Maybelle's fiancé so she could spend her life sorting envelopes? Protecting U.S. property from my brother and me? Did Marvin die so those of us who loved him could suffer while his killers walk around scot-free?*

*What do you think, Vaylie? Do bad things happen because God wills it so? Or is evil something else, with a mind of its own? Like the serpent in the Garden of Eden, or an alligator at the edge of a swimming hole?*

*Down here, people think of alligators as "a necessary evil." "Take the good with bad," they say. Do you think maybe good and bad are stuck together, like two sides of a dime?*

*I'm sorry for going on about this. But every question I come up with just seems to lead to another one. Most days, I feel like a dog chasing its tail.*

*If you come up with any answers, or reasons either, please let me know. And write again <u>soon</u>!*

*Love, Reesa*

*Chapter 14*

S ummer's heat settles on us like a mother hen. We locals know enough to stay in the shade, but the summer tourists, skin white as eggshells heading south, are blistered stiff going north and reeking of Coppertone applied too late.

Today, Mother and I are tending customers in the showroom while Daddy and Luther prune the last of the spring-bearing Valencia trees in the grove out back. The big fruit-processing equipment on the raised platform behind the showroom walls is quiet: the washer with its giant water tank and big bristle brushes; the waxer with its rubber rollers, preservative spray, drying fan and hood; and the long conveyor belts that transport the washed-and-waxed fruit to the sizing bins are all at rest between summer's relaxed, twice-a-week runs.

Mid-morning, the big black pickup truck wheels into the parking lot, oversize tires splaying gravel, large chrome bumper and Confederate flag plate glaring in the sun.

*Local*, I think at my post behind the juice counter; *nobody I know*, seeing the packed metal gun rack behind the seat.

The driver gets out, skinny, on the short side, with an upright stride that's soldier-like. *War veteran*, I guess. Although he's a stranger to me, the two same-size boys with different clothes and identical faces with him are familiar. *The Bowman twins*, I remember, *first graders*, and the only identical twins in the history of Opalakee Elementary. I've helped them find picture books in the school library.

The three of them move quickly into the shade of the front awning, get their bearings, then strut over to me.

"We'd like some of that ice-cold orange juice you're advertisin'," the man says, pulling a forearm across his forehead to wipe back the sweat. He has the flushed red coloring and the slow-rolling accent of people from south Georgia. "Three for a dime, right?"

"No, sir," I say with a smile. "It's all you can drink for a dime, limit three per customer. We say that to keep the tourists from drinking too much and getting sick to their stomachs."

"You tellin' me you want *thirty cents* instead of a dime?" His eyelashes are thick and orangey around pale eyes that have turned suspicious.

"Yes, sir." I smile again. "A dime apiece. After your first glass, you can have two more each, if you want." The boys are staring at me, trying to sort why I'm familiar. The man sees it, too.

"Y'all know this girl?" he asks them.

The boys nod and say, "Yes, from school." "The library, right?" They have the habit of finishing each other's sentences.

"*You* go to their school?" the man asks me, leaning forward to get a closer look.

"Yes, sir. I've helped your boys find their library books."

"That's funny," he says without smiling. A fat drop of sweat pops out at his hairline. It swerves down the flat of his temple, the hollow of his cheek, and hangs off his jaw. "I didn't think we had any *Jew* girls at our school."

"Pardon me?" His tone turns my arm trembly. Without my telling them to, my hands grip the edge of the counter.

"Well, anybody that advertises three glasses for a dime then tries to charge thirty cents *must* be a *Jew*." His glint across the counter is ugly. The drop of sweat falls off his chin and splats on the counter between us.

"*No*, sir, we're Baptists." My heart's pummeling my chest with a fear I don't understand. What if I *was* Jewish? What would be wrong with that?

His eyes sweep the showroom, taking in Mother and the customers in the shell-lamp section.

"Well, looky here, little Baptist Jew girl," he drawls in a voice that pricks the back of my neck. "I think we've changed our minds about that juice. I think we'll just head on down to Voight's for some Coke-Cola. C'mon, you two. *Git* in the truck." His words cut the space between the twins like a knife. The boys quit and run, fast, toward the truck.

The man glares at me across the counter some more, then slowly, like a dare, parts his fat pink lips into an unpleasant smile. He turns, unhurried, on his boot heel, and swaggers away, under and out from the awning. When the sun hits his back, I gasp. Mother, returning to the counter carrying a conch lamp for checkout, turns. "Reesa? What's wrong?"

As the man's boots crunch across the gravel toward the truck, the letters "J.D.," tooled on the back of his black leather belt, get smaller, harder and harder to read.

"Reesa, what is it?" Mother asks, coming close to look me in the eye.

"That man, that's J. D. Bowman, the one who shot Marvin."

"Good Lord, Reesa, are you all right? Did he *say* something? Did he *do* anything to you?"

"He called me a Jew."

That night, the nightmare, the horror where I'm trapped in the crowd and can't save Marvin; that dream changes. Now, one of the men in the center of the circle stops and turns to scan the spectators. In this new nightmare, J. D. Bowman singles me out, points and yells, "Grab her, too. She's a Jew!"

The next day, at the border between two Miami neighborhoods, all hell breaks loose.

Daddy's family, genetically inclined toward quick thinking and fast acting, are the first to call. I answer the phone and Uncle Harry, in a voice that sounds like Daddy's, mistakes me for Mother.

"Lizbeth, what the *hell's* going on down there?" he wants to know.

That night, we hear from Doto and Aunt Eleanor.

"Warren, you've had fourteen years to whip that state into shape. What the hell's wrong with it?" my father's only sister demands.

"The hell" they refer to, the one *every*one's talking about, is the bombing of the Carver Village Housing Project for Negroes in Miami. The story's all over the news. Bombs gutted two buildings in the recently refurbished section of what used to be all-white Knights Manor. "The largest blast ever detonated in the state of Florida," the papers say, "possibly the entire Eastern Seaboard." The boom of it pitched people living five blocks away out of their beds, and rattled the balcony windows of the fancy hotels down at the beachfront.

One picture in the paper shows the garage owner across the street from the project pointing at the mangled cars, which leaped eight feet in the air, crashing their roofs against his ceiling.

Despite the fact that a number of people suffered cuts and bruises from flying glass, block and wood, everybody swears it's a miracle nobody's dead. The lucky thing is, the two eight-unit buildings were empty; their new occupants hoped to move in next month.

"My guess is that the local whites weren't inclined to form a welcoming committee," Daddy tells us grimly. "This thing's got the Klan written all over it."

When the investigators uncover the remains of two 100-pound bundles of dynamite, they find a third bundle of eighty sticks which failed to explode. One war veteran, looking things over, tells reporters it reminds him of "the blockbuster bombs we used to rout the Krauts out of Bastogne and Coblenz."

On the radio, the Miami police chief says he's certain the Ku Klux Klan "had no involvement *whatsoever*"; in fact, he has "reason to believe that *Reds* are responsible." One Negro has been arrested.

*"Idiots!"* Doto rages on the phone (so loud the whole family can hear her) and declares she's calling her Congressman *first thing* in the morning.

After Doto rings off, we hear from our mother's only brother, Gordy, and our other grandmother, Nana. Like Mother, they're the sensitive side of the family:

"We're just a nervous *wreck* over this, Lizbeth. Aren't *you?* Why not pack up the kids and come back to Chicago for a few weeks? We'll have a nice visit while the police settle things *down* down there."

Mother and Daddy hand the phone back and forth, each reassuring the other's family, *"Every*thing's fine, we're all *fine."*

As bad as the bombing appears to be, there is, in fact, the slightest flicker of a silver lining in this storm cloud. In to-day's paper, the remarks of Mr. Harry T. Moore and Mr. Thur-good Marshall are startling:

"I call on Mr. J. Edgar Hoover and the Federal Bureau of Investigation to come to Miami, help us sort this thing out," Mr. Moore, Executive Secretary of the State N.A.A.C.P., is quoted as saying.

"And when they get here, I have a list of other things to look into," Mr. Thurgood Marshall, attorney for the National N.A.A.C.P. said, "including the mistreatment of my clients, Walter Lee Irvin and Samuel Shepherd, in Lake County's Raiford Prison, and the murder of Marvin Cully, a fruit picker, outside Opalakee, in central Florida."

It is the first official acknowledgment of anything to do with Marvin, who was killed three whole months ago. And, to me, it means, it surely *must* mean *something* will happen now.

*Chapter 15*

---

In the middle of July, at the peak of our summer season, here's what *should* have happened:

At six o'clock, Daddy, having placed the big "Closed For The Day" signs out front, should've joined the rest of us at the already bustling party in the back.

Our friends Sal and Sophia Tomasini, having closed their own store an hour earlier, should've been holding court over the stove's steaming, boiling, baking pots, bubbling Italian, brimming laughter. Armetta should've been basking in our communal admiration for her heavenly cloud cake—three light-as-air layers floating in creamy coconut—the very one Marvin calls her "Ain't-None-Betta Cake." Luther and Marvin should've been corralling the boys to take their turns cranking the homemade strawberry ice cream. My parents should've looked and felt young again when, after our dinner, we laughed until we cried at the stories of that other summer thirteen years ago:

They remember the swim in the lake followed by polio's headaches, high fever and paralysis. But it's Armetta who tells the one about Doto best. "Miz Doto was a wildcat. You shoulda seen ol' Doc Johnny go bug-eyed when she tol' him, 'What kinda doctor *are* you? I want those splints off Warren's arm and leg this *minute*! Moist heat and massage is what he needs, you old *fool*!' She was right, too!"

Old Sal should've told the one about the big day itself: the men tending Daddy's muscle spasms in one room; the women helping Mother with her contractions in the next while, downstairs, Doto railed at the doctor on the phone, "They're coming *too close*! We'll never make it to Orange Hospital in Orlando, *get* in your damn car and get over here *now*!" It was serene Sophia who held Mother while Armetta "caught" me on my birth day. Doto was downstairs at the door, hauling in poor Doc Johnny, who luckily arrived in time for cleanup. "It's a wonder he's even speaking to us," Mother should've said.

After dinner and the stories, Marvin should've turned on the radio and coaxed us all out to dance, something lively and fun like Teresa Brewer and the Dixieland All-Stars "Choo'n Gum." This very minute, we should've been howling at Marvin trying to teach a shuffling Sal the latest fancy dance step.

Truth is, all of this *should've* happened and *would've* happened—as it always had on this particular day—if only Marvin hadn't been murdered, and the Klan stayed out of everybody's business in Miami.

Instead of loud music, the radio plays low, everyone half

listening for the latest news update. Instead of funny stories, my parents, Sal and Sophia, and Luther and Armetta sit softly discussing the latest fearful developments. Last month's massive bombing of Carver Village was only the beginning. On the Fourth of July, dynamite bundles were hurled at the steps of the Miami Jewish Center and, just today, a blast blew up the doors of St. Stephen's Catholic Church.

"First da Negroes, den da Jews, now Catholics." Sal's eyes behind thick glasses sink into the shadows of his bushy gray brows. Next to him, Sophia, his wife, bows her silver-streaked head.

"It's the Klan's holy trinity of hate. Nobody else is so obviously ecumenical," Daddy says.

I wonder if it occurs to him how nearly our little group resembles that triangle. Luther and Armetta are Negroes; the Tomasinis, Catholic transplants from New York; and we've been called Jews by the very man who murdered Marvin!

Except for Daddy who's angry, we're an anxious, apprehensive group. As Ren and Mitchell quit us to search outside for fireflies, it's Luther who lays out the night's most troublesome question.

"How long 'fore the Opalakee Klan stirs things up 'round here again?" he asks quietly.

"Hard to say, isn't it?" Daddy says. "Since nobody's doing anything to stop the Miami crowd, this business could easily get out of hand. It's not surprising their police are looking the other way—they're probably half Klanners themselves. We know Thurgood and Harry are doing all they can. But you'd *think* the big hotel owners would be screaming their heads off. It won't be long, it *can't* be long before the wealthy tourists start making other plans. Once the cancellations start rolling in, the Miami bigwigs will be howling for the governor, *some*body, to do *some*thing. Nothing like an endangered pocketbook to help a businessman find his conscience."

"In the meantime . . . ?" Mother's eyes are dark with worry.

"In the meantime, what are *we* supposed to do?" Daddy wonders, his stare challenging the table, his jaw hardened in frustration. "What choice do we have but to sit tight and keep our heads down?" he asks in a tone that tells me that's the *last* thing he wants to do.

I was Mitchell's age when the Japanese bombed Pearl Harbor. I have no memory of President Roosevelt saying the day will live in infamy, but I know he said it. I was Ren's age when we dropped the A-bomb on Hiroshima. These were Acts of War. Everybody knew it. What with Europe, Japan and Korea, my country's been at war with somebody, somewhere, practically my entire life. But it was today, July 14, 1951, that the Klan bombed St. Stephen's Catholic Church and declared war on the people of this state. It was a lousy gift in the worst year I've ever known. It ruined my thirteenth birthday, which, by all rights, *should've* been a happy day.

The one and only bit of good news this month comes from Ren: the Brooklyn Dodgers, who captured first place in their league in April, and held on to it throughout May and June, win ten games in a row in July. At midseason's All-Star break, they're still way ahead of everybody else—which, Ren says, "is a sure sign they'll win the pennant and make it into the Series!" Ren, old Sal, and the fans from The Quarters go crazy when a record seven Brooklyn Dodgers make it onto the National League's All-Star team, including Negroes Jackie Robinson, Roy Campanella and Don Newcombe. These days, what Marvin called "baseball's Heaven on Earth" offers the only hopeful respite from our real lives in central Florida.

*Chapter 16*

The high, humid heat of August presses on us with an unkind hand. This is, officially, the hottest Florida summer on record. Everything, from traffic on the Trail to Buddy's tail-wagging, has slowed to a crawl.

In Miami, denied protection by local police ("We will not make night watchmen out of our officers," the chief says), Jewish war veterans patrol their communities to protect their families from further bombings. In the Negro neighborhood surrounding Carver Village, leaders request but are denied the same privilege.

The F.B.I., citing "no apparent violation of any federally guaranteed civil rights," remains elsewhere. The bombings continue.

This week's explosion is at the Coral Gables Jewish Center, fifteen miles north of Miami. As usual, the police report no suspects. No official actions are taken.

Inside the showroom, the air hangs as limp and damp as a washrag. Daddy brings out the three big pedestal fans, normally in the back, and places them in opposite corners to create a cooling air flow. The fans are noisy. Ren and Mitchell, playing darts in the office, yell to us, "Hey, sounds like there was a wedding in Wellwood!"

The familiar sounds of a squealing lead car followed by a flock of honking well-wishers pull Mother, Daddy and me outside and onto the walkway, peering north.

What we *expect* to see is a pair of newlyweds, their car decorated with ribbons, cans, signs and all, followed by loudly celebrating family and friends.

What appears *instead* stuns us.

In the lead, a sleek black Chrysler New Yorker, speeding wildly, weaves in and out of the slow-moving traffic. No decorations, no signs, four Negro occupants, two in front, two in back, *obviously* in flight. The Hertz logo on the car's front plate tells me it's a rental, probably from the airport. The lockjawed concentration of the driver and the flat-out frantic movements of the others inside makes it clear—*this* is no party game. The four people flying past us in the Chrysler are terrified. When you see what's behind them, you can't blame them.

The first of the three chase vehicles roaring down the Trail is a big black Ford pickup, oversize bumpers polished to blinding brightness. Two men inside wear the ghostly white of the Ku Klux Klan. Out one window, the rider brandishes a double-barreled shotgun. Out the other, the driver waves a high-powered rifle, using his inside forearm to press against the truck horn. Both men are hooded, but there's no mistaking those bumpers and Confederate flag plate. Passing in front of us, pursuing the Chrysler, is J. D. Bowman, the man of my nightmares.

Behind him, about a hundred yards, a red Dodge truck tears toward us. Three riders lean forward in the front. Two more stand in the back, clutching the cab and waving weapons. The sleeves of their robes flap in the wind, the crests of their hoods blow back, flat against their heads. One lets out an eerie, high-pitched cry, the unnerving howl of the Rebel Yell.

In the last truck, a shiny blue Chevy, the white robes of three men glow against its dark interior. These figures brandish no weapons, honk no horns, make no battle cries. These men sit calmly, the driver coolly maneuvering in and around the traffic, the riders patient like observers or judges or law enforcement officials. A large Confederate flag draped and taped to the driver's side covers the logo we all know is there: the golden script of Emmett Casselton's Casbah Groves.

As this terrible parade flies past us, Mother and Daddy look at each other in disbelief. The fearful faces of those in the front car, the hateful menace of their white-robed pursuers leaves me numb. I *know* the Klan is a group of white men capable of doing horrible things; what they did to Marvin is etched in my mind till I die. But to tell you the truth, I'd somehow imagined that adults dressed in sheets might look like a grown-up Halloween party. The sight of them in full pursuit, in broad daylight, sickens me.

Mother pulls me close. Daddy, behind us, grips us both. Mercifully, the boys have remained inside, choosing dart play over the supposed "wedding party." My parents and I stand stiffly together, listening to the horns race out of town. Then two carloads of customers pull into our driveway. We follow them, dazed, into the showroom.

"You see that Big Chase?"

"What was it all about?"

"Was that the Ku Klux Klan?"

"Where were the cops?"

"Who was in the Chrysler?" the tourists want to know, peppering us with the very questions we have for each other. For the next few hours, we collect details like puzzle pieces.

"That car flew past us, doing at least ninety outside Wellwood, nearly scared my wife and kids to death!"

"I don't know where it started. We stopped to get gas in Tangerine and that Chrysler nearly crashed into us when we were pulling out of the station. We stopped, tried to pull out again, and here come the trucks. My wife made me wait fifteen minutes, just to be sure it was safe to get back on the road."

"That black pickup ran the car ahead of us off the road outside Lockhart!"

On Sunday, at church, the congregation is buzzing.

"Did you see—?"

"Where were you when those trucks went through?"

"I recognized that big black truck, didn't you? Blue one, too."

"Any idee who was in the car?"

"Had to be folks from up north. Rented from the airport. Wonder what they did?"

After Sunday's midday dinner, we drive to Opalakee for ice cream. Mother and Daddy buy an Orlando paper and search it for clues. We listen to the car radio. We ask a few Opalakee people (not many out in this heat) what they know.

"Oh, it went right past *here*, smack-dab through the middle of town! Chief of Police was parked over there, front of the bank building. Leaned against his car and watched it with the rest of us. Didn't do a thing."

*Of course not, but who were they? Are they okay?*

It's not until Luther stops by, after that night's supper, that the pieces tumble into place. He comes in carrying a bulging brown paper sack.

"Evenin', y'all!" he beams. "Mah cousin Sylbie was visitin' from Valdosta this weekend, brought us a case of sweet Georgia peaches. They won't last the week in this heat, thought y'all might take some off our hands."

"Luther, there's nothing in the world better than a ripe Georgia peach," Mother says, brightening. "Thank you! You kids want one?"

Ren, Mitchell and I sit at the table smacking through our peaches, catching the sweet juice running down our chins with pink paper napkins, when Daddy asks Luther, "You hear anything about the Big Chase?"

"Well, actually, Ah did." Luther leans back in his chair, his gold dog tooth glinting in a grin.

Daddy leans forward, hanging on his every word.

"Y'see, Mistuh Thurgood Marshall was s'posed to be in Tavares yesterday, filin' for the hearin' on the big *re*-trial. The Opalakee Klan got wind of it, thought they might kidnap Mistuh Marshall, or at least give 'im a scare on his way to the *a*'port. They was waitin' for him to cross the county line. Chased his car all the way down the Trail to O'landah. Lost 'im in the a'port traffic."

"Luther, how in the *world* do you know this?"

"Mist'Warren, half mah choir works in the homes of the Klanners 'round here, *have* since most of these young bucks were chil'ren. Those folks so use to havin' they colored women in the kitchen or workin' 'round the house, they forgit to watch what they say."

"You mean to tell me, you heard all this from your *sopranos*?" Daddy's flabbergasted.

"Well, *some* of 'em are altos," Luther says, "but, yes, Ah did."

"Why, Luther, you're head of a spy ring," Daddy says, impressed.

"Ah s'pose Ah am," Luther nods.

"You know . . ." The corner of Daddy's mouth twitches. "You could call it the Choir Intelligence Agency, your own private *C.I.A.*"

"Oh, that's good, that's real good!" Luther's booming laugh bounces off the kitchen walls. Then he turns serious. "Ah'll tell you somethin' else . . ."

"What?" I ask.

"What those Klanners don't know is that Mistuh Thurgood Marshall wudn't even in that car."

"What do you mean?" Mother asks.

"Mistuh Marshall had to cancel and send his assistants. The people in that car were his staff, plus a couple Yankee reporters hitchin' a ride to the O'landah airport!"

"You're kiddin' me!" "Really?" "Can you believe it!" we exclaim as the implications of this news race around the table.

"But wait a minute . . ." Daddy's tone cuts off our delight. "Luther, if the Klan lost the car in the airport traffic, how do *you* know who was in that car?"

"You a quick one, Mist'Warren." Luther narrows his eyes at Daddy, dropping his voice. "Ah got *that* information from Mistuh Harry T. Moore, who sends y'all his regards, by the way. Mistuh Moore says those redneck Klanners have no idee how much they helped the cause of the Florida Negro yesterday."

In the wake of Luther's revelations, I'm relieved that the people in the black car got safely away. *Maybe* the involvement of two Northern reporters will call attention to a bad situation that's clearly grown worse. "Evil is contagious," Doto told me once. Like some Biblical plague, the Klan's particular kind of evil has taken over Miami and headed north, back up the Trail, parading past our very doorstep.

That night, as my parents enter their bedroom across the hall from mine, I hear Mother echo my worry.

"I thought Marvin's murder was a mistake, the show-off act of a madman," she tells Daddy, "but *this* was *organized,* Warren! If the Klan's grown brazen enough to attempt a kidnapping in broad daylight, what's next?"

I can't hear, I can only imagine my father's stone-faced reply.

*What will the local Klan do next?* I wonder, curled tight in my sheets. There aren't any Negro housing projects or Jewish synagogues around Mayflower. They wouldn't dare dynamite The Quarters or Opalakee's Colored Town, would they? But if they tried, who'd stop them? Not the local law, of course. We learned that last March. Then who? And I find myself praying for the first time in months. *Oh, God, if You're up there, could You arrange a little help down here?*

# Chapter 17

The *he answer is no.* God doesn't care what's happening in Florida. And, apparently, Mr. J. Edgar Hoover doesn't either. (Of course, in little Mitchell's mind, God and Mr. Hoover have become one and the same.)

Without Anyone's intervention, the Miami Klan continues to terrorize that city's non-white and non-Protestant neighborhoods. You can read all about it in the newspaper; though, since the big blast last June, the stories are buried in a back section . . . as if it's perfectly *normal* to have dynamite blow up another Catholic church, or a Jewish synagogue, or Negro housing project.

Everyone says it's a miracle nobody's been killed. *Yet.*

Last Saturday, the Orlando Klan jumped in, blowing up a perfectly good ice-cream stand called the Creamette. We drove over the next day and I could not believe my eyes. What was once a nice little drive-up business is now a heap of rubble, as if a nasty-tempered giant monster stepped on just *that* place and flattened it to nothing.

Daddy talked to the owner and his wife, who were picking through the piles, shaking their heads. "Somebody called us," they told him, "a man's voice telling us we better stop serving white people and Negroes from the same window. We only had the one window to hand out the ice-cream cones. *What* were we supposed to do?"

The Orlando paper says the blast hurled concrete blocks two hundred fifty feet in the air. The lady across the street said she spent the entire day picking up rocks, pieces of metal, paper napkins and the little white wrappers they put ice-cream cones in, scattered all over her yard.

Everybody's talking about it: the people at church, the customers at Voight's, the last of the summer tourists heading home for Labor Day and, of *course*, the ladies at Miz Lillian's Beauty Parlor.

Miz Maggie Brass, wife of Deacon Aldo, is on the same Labor Day–Christmas–Easter perm schedule I am. (Nobody gets a summer perm. The weather's so hot and heavy that everybody's hair frizzes, perm or not, so why bother?)

"It's hurricane season," Miz Maggie says. "Got everybody on edge, doin' crazy things with dynamite."

"No, no, it's the Nigras gettin' *uppity*, movin' into their fancy housing projects," says Miz Opal Taylor, in for her weekly shampoo-and-set. "The Klan's just keepin' 'em in their place. I'm inclined to agree with Mr. Eugene Cox, that

Georgia Congressman, y'all know him? He says it's the *hand of Stalin* behind these Nigra uprisings."

"*Up*risings?" Miz Lillian laughs, coaxing Miz Opal's top curls into place with a red rat-tail comb. "Far as I can see, the Negroes haven't done a thing! It's the Klan that's *doin'* it all."

"And why'd they bomb the Jewish synagogues and the Catholic church? None of 'em have a *single* Negro member," Miss Iris, Miz Lillian's assistant, wants to know.

"Be*cause*, Iris," Miss Opal, sounding aggravated, says, "those left-wing liberals are *a*gitators, givin' the Nigras *ideas* about livin' next to whites. Next thing y'know, they'll wanta be eatin' in our *re*staurants, usin' our toilets," Miz Opal says.

"Maybe even comin' to our beauty parlors." Miz Lillian winks at me in the mirror, aggravating Miss Opal right back.

"Lillian! You're not about to let a Nigra woman in here!" Miz Maggie barks, her voice rising out of the rinsing sink.

"I don't know, Maggie. I never had the chance to work with that kind of hair. Might be interestin'," Miz Lillian says, stifling herself.

At supper, I relate Miz Opal's "hand of Stalin" comments to my family.

"That's ridiculous," Mother says, Miz Opal being one of the church ladies she regularly avoids.

"Devil's trick, my dear," Daddy says, shaking his head.

"What do you mean?" Ren asks, making a face at the spoonful of succotash Mother's placed on his plate.

"If you're the bad guy, people are *against* you, right?" Daddy asks, pointing a fork full of limas in Ren's direction.

"Right," Ren nods.

"Best way to get people rooting *for* you is to accuse your enemy of being something worse than you are."

Ren frowns. "You mean if people think that Negroes are turning Communist . . . that's supposed to make it okay for the Klan to blow up their houses?"

"Exactly," Daddy tells him.

"Mother's right. That's the stupidest thing I've ever heard," Ren mutters, turning his attention to his meat loaf.

"But will it work?" I want to know.

"I certainly hope not," Mother says.

"Depends." Daddy leans forward, both elbows on the table. All of sudden, he's very serious. "Sometimes, this kind of thing starts out small, like a new plant, a vine like kudzu, for instance. If nobody pays attention to it, it grows and grows, and before you know it, it's taken over a whole hillside, choked the life out of every other plant around it."

"Warren," Mother says, in a way that means *quit scaring the children.*

"Forewarned is forearmed," Daddy shoots back at her. "These are devilish times we're living in, Lizbeth. There's no hiding that from anybody, especially these children."

At Daddy's stinging tone, Mother retreats behind her Poker Face, gets up and clears the table. It's their last exchange of the evening.

To tell you the truth, I'm worried about my mother. Ever since we went to visit the Creamette, or rather the place where the Creamette used to be, ever since we toed our way through the rubble of what's left of that other family's business, she's not been herself. Fact is, none of us are.

## Chapter 18

The number eighty-six school bus lumbers to a squeaking stop in front of the post office. The bill of Taddy Carver's green John Deere cap turns profile, nodding toward the steps. Taddy's big hand cuffs and thrusts the handle. The doors split open and the boys—Ren plus Roy and Dwayne Samson—tumble out ahead of me, barking and romping like bloodhounds released from their cages, eager for the woods.

Over the din of their cries for weekend adventure, Taddy's cap dips a silent "See you Monday" to me. The doors swish closed and the bus, clutch complaining mightily, heaves itself back onto the road. The Samson boys cut left toward their house, but I amble right, behind the bolting bird dog that is my brother. *It's a relief to be back in school,* I decide, feeling the first-week jitters crowd out this summer's insanity.

As the front porch door slams behind us, the phone is ringing in that jingle-jangle way that means it's a party-line call. Ren, knowing it could only be Miss Maybelle at the Post Office or Miz Sooky across the street, tears into the bathroom.

"Reesa! Where's your daddy? I *need* him, *quick.*" The voice is Miss Maybelle's and it's urgent.

"He's not here, ma'am, probably at the packinghouse."

"You've *got* to find him. I need his help *now!* Understand?"

"Y-Yes, ma'am." Something is very wrong. There's no doubt about that.

"He must come right away!"

"Yes, ma'am," I say, sensing no time for questions. "I'll find him."

Mother answers on the first ring.

"Where's Daddy . . . something's wrong at the post office . . . Miss Maybelle needs him," I tell her in a rush.

"He's gone over to Winter Garden to pick up a tractor part. Reesa, what is it?"

"She didn't say. Just that he needed to come quick!"

"Weren't you just there, Reesa? Did you see anything wrong?"

"Nothing out of the ordinary." What could it be?

"Robert's due any minute," Mother tells me. "I'll send him along as soon as he gets here."

As I hang up the phone, Ren demands an explanation. Getting it, he turns without a word and heads out the door.

"Where are you going?" I yell, running after him, then, realizing his intent, race to catch him.

The front of the post office is as dead as usual this time of day, at least two hours before the mail is sorted and available for pickup. There are no cars or trucks, front or back, no sign of anything or anyone outside. Carefully cracking the door, we peer inside, then back at each other. One whiff of that musky-sweet scent and we *know*, without asking, what's wrong.

"Damn, need my fork stick!" Ren whispers, tiptoeing in with a hunter's grace. The lobby's empty, but over the counter, in the shaft of sunlight slashing across the backroom floor, I see the diamondback rattler, coiled and spitting at a frozen Miss Maybelle. The rattler whorls in the dusty light, dead center between Miss Maybelle, who's trapped at the front counter, and the room's only exit at the back.

"Where's your daddy?" Miss Maybelle asks us desperately, nothing moving but her mouth.

"He can't come, but Robert's on his way," I assure her, watching Ren size up the situation. Over his shoulder, something in the corner catches my eye.

"Can you use the push broom?" I ask and point.

"Yes!" he says. "Help me up, then hand it to me."

"What are you two doing? Don't come in here!" Miss Maybelle cries out of the side of her mouth, eyes glued to the snake.

I hoist Ren up on the counter and he squirms quickly across it and to the right, out of the snake's line of sight. Quietly he says, "Don't worry, Miss Maybelle, I've caught a *million* snakes. You stand real still now. *I'll* get him."

With great care, I pass him the long-handled push broom, then reach across to put my hand over Miss Maybelle's ice-cold claw clinging to the counter's edge. As Ren mountain-climbs across the wall of mailboxes and steps lightly, gingerly onto the worktable, the snake senses something and bobs his hood. Miss Maybelle's bony fingers find mine and crush them so tightly I cry out, a sharp yelp of pain.

Ren raises a finger to his lips, then inches down to his knees. He twirls the broom into position, brushes up, rail-side down. Holding it like a pool cue, eyeing his mark, he rams it down onto the back base of the snake's skull, pinning it, tail wildly flopping, to the floor.

He looks up, grinning ear to ear. "Can you toss me an empty mail sack, Miss Maybelle?" he asks her.

"Is it safe to move?" she wants to know, still clutching my hand.

"Perfectly," he tells her.

Miss Maybelle lets go, grabs a soft canvas sack from under the counter and with a nervous jerk heaves it Ren's way. Catching it with one hand, maintaining pressure on the flat, trapped head with the other, Ren slides off the table and scoops up the writhing body, tail first into the sack. With a practiced flick, he lifts the broom and yanks the drawstring, securing the rattler inside.

"Safe and sound, Miss Maybelle," he says, holding the sack, like a prize, up in the air.

Relief wilts her. "Oh, my dear boy, thank you, thank you," she says.

"No problem," Ren tells her. "How'd he get in, in the first place?"

"Must have snuck in during the afternoon delivery. I turned around and it was just *there*." She shudders. "Will you take it out and kill it?"

"*Kill* him? He was just looking for a safe place to sleep. Naw, I'll let him go, out in the scrub where he belongs."

Out front, we hear the sudden rumble and heave of Robert's motorcycle. The big front door bangs open. "Miss Maybelle, Miz Mac says there's trouble. What's wrong?" Robert growls, ready for action.

"Not a thing," she answers, her eyes lighting on Ren. "Not anymore."

Ren, still holding the squirming sack, recounts his heroics for Robert. The sun streams through the window, bathing Miss Maybelle in light. As she thanks us again, I find myself blinking at her powerful resemblance to the pretty bride-to-be in the photo in our attic.

V aylie's postcard arrives the following week, her choice an unfortunate one for our postmistress. The picture on front shows a coiled diamondback rattler, tail and triangular head erect, pointy fangs like drapery hooks ready to strike. Red letters on the front say GREETINGS *from the Natural History Museum, Washington, D.C.*

On the back, she writes:

*Guess who's on tour again? Is Junior High great? I hate missing the first few weeks, takes forever to catch up. Did you know a rattlesnake is part of the Pit Viper family? I told Mamma that since she always calls Daddy's mamma "the old viper" that must make me part rattler. Maybe I'm related to the bunch we saw in ol' Dry Sink. If you see one, tell 'em "hi" from Cousin Viper! Will write more when I can.*
                                                    *Love,* VAYLIE

You've got something there, Vaylie, I think. There's a bit of the rattler in all of us. But as far as I've seen, human snakes are a whole lot meaner than the reptile kind.

*Chapter 19*

Otober third is a summer day with an autumn date. Ren and I spent the morning helping Sal and Sophia get ready for this afternoon's crowd. In the scrawny shade under the scrub pines behind Tomasinis' store, over a hundred people are assembling to cheer their beloved Jackie Robinson, and the Brooklyn Dodgers, to pennant glory over the nasty New York Giants.

After a season that, according to Ren, was pretty much a one-horse race, with the Dodgers in the lead April through September, the Giants came out of nowhere to force a pennant play-off, the three-game cockfight that, one way or the other, ends today.

Already, we've raked the dirt free of pinecones and rearranged the rough-sawn benches into semicircles facing the back of the store. Against the wall, Sal's perched his small black-and-white TV set on a plywood shelf, suspended by ropes out of the window of their upstairs apartment. We've stood on the ground below while Sal fiddled with the twenty-five-foot antenna, yelling our opinions on the screen's reception from the faraway Atlanta station. We've stocked the Coke-Cola cooler and arranged the charcoal in the side-split fifty-gallon barrels where Sal will barbecue, and we will serve, his secret-recipe, all-beef frankfurters, "like da Stahl-Meyers at Ebbets Field, only betta."

Luther and Armetta are among the first to arrive just after noon, with Reverend Stone from St. John's A.M.E. I see Jerry Tee, Jimmy Lee and Natty and others who work on our picking crew are here, and old ladies and young mothers and children who, lacking real Dodger baseball caps, wear blue cotton kerchiefs tied to their heads. They race around like a band of miniature pirates.

The hot dog work before the game is fast and furious. The talk around me is all baseball. *Marvin would have loved this*, I think with an ache around my heart, as old Sal, the only person present who's actually been to Ebbets Field, holds court: One boy asks, "Mistuh Sal, Big Nate says they usta be the Trolley Dodgers? What's a trolley, anyway?" Some young men challenge Sal to "tell Willie 'bout Babe Ruth's fastball in the 'sixteen Series 'gainst the Red Sox." A man in an old brown Grays cap wants to argue: "Babe Ruth? Smokey Joe Williams could outplay Ruth any day of th' week!"

At five minutes before game time, in a move that's an important part of this behind-the-store ritual, Reverend Stone rises for the opening prayer. Reverend Stone is a wiry man with a big, booming voice. He holds a blanched palm high above the crowd and we all, even the youngest children, respectfully bow our heads.

*"Lawd,* **Lawd,** *we thank You for Your son* **Jesus,"**
the Reverend says, and a chorus of scattered voices say, "Amen."
*"And, on this day especially, we thank You*
*for our* **people***'s son,* **Jackie."**
At this, the "Amens" become noticeably more enthusiastic.
*"Now, Lawd, we know* **better** *than to ask*
*Your involvement in* **petty** *sports.*
*But in Your Son's* **glorious** *Sermon on the Mount, He told us*
*'Enter ye in at the* **straight** *gate.*
**Straight** *is the gate, and* **narrow** *is the way,*
*and* **few** *there be that find it.'*
*We ask, Lawd, Your blessing on young Don Newcombe,*
*our starting pitcher.*
*We ask that* **his** *gate be straight and narrow,*
*and that there be* **few** *today that find it."*
Amens and muffled laughter ripple through the crowd.
*"Lawd, we thank You for the four apostles who*
*spread Your good word—***Matthew, Mark, Luke and John.**
*And we praise You for the good wood of four*
*others—***Jackie, Campy, Duke and Gil.***
*May their bats ring loudly the gospel of hope, faith, fairness*
*and the equality of* **all** *men at the plate!"*
"AMEN!"
*"We know it's best, Lawd, not to hope too high."*
Reverend Stone pauses to eyeball the zealots in the crowd.
*"And we* **promise** *You, Lawd, that,* **whatever** *today's outcome,*
*we* **will—***now and forever—praise Your* **holy** *name!"*

"AMEN and PLAY BALL!" the crowd yells enthusiastically.

Jerry Tee clambers up the stepladder to turn up the TV's volume, loud, and the game begins. It's a shock to hear a voice other than the honey-toned Red Barber's, but Ren explains to me, since they're playing at the Giants' Polo Grounds, their man Russ Hodges is announcing the game.

Because I don't follow baseball as fanatically as the people around me, I find myself watching them for clues as to what's going on. Throughout the early innings, the fans are nervous, wringing their hands, shaking their heads over every pitch, hit and play. By the end of the seventh inning, the teams are tied at only one run apiece. People cast worried eyes at the TV screen and each other.

In "the top" of the eighth inning, when Maglie—the Giants' pitcher who nobody likes—makes a mistake, a bad throw, and a Dodger named PeeWee runs home, 2–1, the fans cheer loudly. Then Maglie walks Jackie Robinson, and the crowd erupts. "Steal second, Jackie!" they holler. "Steal 'em all!" Miz Coralie Brown—the tiny old lady with a face as round and crinkled as a walnut, sitting next to Armetta—crows. But before Jackie can steal anything, batter Billy Cox hits a two-run homer and stretches the lead to 4–1. The fans are *thrilled* by that, and by the fact that in "the bottom" of the inning, the Giants don't score a thing.

Now, in the ninth inning, the Dodger batters don't score either. But the fans are hopeful as the teams change places. "Three more outs and we get our Series!" Ren yells in my ear, then, turning back to the screen hunched over and intent, wipes wet palms on his pants. Reverend Stone dabs his upper lip with a huge white handkerchief. Old Sal nervously taps his false teeth. And Miz Coralie holds up crooked arthritic fingers, double-crossed for luck.

The crowd is hushed and unhappy when first one, then another Giant batter gets on base. A third batter hits the first one home, bumping the score to 4–2, with two men still on base. Suddenly, there's a great roar of disapproval as the

Dodger manager walks out to remove Don Newcombe from the pitcher's mound. "Leave 'im in!" Jimmy Lee and many others holler. "Let 'im be!" Miz Coralie wails.

The announcer Hodges identifies Newcombe's replacement, a young pitcher named Ralph Branca.

Beside me, Ren is stunned. "Branca? *Nooooo!*" he howls as, beside him, old Sal mutters, "Is no good, Dressen, no good."

The crowd is still grumbling as the Giants' next batter, Bobby Thomson, comes to the plate. "Shhhhhhh, hush, now," the old people hiss, some watching the screen, some merely listening, seeing the game inside their heads. Branca's first pitch is a good one. "Strike one off the knees," Hodges says. Ren and Sal eye each other in guarded relief. At the second pitch, the voice from the Polo grounds says, "Here's a long fly . . . it's gonna be . . . I believe . . ." And, then, a pause and the unbelievable, heart-stopping news, "The Giants win the pennant! The Giants win the pennant! The Giants win the pennant!"

Ren jumps up, slams his fist against the wall. "No," he cries, "*no, NO!*" Old Sal buries his head in his hands, hiding his tears but not the moan in his throat.

Several people, including Miz Coralie, openly weep. Armetta turns to her with shiny wet cheeks. Luther and Reverend Stone stand to comfort them; Luther with a soft squeeze on his wife's shoulder, the Reverend with a sorrowful "The Lawd giveth, and He taketh away."

As the dejected young men, the disappointed parents and their silent children, the pairs of old people rise and turn to tread sadly home, I want to protest.

It would have been divinely *right* for these Dodgers, seven All-Stars among them, to have won this pennant. But apparently, Marvin has no damn pull in heaven. It would have been morally *just,* for Jackie Robinson especially, to have played the Series, and shown the world that Negroes are the equal of anybody. But, instead of the Dodgers' brilliant Don Newcombe standing victorious, today black-hearted Sal Maglie—who viciously bean-balled Robinson all season—is the pennant-winning pitcher.

To my mind, because of Marvin, God owed us this win, owed the Dodgers their stay in Heaven on Earth. But, for reasons beyond me, God came down on the wrong side of right. And made baseball, as Red Barber says, "just like life."

The late-afternoon sun pierces the pines with sharp orange swords of light. The departing fans trail long, lonesome shadows. Dusk comes fast and is wintry red.

# Chapter 20

On Monday afternoon, November fifth, Mr. Thurgood Marshall wheels his rental car into the packinghouse lot. Leaving his suit coat in the car, he strides into our showroom, tie loosened, starched white shirtsleeves rolled back against the heat.

"Did you hear about the cold snap in New York?" he asks, patting his forehead with a folded white handkerchief. "There were icicles hanging off our front stoop when I left," he tells us with a throaty chuckle.

"Welcome to paradise," Daddy says, turning the small electric fan on the counter in his direction. "Time for another tango with Sheriff McCall?"

"Ackerman, the defense counsel, has filed for a change of venue; Judge Futch is going to rule on it day after tomorrow," the big man tells us. News of the Supreme Court-ordered retrial—of the two young

Negroes accused of raping a white woman up in Groveland—
has been all over the papers for months.

While I pour Mr. Marshall some fresh-squeezed juice, I
listen to him tell Daddy they're hoping to get Prosecutor Jess
Hunter removed for calling the N.A.A.C.P. "a subversive and
Communist organization." He wants to transfer the proceed-
ings to Marion County, where Lake County's notorious Sheriff
McCall "has fewer friends."

"Better there than Miami," Daddy says, and the two men
shake their heads over the most recent string of bombings—
three more since Labor Day.

"What the hell's taking the F.B.I. so long?" Daddy rails.

Mr. Marshall's face falls. "Your guess is as good as mine.
We've called everyone we can think of, *twice*. And that in-
cludes the President and the former First Lady!"

"And, unfortunately, old give-em-hell Harry's up to his
eyeballs in Communists?" Daddy asks, raising an eyebrow.

"We're standing in a line that's gets longer every day,"
Mr. Marshall tells him sadly, finishing his juice. "If you have
the time," he adds, "you're welcome to attend Wednesday's
hearing in Tavares."

"Really?" I say, avoiding Daddy's eye. "Me, too?" I ask,
hoping to confirm my seat from Mr. Civil Rights himself.

Far too smart to be caught between a teenager and her
parents, Mr. Marshall shakes his head. "That's for your parents to decide, Reesa."

After he's gone, my begging begins. The trick is to press
hard enough to get a yes, but not so hard I get a no. "Please,
Daddy, please. After all I've read, all the things the paper's
said, you have to let me go! It's history!"

My father, no slouch at smartness either, gives me the sly
eye. "We'll discuss it with your mother, later."

I t should have been, it *would* have been, something to see Mr. Marshall at work, defending Walter Lee Irvin and Samuel Shepherd, two of the four young Negroes who stopped their car to help a white couple and were later accused of raping the woman. But, on November sixth, on their way to the courthouse, both Walter Irvin and Samuel Shepherd were shot. Shepherd was killed. What happened that night, on a lonely road in Lake County, depends on who you choose to believe.

In the local paper, Sheriff Willis McCall tells his side of things:

In the late afternoon of November sixth, the sheriff and his deputy James Yates drove up to Raiford State Prison to pick up defendants Irvin and Shepherd. The lawmen's court-ordered task was to deliver the two Negroes back to the county court in Tavares. When they left the prison, the defendants were handcuffed together in the front seat next to the sheriff. Deputy Yates sat in the back.

"Fearing interference from a lynch mob," Sheriff McCall explained, he drove Deputy Yates to Weirsdale to pick up a second car. "By that time, it was dark, so I sent Yates ahead to watch for roadblocks. On the way," McCall said, "a tire went flat and needed fixing. When I opened the car door to get the prisoners out, Shepherd grabbed my flashlight, smashed me on the head with it, and yelled to Irvin to get my gun." Sheriff McCall pulled his revolver and shot each prisoner three times. Then he radioed for Deputy Yates to come back and to call a doctor. When the doctor got there, Samuel Shepherd was dead. Walter Lee Irvin looked dead, but was not.

Instead, Irvin's in the hospital with tubes draining blood

from his chest cavity, and a bullet lodged forever in his kidney. Miraculously, he's able to talk. In an interview, headlined "Who Lied?," twenty-three-year-old Irvin tells his story:

"The sheriff and the deputy began talkin' on the radio a little bit. The sheriff told him to 'go ahead and check' and so the deputy sheriff went on a short ways in front of us and he says, 'Okay' . . . The sheriff shimmied his steering wheel and said, 'Something is wrong with my left front tire.' "

Irvin said McCall reached under the seat for his flashlight, got out and kicked the front wheel. "Then he opened our door and said, 'You sons of bitches get out and get this tire fixed.' . . . So Sammy—he was by the door—he takes his foot and put it out of the car and was gettin' out, I can't say just how quick it was, but he shot him. It was quick enough, and he turned, the sheriff did, and he had a pistol and he shot Sammy right quick. Then he shot me. He reached and grabbed me, and snatched me, and Sammy, too. He snatched both of us and then threw us on the ground.

"Then I didn't say anything. I didn't say nothin'. So later he snatched us, he shot me again in the shoulder, and still I didn't say anything at all, all that time. And I knew I was not dead.

"In about ten minutes, the deputy sheriff was there. And the deputy he shined the light in my face and he said to the sheriff, 'That son of a bitch is not dead.' And then he said, 'Let's kill him.' The deputy sheriff pointed his pistol on me and pulled the trigger, snapped the trigger, and the gun did not shoot. The deputy took it around to the car lights and looked in it and shined the light in it. He turned it on me again and pulled it and that time the gun fired. It went through me here," indicating his throat, "and then I began to bleed out of my mouth and nose. I didn't say nothin' and didn't let them know I was not dead. And some people came . . ."

There isn't a doubt in my mind that Walter Lee Irvin is telling the truth. And that Sheriff McCall is, like Daddy says, "a lying sack of cesspool slop."

But, like Daddy also says, "These are devilish times."

At the end of the week, an all-white Lake County Coroner's Jury hears nine hours of testimony and decides, after just thirty-five minutes of deliberation, that Samuel Shepherd's death was "justifiable homicide," and that Sheriff McCall fired "in self-defense and the line of duty."

Even the most conservative people we know can hardly believe it. But no one is more disgusted than Harry T. Moore.

"This thing stinks to high heaven," he tells Daddy, asking us to join him in a statewide letter-writing campaign demanding that the Governor suspend Sheriff Willis McCall.

"A total whitewash!" Daddy agrees, reading a copy of Mr. Harry's own letter to Governor Warren.

"Florida is on trial before the rest of the world! Only prompt and courageous action, by removing Sheriff McCall, can save the good name of our fair state," the normally reserved schoolteacher warns our Governor.

"This is great, but, Harry," Daddy locks eyes with the soft-spoken leader of the state N.A.A.C.P., "I hope you're watching your back."

*Good Lord*, I think, stunned, *who would even think of harming Mr. Harry?*

"There have been threats," Mr. Harry says, jutting his chin, "but I've got a .32 caliber in my car, and, if it comes to that," he declares, "I'll take a few of them with me."

## Chapter 21

December snuck up on me. I should've seen it coming but I was busy with other things.

From the middle of November to the end of December, the packinghouse is a crazy place. We have long lists of standing mail orders to pack and ship, big wooden baskets of Florida Sunshine, fresh-wrapped fruit, to get to somebody's Aunt Mabel, or Cousin Larry, or, my special favorites, the children's wards of quite a few hospitals.

Aside from school, we do everything but sleep in the big back work area behind the showroom, helping our parents "make pay while the snow falls."

The radio is constantly on, providing a rhythm to our work, and there must have been a time when the Christmas carols began, but I didn't notice it. I did notice, however, the point at which my mother, planner of picnics, singer of songs, initiator of card games, disappeared, permanently it seems, behind her Poker Face.

The radio announcement on the morning of December fourth was brief: In Miami, at three A.M., an explosion blew up yet another Carver Village apartment building. Thirty minutes later, another building in that very same housing project exploded and fell in the night. Half an hour after that, a blast at the Miami Hebrew School and Congregation shattered forty-four stained-glass windows, a memorial to family members lost in Hitler's Holocaust. Exactly thirty minutes later, a fourth blast destroyed a Jewish community center, sending nearby residents screaming into the street.

"What a nightmare!" I say, mad as can be.

"When will it end?" Mother says, but she's not asking me.

And I watch it happen: As if somebody pulled a plug, her brightness fades, her dimple disappears. Only her Poker Face—the careful, studied expression, the hazel eyes that see everything and say nothing—remains. She shifts her attention back to the task, wrapping and packing fruit in the basket between us, working as hard, harder, than anybody. But she has drawn the curtains and retreated to some private, inside place.

Even a week later—when U.S. Attorney General Howard McGrath decides, *finally*, to act, ordering Florida's F.B.I. agents to "investigate to see whether they can investigate" violations of anyone's federally guaranteed civil rights—my real mother does not return.

Even when we hear that Mr. Harry T. Moore—the F.B.I.'s most vocal critic, the Negroes' most powerful advocate, the compiler of civil rights case files that local law enforcement conveniently overlooked—has been invited to Miami to brief the federal agents. Even then, she doesn't respond. Not really.

Even as the rest of us sit around the break table, expressing our hopes that, maybe now, the bombings will stop. Maybe now, the tidal wave of evil will ebb. Maybe now, Marvin's murderers will be brought to justice. And the winter tourists, who should be choking the Trail with traffic by now, will change their minds and decide it's safe to come to Florida after all. Even now, she holds herself apart, playing Solitaire at the table's other end.

I wonder, I worry, I even think about asking her directly, "What's going on behind that Poker Face of yours?" But it wouldn't do me a bit of good. My mother, the expert card player, never tips her hand. "You think *I've* got a Poker Face," she told me once, "you should have seen my *father's!*"

My mother adored her father, the soft-spoken accountant whose thick spectacles and thinning hair made him look older than he was. He taught her everything there is to know about card playing—from how to count the cards to how to calculate, in her head, statistical probabilities. The summer she turned sixteen, a bad strep throat kept her daddy home from work. She helped him pass the hours, that stretched into days, with their own special versions of Pinochle, Gin Rummy and double-handed Bridge. While she sat by his bedside playing by the rules, and he did everything the doctor ordered, that strep throat turned into scarlet fever, a child's disease, that somehow became rheumatic and masked the pneumonia that, in the middle of the night, stole him away from her forever.

I know, from my own father, it was a terrible shock and a devastating loss for her. And, I can't help but wonder if it's playing on her mind now, the way it is on mine. Is she worried, too, that something awful is sneaking up on us the way that pneumonia did? I'd like to ask her about it. But I have the distinct feeling she'd tell me to "breast your cards," which is cardplayer talk for "mind your own business."

*Chapter 22*

In the store windows and on Christmas cards, Santa Claus shows up as a round little man with a white beard and a red suit. At our house, Santa is a feisty old lady with silver-toned cat-eye glasses and mink-colored hair.

"You're a sorry sight for sore eyes," Doto tells us and she's probably right. The events of the past seven months, since she left us last May, have made us "all hollow-eyed" and "too thin," she declares. Mother's "just skin and bones" and "obviously, these children need more ice cream."

Doto's like a tonic. In the span of a single week, she's bullied us out of the backroom to cut down a Christmas tree (a Florida pine from the woods off Wellwood Road); she's unearthed the decorations, opened her pack (from the trunk of the DeSoto) and infused our lives with much-needed holiday spirit.

Heaped under our tree are gifts from her and from our cousins in Montana and Maryland. There are gifts from our mother's side, our cousins and grandmother outside Chicago. And there are the small gifts which we children have for our parents and each other, thanks to Doto carrying us off for an afternoon's shopping at Woolworth's and the Opalakee Five-and-Dime.

On Christmas morning, we plow through our presents like half-starved entrants in a pie-eating contest. Afterwards, our opened piles are full to bursting with possibilities: board games, science sets, puzzles, new underwear and outfits for all, plus a bright red Radio Flyer wagon for Mitchell, a Schwinn bike for Ren, and a pink portable record player for me. For the first time in recent memory, it feels like some kind of normal has returned.

The last gift to be opened is a very large box tagged *To the whole family. Love, Doto.* My brothers and I have been eyeing it ever since she arrived, trying to guess what it could possibly be. Daddy drags it from behind the tree to Mother, who invites us to help her unwrap it. With each of us posted on a different side, we tear back the colored paper, racing to see who will solve the mystery first. It's Mother who realizes it's a television, a beautiful dark-wood cabinet with an oval screen the size of a turkey platter, the much-talked-about black-and-white eye on the rest of the world. Doto has topped herself! We surround her, hugging her, calling our thank-yous.

"Hurray! Now we can see *Howdy Doody!*" the boys cry.

"And *I Love Lucy!*" I say.

"What's *I Love Lucy?*" Doto wants to know.

"It's new. Miz Lillian says it's her favorite," I explain. "Miz Lillian never goes *any*where on Monday nights anymore because she doesn't want to miss Lucy."

"We'll just have to check it out then, won't we?" Doto grins.

As Daddy looks over the manual for hooking up the television, Ren, Mitchell and I organize our gifts into individual piles under the tree. Doto and Mother clear away the box of wadded-up wrapping paper and curled ribbons, then head into the kitchen to check on the turkey, already in the oven.

At noon, Sal and Sophia arrive carrying a round box of panettone, Italian Christmas cake, for the adults and a red tin of Amaretto cookies for us. I know that later, after dinner, Sal will show us how to twist the paper cookie wrappers and light them so they take off and fly like tiny angels.

During dinner, the adults entertain us with their favorite Christmas stories. Doto tells about the morning she received her very own pony, complete with wagon. Doto was one of two children, but after her only sister, Hettie, died of scarlet fever, her parents spoiled her *terribly*, she says. Shy Sophia, egged on by the rest of us, tells about the time when, as a child in Rome, she attended midnight mass at St. Mark's Cathedral. But old Sal's story is my favorite. It's about a big fire on Christmas Eve that destroyed his apartment building off Brooklyn's Flatbush Avenue, how all the people and families from his building were adopted by other big families on the street, who shared their dinner, clothing and gifts with those who'd lost everything. At the end of the story, both Sal's and Sophia's eyes are watery.

"That's really what Christmas is all about, isn't it?" Daddy says, smiling around the table.

"Yes, is about good neighbors," Sal agrees, "and about moving on, what Sophia and me, we must do."

The crack in Sal's voice, the look on his face, prompts

Daddy, who's all of a sudden solemn, to ask, "What do you mean?"

"Sorry." Sal drops his eyes and shakes his head. "I didna mean to speak of this in fronta the children."

"Please, Sophia, are you moving?" Mother's tone is urgent, concerned. Doto is frowning.

Sophia closes her eyes, unable to speak. She puts a shaking hand on Sal's arm, a mute request for him to explain.

"The phone calls," Sal tells us, nearly in a whisper. "They started lasta month. First, justa name-calling, a man with a Southern accent saying, 'Fish-eaters!,' 'Pope-lovers!'—baby stuff nexta what I heard in Brooklyn as a kid. Then, the calls, they got worse. Insults, threats about us and the coloreds, saying leave, 'or else!' Lasta night, a stick wrapped in paper thrown through our big window. We hearda the crash, ran downstairs, and found—the stick was dynamite. On the paper, the words: 'Next time, this will be lit.' "

Across from me, Ren goes bug-eyed. Beside me, Doto gasps.

Mother's eyes fill with tears. "Oh, Sal, Sophia, how horrible!"

"Have you talked to anyone else about this?" Daddy asks Sal.

"I called the Constable's office lasta week, also the week before. Constable Watts came, but when I talked, he kept interrupting. 'Speak English! I can't understand you!' he says. Then he shrugs. 'A little phone call never hurt nobody,' he says. I think now, if I showed him the dynamite, he'd shrug again and say, 'It don't hurt if it ain't lit.' "

"What will you do?" Doto, angry, wants to know.

"If I was a younger man . . ." Sal's voice trails off. His eyes find Sophia's, then return to Doto. "Sophia and me, we boarded up the window and putta sign on the front door, 'Closed, Out of Business.' We called her sister in Tampa. We go there, for now, this afternoon. Afterwards, who knows?"

Sophia is sobbing into her napkin. Mother moves to put arms around her and leads her away from the table, into the kitchen. In the silence, Doto stands. "Children, it's time we took a look at Reesa's new puzzle. Everybody out on the front porch, *now*!"

We drop our napkins beside our plates and follow her quickly out of the dining room, leaving Daddy and Sal alone. Looking back, I see my father, stony-faced and rock-hard, turning slowly in his chair to face his old, suddenly frail-looking friend.

*This place has gone to hell in a handbasket*, I fume inside my head to Whoever's listening, which, as near as I can tell, is nobody.

T he morning after Christmas, the rumble of Daddy's truck engine wakes me. I hear women's voices in the kitchen, Mother's, Doto's, and, surprisingly, a third one with an accent. Sophia, I remember. She and Sal spent the night in Mitchell's room, the boys camping out on the couch in the living room. The Plan.

Instantly, it comes back to me. My parents persuading them not to leave for Tampa yesterday afternoon; Daddy and Sal's trip to The Quarters to meet with Luther, Armetta, Reverend Stone and the elders from St. John's A.M.E. Last night, after Doto led Sal and Sophia upstairs, my parents explained The Plan. It goes like this:

Sal and Sophia wanted to leave town immediately, abandoning everything, walking away from the contents of their beloved store, and the sunny, furniture-filled apartment above it. Daddy convinced them to wait one day, to attempt to salvage as much of their lives as possible.

Their Christmas night meeting in The Quarters proved fruitful. Luther and Reverend Stone agreed to rally the residents to purchase as much of the store's perishable goods as possible in a special sale this very morning under the big oaks behind the church. Daddy and Sal left early to load the truck with the store's stock of dairy, meat and produce. The elders of the church will oversee the sale. Luther and the Reverend offered to stock the church's choir room with the store's canned goods, sell them to the locals as needed, then turn over the proceeds to Daddy for forwarding to Sal and Sophia in Tampa. On top of that, Armetta volunteered to take on collecting from their credit customers in The Quarters.

The Tomasinis seemed overwhelmed by the willingness of their customers to help them. "We know all about the Klan, Mistuh Sal," the elders said. "You and Miz Sophia have been nuthin' but good to us ever since y'all came here." By way of thanking them, old Sal presented Reverend Stone with his hastily disconnected twenty-five-foot antenna which, the Reverend told him, would make a fine addition to St. John's steeple.

I head into the kitchen where Sophia sits at the table, fingering her black rosary beads. With her big eyes, made larger by dark, worried circles, and her long hair hanging loose instead of in her usual bun, she looks like a little lost soul instead of our Sophia.

"Everything will be fine," Doto tells her, patting her shoulder. "Warren said they'll be home by noon."

"Mother, Doto, look at this!" "Come here, quick!" The

boys' cries pull us out of the kitchen and into the living room, where they point wildly to the television.

On the screen, a man is talking: "*. . . from Mims in Brevard County. Agents from the Federal Bureau of Investigation arrived this morning and cordoned off the scene of last night's explosion. Local lawmen suspect dynamite destroyed the home of the state's N.A.A.C.P. leader and his wife. According to relatives, Harry Tyson Moore died on the way to Sanford Hospital. Doctors report his wife suffered severe internal injuries. Her condition is critical.*"

"Santa Maria, Madre di Dio!" Sophia cries, beads to her chest. Tears slick her face.

"*Relatives say the blast occurred after the Moores returned home from a family party celebrating Christmas and their twenty-sixth wedding anniversary. The Brevard County Sheriff's Office states that although the F.B.I. has no jurisdiction in this case, murder being a state crime, the local authorities will give Mr. Hoover's G-men their full cooperation. At this time, there are no known suspects.*"

"This is a nightmare," Doto rages.

"That poor man and his wife," Mother murmurs, to none of us in particular.

*Mr. Harry. Dead?* My mind flashes with pictures of him, vibrant and alive: His first visit to our house with Luther and Mr. Marshall; his patient help with my homework ("Democracy is the fairest form of government on earth," he'd said); the jut of his chin when he told Daddy about the death threats and the .32 caliber under his car seat.

I remember telling Daddy once it didn't fit, the soft-spoken schoolteacher with the loaded gun under his seat. But Daddy said Mr. Harry was *made of steel.* "Any man who travels up and down this state registering Negro voters right under the noses of all these Klanners is *solid steel*, through and through," Daddy told me.

As we stare at the screen for more information, it's obvious the reporter cares more about the arrival of Mr. Hoover's G-men than what happened to Mr. Harry. Doto fiddles with the knobs and the V-shaped wires she calls rabbit ears in search of another station. Frustrated, she and Mother move into the kitchen for a radio update.

Ren and I run out front to retrieve the morning paper which, because everyone was worried about Sophia and all, lies forgotten in the driveway. Outside, we rip off the rubber band, scan through the sections for something, any kind of mention of the Moores. Nothing. Ren runs to take the paper in to Mother, but all of a sudden, *I can't move.* Just then, at that very moment, all of it, every single, stinking, heart-hurting detail of Marvin in the bed of Daddy's truck comes bolting back on me.

Collapsing on the lawn, I see it *all,* all over again—the cuts, the wounds, the striped blood-soaked turban hiding his eyes. I hear his raggedy breath, bubbling on bleeding lips, knowing now what I couldn't know then, that it was one of the last breaths he'd ever take on this earth. And I smell, in a memory more sharp, more painful than all the others, the smell of his life's blood oozing out of him onto the filthy truck bed.

*For what?* I want to know. *For WHAT!* I rage at the Rock of Ages who, as far as I can determine, has turned His back on this whole stupid mess called the State of Florida. *When will this nightmare end? And why, WHY is ALL this happening?*

Sophia stands on the front steps, frantically fingering her beads, watching the driveway for signs of the truck. We hear it, she from the steps, me from the lawn, roar onto the property. I watch her fly down the walk to the far side of the drive, and, as Sal climbs from the truck, fling herself into his arms.

The minute I see Daddy's face, I can tell he's heard the news. Wrenching his door open, he strides right past me, asking, in a voice like granite, "Your mother in the house, Roo?" But he does not look or, taking the steps two at a time, listen for my reply.

*Chapter 23*

The most frightening part of a hurricane is its eye.

Like the giant blade of a buzz saw broken loose, a hurricane spins wildly; its outer edges blow and bite and dump barrels of water and dangerous, wind-whipped bits of wood and trash. After that, closer in, comes the *real* rain and the horrible sound of the wind cracking hundred-year-old oak trees in two. If you're lucky, locals say, the hurricane only glances in your direction and whirls off, moving on to the next community, the next state or, better yet, back onto the ocean where it came from.

If you're *not* lucky, if you have the unfortunate luck of living *directly* in its path, the center of the storm, *the eye*, engulfs you in terrifying silence. You wait, and watch, and wonder *when* it will pass, when the crack of old trees, and the rain, and the winds, and the barrels of water will return, all over again. It always does.

In the ten terrible days after Christmas, after the murder of our friend Harry Moore, after Sal and Sophia left Mayflower for good, the Klan's silence is deafening. Not a word, not a *sound* from the men in white who, everybody knows, spent the last nine months whipping the state into frantic frenzy.

For ten days, during which the F.B.I. sorts and sifts through the Moores' ripped-up floorboards, the shattered ceiling planks, the tinsel of Christmas glittering in the yard, and finds too few clues as to *who* did *what*, we wait. Ten days after her husband died, the day after his funeral (where Reverend J. W. Bruno pronounced "You can kill the prophet but you cannot kill his message"), Mrs. Harriette Moore dies, too.

Mrs. Moore's death is the first sign that this hurricane's overquiet eye has passed. A flurry of increasingly loud events follows:

M r. James Ferris, the wealthy Chicago retailer whose family owns the winter estate just south of town, calls Daddy to ask if "there's still martial law in Miami."

"No," Daddy tells him, "never was."

"Ruthie's been after me to visit the Bahamas," Mr. Ferris tells Daddy. "We thought we'd try there this year, put off Florida 'til next year, when things are more settled." His is the first of many calls from longtime big-spending customers who "just aren't comfortable" coming to Florida this year.

A fter that, we have an odd, unsettling encounter with Mr. Barrett of Barrett Hardware in Orlando:

Daddy has dynamite. He and most citrus growers around

Mayflower use it to blow the stumps of old dead orange trees in preparation for planting new seedlings. The powerful variety, called ditching dynamite, is also used to rout the stubborn tentacle roots of a stand of palmetto. Above ground, there's nothing friendly about a palmetto. Underground, its roots are as mean as an army of octopi, thick as a man's arms and impossible to dig up.

On a Saturday afternoon in mid-January, Daddy and I drive down to Orlando to the big Barrett Hardware Store. Daddy, an avid subscriber to *Popular Mechanics*, read about a new kind of electric fuse which makes igniting ditching dynamite "a heck of a lot safer.

"Usually, you just dig a hole as close to the root center as possible, put in the sticks, light the fuse strings and let her go," Daddy explains to me. "A fuse string burns at three seconds a foot, so you have time to run away before it blows. Sometimes it fizzles, or you think it has. If you walk in too soon to check it, you risk getting yourself blown up or blasted by flying palmetto. These new electric fuses are expensive but a lot more reliable than the strings."

"Is that what you think the Klan used on Mr. Harry?" I ask him.

Daddy takes a deep, raggedy breath. "Maybe. Especially since the boom sticks were hidden under the house."

"Daddy," I say, feeling my tongue grow thick, "I can't believe they did that to him."

Daddy is quiet a minute. Then he says, "He knew there were risks, honey."

"But his wife . . ." The words get stuck in my throat.

"There's no accounting for that level of cowardice," Daddy says, wheeling abruptly into the parking lot, his eyes clouding with contempt.

I trail him through the front door of Barrett Hardware, through the big aisles, to the back counter where Mr. Barrett handles special requests. Mr. Barrett is very tall and thin with a helmet of white hair, "a real Southern gentleman," my father says.

He listens patiently to Daddy's request, nodding in recognition and understanding, but in the end he shakes his head. "I know what you want, young man, but I can't help you."

"Is it something you could order for me?" Daddy asks.

"As of this week, as the result of a visit by high law-enforcement officials, I am out of the powder and explosives business. And you should be, too."

"What do you mean?" Daddy asks.

"Just what I said. My basement which has, in the past, been stocked with powder and explosives to meet the needs of my agricultural customers is now empty. My purchase records have been appropriated."

From the sweep of Mr. Barrett's hand, I gather "appropriated" means taken away.

"Who was it? The F.B.I., the County Sheriff, who?" Daddy asks, immediately curious.

"I'm not at liberty to say, young man," Mr. Barrett says. "Only that these items are now in the possession of *high* law-enforcement *officials*." Mr. Barrett lifts up his open palms in that way that means *I've said all I care to.* "Like I said, *I'm* out of the dynamite business and *you*, sir, should be, too."

Daddy's always said that the reason they called Stonewall Jackson "Stonewall" was because it's near impossible to get a Southerner to do or say anything he doesn't want to.

Daddy and I walk out, unanswered and empty-handed.

A week later, when the plain black Ford pulls into our parking lot, Ren and I watch it through the office window. Both doors open at the same time and two white

men in white shirts, dark ties and pants step out of the car
and shrug themselves into their suit jackets.

"Definitely not tourists," Ren says.

"Salesmen, maybe?" I wonder.

"Naw, salesmen are usually alone. Mormons?"

"No Bibles or books," I point out.

We watch the men cross the gravel, enter the showroom
and approach Mother at the counter.

"Mornin', ma'am," the older one says. He's got a wide red
face atop a body shaped like a barrel. His shoes are very shiny.

"Good morning," she replies. "May I help you?"

"We're lookin' for a Mistuh Warren McMahon. This his
place?"

"It's ours. Warren's my husband and he's in the back. May
I tell him your business, please?"

The older man puffs out his chest and hikes up his belt,
like it ought to be obvious his business is important. He
reaches into his coat pocket and flips out a black leather wallet. "Agent Thomas Elwood of the Federal Bureau of Investigation. This here's Agent Odom."

"Ma'am," the younger man says, dipping a pointy chin at
Mother.

"Reesa, Ren, please get your father off the platform," she
calls in our direction as the agents' eyes skim the showroom
for our hidden location.

Without a word, Ren and I fly out of the office, across the
showroom to the side door, up the steps, around the big
waxer to the washer machine, where Daddy's upending boxes
of grove fruit into the cleaning tank.

"Daddy, the *F.B.I.'s* here! Two of them. In the showroom
with Mother!" we pant.

"What?" he says, looking at us like we're crazy, like we've
just told him the Martians have landed in Mayflower.

"Mother wants you *now*. They've got badges and everything!"

We follow him off the platform and into the showroom.

"Gentlemen, Warren McMahon," Daddy says, extending his hand with a smile. "My children tell me you have F.B.I. badges. I have to tell you, they won't sleep tonight if they don't get a good look at one."

Young Agent Odom grins at us, pulls out his wallet, flips it open and lets us see. *Agent James S. Odom,* the card says beside the shiny silver shield that spells out *Federal Bureau of Investigation.*

"You a G-man?" Ren asks him.

"Yessir, I am!" Agent Odom seems hardly old enough to be anything.

"Ever met Mr. J. Edgar Hoover?" I want to know.

"Not personally, but we teletype a report to 'im every night."

"Okay, you two, thank the gentlemen, then make yourselves scarce," Daddy says, waving us off, away from the counter.

Kneeling on chairs inside the office, Ren and I quickly fold ourselves over Mother's desk, straining to hear the adult conversation.

"I didn't catch how you happened to know my name?" Daddy asks the two agents.

I catch my breath, sure the G-men will say that it was Mr. Hoover himself who sent them, because of Daddy's long-ago letter about Marvin's murder.

"We understan' y'all have some dynamite." Agent Ellwood's clearly the boss. "We had an interest in knowin' what y' plan to do with it?"

"Same thing every other citrus grower in the county does with it—blow stumps, try to win the war against palmettos."

All of a sudden, Daddy's got his guard up and I think I know why. For years, Ren and I have played a game called "Accents," where we listen to the way customers talk and guess where they're from. Some accents are harder to peg than others, but Agent Ellwood's is pure Florida panhandle, the heart of Cracker country.

"Would y'all have any other uses for it?" Agent Ellwood drawls.

"You mean, like blowing people up, or destroying private property? Gentlemen, my wife and I aren't Klan members. In fact, you can probably tell from our accents, we're not even Southerners," Daddy says, throwing his arm protectively around Mother.

"But y'all are familiar with Klan activities 'round here?"

"Well, they killed a young friend of ours last March. I wrote your boss a letter about it but never heard anything back. At Christmas, the Klan ran the only other Northerners in town out of here because they were Catholic and made the mistake of being too nice to the local Negroes."

*They killed Marvin in Emmett Casselton's lemon grove! They scared old Sal and Sophia into leaving here forever!*

"What was it y' say the Klan did 'round Christmas?" Agent Ellwood asks sharply, his fat blue pen poised over his small black notebook.

*Just like that, they've brushed past Marvin's murder as if it doesn't count!*

"Christmas *Eve*," Daddy says, "which is twenty-four hours before the event I imagine you're interested in. On Christmas *Eve*, they threw an unlit stick of dynamite through our friends' store window, warning the owners that if they didn't leave town, the next one would be lit."

"What'd the owners do?" Ellwood asks, putting his pen down.

"They left," Mother says quietly.

*It's clear their only interest is the Moores' murder. To hell with anybody else.*

"Mistuh McMahon, you friends with local Klansmen?"

"I know a lot of the local men, do business with them from time to time, and, in general, try to get along with everybody." Daddy's tone is even more guarded than before. "We have property here, a business, and—as you can see— children who attend the local school. We get along. But we're not what I'd call *friends.*"

"Looky here, Mistuh and Miz McMahon, we're on a sort of fishin' trip, officially to determine if all citizens are re- ceivin' equal protection under the law. Unofficially, we got some suspicions 'bout the Opalakee Klan. Y'all be willin' to speak with our supervisor?"

"Regarding?" Daddy asks, politely.

"Oh, jus' the general lay of the land 'round here, how things work in Orange County and Opalakee?" Ellwood says.

"I'd be willing to speak *generally* about just about any- thing, Agent Ellwood. What's your supervisor's name?"

"Jameson, sir, James Jameson's his name. Can he call y'all at this number?" Ellwood says, pocketing one of our business cards from the little plastic holder on the counter.

"I'd prefer to speak with the gentleman in person," Daddy tells him. "I like to see who it is I'm talking to."

"I'm not exactly sure when he'll get up this way. He's operatin' outta Orlando, though, and he jus' might want to stop by."

Daddy shrugs. "We'll be here."

Agent Ellwood hikes his pants again, an important man off to more official business. "Thank y' for your time, Mistuh McMahon. Ma'am. Y'all have a real nice place here."

"Thank you." Mother nods stiffly.

Agent Ellwood and Agent Odom, who hasn't said a word since showing us his badge, turn and walk out into the sun. At the Ford, they shrug off their jackets and lay them on the back seat like they were babies. As the frowning Agent Ellwood starts the engine, Agent Odom shoots a shy smile and a small wave in our direction.

*Florida Crackers bearing the badges of Mr. Hoover's F.B.I. . . . it's clear the other side of this hurricane has begun to blow.*

# Chapter 24

The word is out. You'd have to be a hermit not to 've heard that Florida has "race troubles."

I sit in the showroom office, flipping through the clippings sent from our far-flung relatives. It doesn't matter which one you look at—*Time, Reader's Digest, Saturday Evening Post*, newspapers from Maryland to Montana—they all say the same thing. Under the swaying palm trees, inside the orderly orange groves, Florida leads the nation in cases of race prejudice and violence. Also, despite six weeks of intense investigation, the F.B.I. has not a single suspect in the Christmas night murders of Harry and Harriette Moore.

I study the pictures of Mr. Harry and his wife. She was a schoolteacher, too, he'd said. We never met her, but she has a pretty face and the same kindly look in her eyes that he always had.

In the showroom, I hear my mother sidestep questions from the troubled tourists.

"You expect this sort of thing in Mississippi or Georgia," a lady with an up-east accent is saying. "But Florida?"

"Hard to believe," my mother lies.

In my hand, a Chicago clipping tells the truth: "Even in the 1920s, Florida, not Alabama or Mississippi, led the South in lynchings in proportion to population." I wonder who did the math.

The husband and wife driving the big Pontiac Chieftain with New Jersey plates exclaim, "It was front-page news in the *Times*. We almost didn't come!"

"We're glad you did," Mother, wearing her guise of Cheerful Saleslady, assures them.

We are, after all, a family of shopkeepers; like Daddy says, "merchants on the South's most lucrative trade route." In exchange after exchange, my mother models "proper showroom behavior." The rules are simple, and older than I am: These people are on vacation, they've left their real lives behind and have no interest in ours. Never complain, never explain, just politely present the Florida of their fantasies. It makes me sick.

Isn't it wrong, I used to ask Marvin, to pretend niceness you don't feel? Especially to people who are rude, or, sometimes, downright mean?

"Cock-a-doodle, li'l Rooster!" Marvin mocked, narrowing his eyes at me as if I was a fool. "Try being colored," he'd grinned. The truth—that my complaints were ridiculous, his, impossible—popped up between us like some jeering jack-in-the-box. We both laughed, shamefaced, and hastily, awkwardly, moved on to other things.

*Oh, Marvin, things are much worse now than they were then.*

*Some days, I'm glad you're not here to see it. Most days, though, I'd give anything to have you here to talk to.*

At Mr. Marshall's invitation, Armetta joins a group of over two hundred N.A.A.C.P. representatives from fifteen states at an emergency meeting in Jacksonville.

"They're hoping," Daddy tells me, "to turn their outrage over the Moores' murders into something meaningful."

Together, the group creates and unanimously adopts the Jacksonville Declaration, a single sheet of demands for "seven basic rights of full citizenship."

Proudly, Armetta thrusts mimeographed copies of the document into our hands. The Declaration calls for:

"One—the right to security of person against the organized violence of lawless mobsters or irresponsible law-enforcement officers;

"Two—the right to vote as free men in a free land;

"Three—the right to employment opportunities in accordance with individual merits;

"Four—the right of children to attend any educational institutions supported by public funds;

"Five—the right to serve unsegregated in the armed forces of the country;

"Six—the right to travel unrestricted by Jim Crow regulations;

"And seven—the right to go unmolested among fellow Americans as free men in a free society."

Daddy calls it a *manifesto*. He ribs Armetta that "all good Communists have to have one." I sit, dumbfounded by my own stupidity.

Nothing, not *one* thing, on their list seems the least bit

unreasonable to me, but the fact that the list exists must mean, can *only* mean that these things are not currently available because, and only because, of a person's *skin* color? Does the entire country—the land of the free, the home of the brave—*know* this? Is ignorance like Miz Sooky's, arrogance like Emmett Casselton's, outright lunacy like Sheriff Willis McCall's so widespread that people like us, *we* are in the minority?

To tell you the truth, it had never occurred me. The signs were all around and I never saw them. I knew we lived in a place, a state, gone crazy, where good people had been killed for no good reason. I knew our nation's leaders had been preoccupied with other things. But the reality, the day-to-day dangers and restrictions that define a colored person's life anywhere in this country, had never struck me before. The shock and shame of it leave me staring, flabbergasted, at Armetta's proud document.

"Try being colored," Marvin had told me. And I couldn't. Even in my wildest imaginings, I wouldn't have come up with the picture painted by Armetta's seven points. And that sickens me, truly.

For her part, Armetta is *transformed*. The weary, weeping soul who attended both of the Moores' funerals in Mims has become someone else. She's fired and filled up. Seeing the change, feeling my own sense of fear and frustration, I can't help but ask her, "Armetta, how *can* you be so hopeful?"

She looks at me steady, without smiling. "Hope's like food, Roo, like air . . . there's no real livin' without it. This world's not perfect, not even close. But everythin' we want, everythin' we're hoping for," she says, "is ahead of us. You can't move forward lookin' back."

S he's right," Doto tells me later when I show her the Jacksonville Declaration. "We *can't* change the world overnight, Reesa. But we begin by changing the way we *choose* to live in it."

T hat same week, I'm relieved to hear, at last, from Vaylie.

*Dear Reesa,* she writes.

*Thanks so much for the silver friendship bracelet. I* love *it! It was my favorite part of a very crummy Christmas.*

*Mamma and Daddy got into a big fight on Christmas morning. Over me, of course. Well, actually, it was over their presents to me. Mamma gave me a whole new wardrobe specially ordered from New York—I was hoping for a pink shirt with matching poodle skirt or maybe something with polka dots. Anyways, everything I got is either bright red, blue or green. My looks are "coltish," Mamma says, and with my freckles, I'm so polka-dotted already, she says, I can only wear solid bright colors like "racing silks." I hate every single thing she got me, Reesa, and I wouldn't be caught* dead *in any of it!*

*Daddy's gift was a small box with a little porcelain pony inside. It was his way of telling me that he'd given me a horse! My very own Tennessee Walker! I was so excited but Mamma about blew a gasket. "I told you absolutely* NO *on this horse thing, Gerald!" she yelled. "I can't believe you did this to me!" and started crying up a storm. Daddy just looked at her, kind of squinty eyed, and hissed, "If you're gonna make the girl dress like a goddamn jockey, the least you could do is give her a goddamn horse to sit on!" I'll spare you the details except that,*

*after they quit yelling at each other, Daddy dove into his
Bloody Marys and Mamma took a couple of her nerve pills and
they both passed out before we'd even had our breakfast. I had
to call my daddy's mamma and tell her they were "too
indisposed" for us to make it to Christmas Dinner. Fortunately
for me, Claudette came by with a pan of her Christmas
gingerbread. She knows it's my favorite. When I told her what
happened she called Whit and he came all the way from
Colored Town with a plate of their Christmas dinner just for
me. Claudette and Whit both sat down with me in the kitchen
while I ate and it was so good! Ham, sweet potato pone,
collards with fatback and a huge slice of pecan pie after. This
might sound crazy but I think I'd be a whole lot better off if
Whit and Claudette were my parents instead of the ones I got
stuck with. (And, wouldn't my daddy's mamma have a big fat
cow if she heard that one!)*

*Have you made your New Year's resolutions yet? I have two
but you're the only soul I'm telling them to. The first is to catch
up with my school work. After missing the whole month of
September, plus two weeks in November "on tour," my grades
are just awful. My daddy's mamma got a look at my report
card and suggested I might be better off at a school for slow
kids! I wanted to tell her I know I'd make honor roll if I could
stay in town for more than a couple months at a time, but she
won't listen to anything that has to do with Daddy's "spells."*

*My other resolution—well, wish is more like it—is that
Mamma and Daddy will just stop fighting and get a divorce.
Reesa, I hope I don't get struck by lightning for saying this, but
I think we'd all be a lot happier without each other. 'Course,
Mamma would have to change her ways without all Daddy's
money, but we'd get by. And Whit and Claudette would take
care of Daddy just like they always have. The thing is, right*

*now, Daddy and Mamma and me are just like those three*
*rattlers in your clearing, coiling and rattling and hissing at*
*each other, then racing away as fast as we can to get out of the*
*big old hole we're stuck in.*

*It's a New Year, Reesa. I wish I could believe it'll be a*
HAPPY *one. Write* SOON*!!!*

*Love,* VAYLIE

Grabbing paper, pen and a jacket, I head out of the house.

*Dear Vaylie,*

*Do you remember the big old oak tree next to Dry Sink? I'm*
*sitting in it now on the same big branch we sat on last spring.*
*My friend Marvin told me everybody ought to have a tree and*
*this one's been mine ever since I can remember; especially after*
*Marvin told me about its heart. You didn't get to see it when*
*you were here but it's carved in the trunk about ten feet higher*
*up, a small heart with the letters "R.S. + M.M." in the center.*
*All my life, I've thought that heart was some kind of magical*
*message just for me. Marvin told me he found it when he was a*
*boy, but I've always been sure that M.M. was for me (Marie*
*McMahon) and that R.S. was a sign, the initials of the man*
*I'd marry someday. But, just now, thinking about our day here*
*and in the attic, it hit me that M.M. wasn't me at all, that*
*the letters stood for Miss Maybelle Mason and her dead fiancé,*
*Richard Swann!!!*

*Oh, Vaylie, aren't a whole lot of things not at all what they*
*seem? Like your grandmother thinking you're slow when you're*
*as smart as can be. And like Whit and Claudette acting more*
*like proper parents than your real mamma and daddy. It's*
*happening here, too, in the way a whole lot of white people*
*think their skin tone makes them better than colored people—*

when the truth is some of the finest people in the world aren't the least bit white!

My daddy calls the whole rotten mess "growing pains." "No pain, no gain," he says. Personally, I see the pain, but where's the gain in your mamma and daddy being so mean to each other, or in Miss Maybelle's heartbreak, or innocent people like my friend Marvin shot, and others—a colored couple named Harry and Harriette Moore—killed in their beds? I don't get it.

Mother sees things different. She tells me God's like the dealer in a giant card game. Because of luck, some people wind up with better cards than others, but the important thing is to do the best you can with the hand you're dealt. That's what you're doing, Vaylie—the best you can!

One thing for sure (I know because I've tried it both ways) is we can't give up hope. Marvin's mother says hope keeps us going, Vaylie. My mother says it keeps us in the game. 'Til luck, like the tide, turns. It always does, she says.

Give yourself a Happy New Year's hug from me, Vaylie. And know I'm sending you all the love and hope and luck I can spare!

                                        xxxooo, Reesa

# Chapter 25

To celebrate George Washington's birthday (and show off her new swimming pool), May Carol Garnet's invited our entire seventh-grade class to a Pool Party at her house.

"I don't want to go," I tell Mother. "Just yesterday, I heard our teacher scolding the boys for playing *eeny-meeny-miny-mo, catch the nigger by his toe, light the sticks and watch him blow.* If they try that in front of me, I'll have to hurt somebody," I warn Daddy.

But my parents are insisting I attend the party. "It's the entire class, so your absence could appear an affront, Reesa. Besides, Lucy Garnet will keep the boys in line. You'll be fine," they say. "Just go on and get along."

When Doto drops me off at May Carol's in Opalakee, she reminds me that Daddy and Luther will pick me up at three, on their way home from checking out a grove for sale, south of town.

May Carol's house is a split-level, with wall-to-wall carpets and sliding glass doors. The pool's what they call kidney-shaped with curved steps at one end and a big slide and diving board at the other. (Mr. Reed Garnet's in real estate and does *real* well.)

Since it's practically against the law to live in Florida and not know how to swim, most of us are good swimmers and divers, too. I join Joan Ellen Marks, who's sitting on the side, feet dangling in the shallow end, watching the boys show off. Their goal, of course, is to leap off the diving board, wrap themselves into a "cannonball" and create a big enough splash to get the girls at our end wet. I don't know the blond-headed boy climbing up the ladder.

I poke Joan Ellen. "Who's that?"

"He's May Carol's cousin Randy, Randall Jefferson Holt the third, a real Georgia jackass."

I love Joan Ellen. She's the only girl I know who swears out loud and gets away with it. She gets it from her mother, who's foul-mouthed but so funny about it and so well connected around town that nobody seems to care.

"Kind of favors her, don't he?" says Lottie Ann Louis, meaning that Randy's pointy features and pale skin tone's a lot like his cousin's.

Randy proves to be the king of cannonballs, splashing every single one of us.

"Told you, didn't I?" Joan Ellen says as we peel off our cover-ups and spread them on the grass to dry in the sun.

Miz Lucy Garnet appears on the patio with a large platter of fried chicken. Behind her, a short, yellow-skinned woman uses pot holders to carry a pan of baked beans, long strips of bacon still sizzling on top.

"Anybody hungry?" Miz Lucy calls. "We got a bunch of Selma's fried chicken here and, boy, is it good!"

Selma is the Garnets' new maid, hired last spring to replace Armetta. Selma lives in Opalakee Colored Town, west of the train tracks that divide the white area and downtown businesses from the Negro community.

All the boys rush forward to the table where Miz Lucy's placed the platter of chicken beside the heaping bowls of potato salad and cornbread and the stack of paper plates and napkins.

"Gentlemen, step back now. It's ladies *first* at our house, as I'm *sure* it is at yours," Miz Lucy chides the boys with a smile.

"Ain't no ladies at *my* house," Cousin Randy yells.

"No gentlemen, neither," Joan Ellen tells him, grinning at me.

The boys shuffle to the end of the line which we girls have politely formed.

Filling my plate, I decide that fried chicken and bacon-topped baked beans are only two of the many differences between my family and that of my Opalakee classmates. My mother bakes, never fries, our chicken. Our beans are "Boston-style," cooked in a round brown pot and served with round dark brown raisin bread instead of the buttery yellow cornbread Miz Lucy serves.

After lunch, May Carol and Miz Lucy organize a game of Pin the Tail on the Donkey.

Still enjoying her jackass joke, Joan Ellen looks from the game Donkey to Randy and asks "Which one?"

The boys win that game.

Next, we play Simon Says in the pool and, fortunately, we girls win that one. The tie-breaker game is a relay involving diving and swimming the length of the pool to hand off the baton to your team members at the opposite end. We put Lottie Ann, our best swimmer, last. Even though she narrowly beats out red-faced Randy, Miz Lucy calls it a tie.

Since it's ten 'til three and Daddy's due soon, I get out of the pool, visit the bathroom, grab my sun-dried cover-up from the lawn, and hunt for May Carol and Miz Lucy to thank them for inviting me. They're not in the pool area or the kitchen, where I see Selma and thank her for the delicious fried chicken.

"Thank you, honey," she says. "You're that McMahon girl, aren't you, from Mayflower? Your family helped out Armetta after she left here?"

"I think my parents would say that Armetta helped *us*; but, yes, I'm Reesa McMahon. Pleased to meet you," I say.

"Pleased to meet *you*, Reesa! You see much of Armetta and her husband Luther?"

"Well, actually, Luther and my father are picking me up any minute, which is why I was looking for May Carol, to say goodbye."

"I b'lieve you'll find Miss May Carol and her mamma in the back bedroom. And, Reesa . . ."

"Yes, ma'am?"

"Would you ask Luther to have Armetta give me a call?"

"I'll tell him as soon as I see him. Thanks again for the chicken. Bye!"

Racing down the hall, I hear Miz Lucy lecturing May Carol loudly, something about "conduct unbecoming a lady" and then the sound of a stinging slap. I rap loudly on the door and, without opening it, make my goodbye quick. "May Carol, it's Reesa! I'm going now; thanks for inviting me!"

"You're welcome, honey," Miz Lucy calls back, in a voice like sugar.

I turn and walk quickly down the hall, thankful for yet another difference between my mother and May Carol's.

Passing through the living room on my way out the door, I hear that Cousin Randy's organized the boys into a pool game like one I've played with my Chicago cousins. It involves one shut-eyed person calling out the word "Marco" while the others, trying to keep from getting caught, call back "Polo!" The big difference, however, is that shut-eyed Randy is calling out "Nigga!" and the others are calling back "Massa?"

*Jackass is right*, I decide, remembering Joan Ellen's words, and feeling my blood boil. Through the dining room, I see Selma in the kitchen—*no doubt she's hearing him, too*—and all of a sudden, as a loud "Nigga!" bursts through the house, this is *more* than I can *stand*!

A large green watermelon on the kitchen counter gives me an idea. I tear through the dining room, rush into the kitchen, scaring Selma, and say, "Knife! Grab the biggest knife you can find and follow me!"

Lunging out onto the patio, I yell, "Randall Jackass Holt the third, think *fast!*" and hurl the big melon straight at his stupid chest. It lands, just inches in front of him, with a huge splash that shocks him silly. On reflex, he scoops it up and now stands cradling it like a baby, glaring up at me from mid-pool.

For the briefest moment, I glare back, then smile real sweetly and say, with my best fake simper, "Miz Lucy says it's time for the seed-spitting contest out back. She's put Selma in charge of cutting and wants you to carry it out for her, please." "Bye, now," I call to the girls on the lawn and to Selma who, giant knife in hand, grins back at me, eyes very bright.

On the drive home, I tell Daddy and Luther all about it.

"Lawdy, you a bold little Rooster," Luther tells me. "Wonder where you got *that* from?"

"She's her grandmother's granddaughter, I'm afraid." Daddy shakes his head.

Luther chuckles. "Wait'll Ah tell Armetta. Better yet, think Ah'll let Selma tell her."

"Boy, can *she* cook," I tell him. "Selma's was the best fried chicken I've ever had."

"Uh-oh, you turning Southern Belle on us?" Daddy teases.

"No, sir, not if that's what Miz Lucy's trying to make May Carol."

"You *know*," Luther says, raising his eyebrows, "Armetta could tell some *tales* 'bout Miz Lucy . . . that woman is *high strung!*"

"I sure wouldn't want to cross her," my father agrees.

"Oh, she'd pull your hair out, for *sure*," Luther tells him.

Daddy's chuckling as he turns to back the truck up to the packinghouse platform, but all of a sudden, his look changes. "What do we have here?" I hear him ask under his breath.

A man, a stranger, is standing on our platform. He's medium-built, with the untanned look of someone who spends his days indoors. He's dressed for business in a white shirt, dark pants, and a tie that's been loosened in the afternoon heat. In his hands is a notebook and he's watching our truck.

# Chapter 26

Mother, spotting us from the showroom, appears tense-faced on the platform. As we pile out, she says, "Warren, this is James Jameson from the F.B.I."

"Warren McMahon," my father tells him, extending his hand. "This is my daughter, Marie, and our friend, Luther Cully."

"Jim Jameson, sir, in the flesh, as requested."

"Excuse me," Mother says, "I've got customers in the showroom."

Mr. Jameson smiles at Mother and says, "Thank you, ma'am."

"Reesa?" Mother says, meaning I'm to come with her.

"I'll be right there," I tell her, stalling for time.

"Mr. Jameson, my assistant, here," Daddy says, nodding to me, "doesn't let me talk to law enforcement without seeing some identification."

"I heard about that. Miss McMahon, my badge," he tells me, not smiling, and flips open the black wallet from his back pocket. "And here's my card," he adds.

I examine his badge and the small white rectangle. "Says here he's official, Daddy."

"Where's he from?" Daddy asks, catching my eye.

*Daddy heard it, too.* Mr. Jameson's accent—the shape of his vowels especially—is a revelation, and a relief.

"Well," I say, "his address is Orlando, but he sounds like Ohio to *me.*"

"Cleveland," Mr. Jameson nods.

"Can we talk to him, then?" Daddy asks me.

"Fine by me," I tell him. *Ohio, I think, is a definite step up from those other two agents who were here before.* We have many long-time customers from Ohio. Mother loves them because "they order early and their checks are always good. Ohioans," she always says, "are as *good* as *gold.*"

"Well, thank *you,* ma'am," Mr. Jameson tells me, very serious. "Okay to sit here?" he asks Daddy, pointing to the bench by the washer's big water tank. "Can Mr. Cully join us, too?"

Daddy and Luther nod, grab chairs and sit, facing the agent on the bench.

"Your deputy staying?" Mr. Jameson asks, meaning me.

Daddy studies me a moment. Then he says, "Reesa, your mother's expecting you in the showroom."

I leave them real reluctantly and walk slowly around the waxer's large metal hood that runs sideways to the washer, six feet high and eight feet long. On the far side, I can hear their voices through the hood's air vent. If I peer through the vent,

I can just see Daddy's and Luther's profiles through the other air vent on the opposite side.

"Mr. McMahon, Mr. Cully, I'm here to tell you that you have friends in high places," Mr. Jameson of Ohio says, rustling his papers.

"Really? Who would that be?" Daddy asks.

"Well, let's start with my boss, Mr. Hoover. And while we're at it, let's add a Mr. Thurgood Marshall of New York City."

"Okay . . ."

"And, Mr. Cully, you're the father of Marvin Cully, shot and killed last March?"

"Yes, sir." Luther sounds nervous. He glances at Daddy.

"Don't worry, Mr. Cully, you're not in any trouble. In fact, truth be told, *I'm* the one in trouble," Mr. Jameson tells him.

"What do you mean?" Daddy asks. Luther stays silent.

"Well, as you know, two people were assassinated, by dynamite, over six weeks ago. So far, my elite corps of crackerjack agents have produced precious little evidence, and not a lot of suspects. Mr. Hoover is, shall we say, not happy; particularly since Mr. Truman of the White House, Mr. Marshall of the N.A.A.C.P., assorted influential people from the Civil Rights Congress, the Anti-Defamation League of B'nai B'rith, and the Florida Board of Tourism are all breathing down his neck."

"Is that so?" my father says mildly.

"Believe me, it is very much *so,*" Mr. Jameson says.

"What's this have to do with us?" Daddy asks him.

"We're operating in a bit of a vacuum here. Although your state's assorted departments of law enforcement promised 'full and complete cooperation,' they've done nearly nothing to help us get to the bottom of anything. In spite of that, we have some extremely compelling reasons to believe that the Opalakee Klan has direct knowledge about the murders of Mr. and Mrs. Moore. The problem is, we have no inside sources. According to Mr. Marshall, you have a very clear handle on things around here, Mr. McMahon. I don't suppose you'd consider joining the Klan for us?"

"Me? A Klanner? Mr. Jameson, I'm a Yankee, for starters, and a man who speaks his mind pretty clearly. Even if they'd *have* me, which they wouldn't, I couldn't do it. It would take me—what d'you think, Luther—three, maybe four, minutes to blow my cover?"

"I figured you might say that. But here's the *real* reason I've come . . . Mr. Marshall says that between you and Mr. Cully, you have a circle of friends who, let's see, how'd he say it, 'would put the F.B.I and the C.I.A. to shame.' "

In my narrow view, I see Luther stiffen. At his side, Daddy shoots him a quick look, then turns back to face Mr. Jameson, who says, "What I'd like to ask you is this . . . I have a list of names we believe to be members of the Opalakee Klan, cross-referenced from several other sources. What I'd like you to do, and you don't have to say yes or no this minute . . . what I'd like you to do is look over this list and have your circle of friends look over it, too, and simply cross off anyone who's not a known Klan member. Of course, if you see any glaring omissions, and you'd like to add a name or two, that would be fine. But at this point I'm merely looking to delete anybody who's not a Klan member. Is that something you might be willing to do to help us catch young Cully's and the Moores' killers?"

"*If* we agree to look at your list, Mr. Jameson, what happens to it when we're done with it?" Daddy's tone is careful, not saying yes or no.

"Well, I've thought about that. I've placed two pieces of paper in this envelope." I hear the rustle of more papers. "The first sheet is the list we've been discussing. The second is a short summary of an event that occurred last August fourth. A high-speed chase between a black Chrysler and three pickup trucks. Did you see it?"

"Didn't everybody?" Daddy replies.

"The second sheet merely describes the incident. You may write in any comments you deem appropriate. As you can see," Jameson says, handing the envelope to Daddy, "it's already stamped and addressed to Mr. James J. Smith—that's me—at P.O. Box 12 in Orlando. All you have to do is look things over, make your comments, then seal it and mail it as soon as you can."

Daddy turns again to face Luther. Slowly, without moving, Daddy raises an eyebrow and, it appears, Luther drops his chin in a nod.

"We'll take a look," Daddy says, standing up. Luther and Mr. Jameson stand, too.

"And mail it?" Mr. Jameson asks.

"I'll deliver it myself into the hands of our lovely post-mistress," I hear Daddy promise as I duck hastily out the side door and into the showroom.

After Mr. Jameson leaves, Daddy and Luther want to tell Mother what happened. But she stops them.

"Why," she wants to know, "didn't you send Reesa down here with me?"

"I did," he says.

"Well, she wasn't here," Mother tells him. All three adults turn their eyes on me.

*Uh-oh*, I think. I was hoping she hadn't noticed.

"But . . ." Daddy's stare is turning to a glare.

"But little Miss Big Ears stood on the other side of the waxer spying on you and the F.B.I.," Mother says in that tone that will brook no excuses.

"Well, why not?" I say, blistered by her calling me Little Miss anything! "It's about time Mr. James Jameson showed up. And what could he possibly say that would be any worse than what I've seen or heard already? I saw what the Klan did to Marvin, same as you. I heard that deputy in Mount Laura tell how it happened. I heard him say how, if Mr. Reed Garnet hadn't shown up late, Marvin might still be alive. And *I'm* the one who had to go make nice at the Garnets' house this very afternoon! It's not fair for you to treat me like a baby. I'm *not* one—not anymore!"

I realize, when I finish, that I've embarrassed Luther, who's now studying his shoes, and I feel bad about that. Daddy's looking at me with admiring eyes, but Mother's face stays a blank.

"She makes a good point," Daddy says softly, but in that way that leaves everything up to Mother.

"Oh, Reesa, when I was your age"—she shakes her head sadly—"it was the middle of the Depression. I worried every single day that my father would lose his job and we'd wind up in the soup lines. My mother told me not to worry, that worrying was her job, that children should have fun, and I should be carefree. But I worried anyway. So I guess it wouldn't help for me to tell you the same thing. I'm just sorry we didn't do a better job protecting you from all this. And for the record," she says, "you're not full grown, just more than halfway."

"Yes, ma'am," I say with as much earnestness as I can muster, considering Daddy's winking at me behind her back.

At his suggestion, the four of us go into the office off the empty showroom. It's late in the afternoon and doubtful that we'll have any more customers today. As we gather 'round his desk, Daddy opens Mr. Jameson's envelope, pulls out two sheets of paper, and sets them side by side on his blotter.

Luther responds to the first one with a low whistle.

*Daddy was right,* I think, *when he told Mr. Marshall that a list of Opalakee Klan members would read like the local social register.* Most of the two dozen or so names are all too familiar.

Across the desk, Mother's eyes meet Daddy's. For the first time in a long time, the curtain of her composure parts. In her face, I see fear and the flare of resistance, like a little flame leaping up.

"You agreed to do this?" she asks him carefully.

Daddy's jaw juts. "We both did," he tells her, nodding in Luther's direction.

Her eyes drift back to the paper on the desk. She stands very still, then looks back up at Daddy. His face is firm, his eyes steady. With the slightest shake of her head, she registers her worry and retreats from a fight. The curtain drops, closing us out again. Closing herself in?

*Don't worry,* I itch to tell her, but it's clear she will. *Besides, we can't back out now. This is important! Mr. Marshall himself sent Mr. Jameson our way. Mr. Marshall and the F.B.I. wouldn't put Daddy, Luther and the maids in any danger, would they?*

The list is arranged alphabetically. As Daddy and Luther pore over it, the most obvious omission is at the top. With a ballpoint pen, Daddy adds: *Bowman, J.D.*

"How the hell did they miss *him?*" he wonders aloud.

*Exactly what I was thinking.*

Beside the name of *Casselton, Emmett* are the initials *E.C.*

"For Exalted Cyklops. The big cheese," Daddy explains to me.

The second change is further down. There are three entries with the same last name, a prominent father and his two sons. Daddy crosses off the younger son's name. He lives down the road from us and is a deacon in our church, always has a roll of Life Savers in his pocket in case somebody gets a coughing attack. His father and older brother live further south and attend Opalakee First Baptist.

"I've had many conversations with him," Daddy tells Luther. "He's a good Christian and absolutely against the Klan's tactics. Even told me once that the rest of the family kid him about it, calling him 'medium rare.' "

"What's that mean?" I've never heard the term applied to a person before.

"That's their way of saying he's soft and a little pink, meaning Communist."

"He's a *Communist*?" I ask quickly, balking at the idea.

"Of course not," Mother says. "It's just their way of insulting him because he's chosen not to join the Klan."

The second sheet is a lot more interesting. At the top, the title says "Attempted Abduction, 8/4/51." A paragraph about the Big Chase follows. Below that are four numbered sections.

The first section is about the Chrysler New Yorker and the four people who were in it—two N.A.A.C.P. attorneys and two Northern reporters.

The other numbered sections contain descriptions of each of the three pickups. All three sections say "occupants," followed by blank lines. There is a question mark at the beginning of each line. All three truck sections have an area marked "vehicle owner." Two of the three have the owner's name filled in correctly. (We aren't the *only* ones who know an Emmett Casselton Casbah Groves truck when we see one, even with the name covered up.) In the section for the big black Ford pickup, the "vehicle owner" line is blank with another question mark. Daddy fills in the name: *J. D. Bowman.*

"That's it for us, Luther," he says, carefully replacing the two pages into the envelope and handing it over. "The rest is up to the ladies of your C.I.A."

Luther takes the envelope and nods. "Looks like there'll be a special choir practice after church tomorrow."

# *Chapter 27*

---

**B**loom time, which used to be my favorite time of year, is back. For most people, it's the perfumed time of new beginnings. For me, it's the anniversary of Marvin's death. I am in gloom time. And, most certainly, *not* the girl I was last time the tangerine tree outside my window wore its band of Angel Blossoms. I can never be that girl again, so safe, so sure of everything and everyone. I long to feel that comfortable inside my skin, but I will never be *her* again.

It's been one whole week since Daddy and Luther mailed Mr. Jameson's envelope to his Orlando P.O. Box. I felt sure we'd have heard something by now. But as the days drag by, as the date Marvin died comes and goes with no hint of resolution, the nightmare I thought I'd outgrown returns.

I wake screaming. The run through the grove, the crowd on the hill, the flashing red lights are all the same. But this time, after I kick and claw my way to the front, after J. D. Bowman sees me and yells "Grab her, too!" because "She's a Jew!," the men in the circle yank me between them. Their faces, now familiar from the F.B.I. list, surround me, contorted in anger, eyes hard, teeth bared, as a hideously laughing J. D. Bowman raises a rattlesnake whip high above my head . . .

This night, Mother and Daddy are out for the evening. It's Doto who hears me and holds me tight. Turning on the light, she sits down beside me and we talk quietly for some time, going over every awful detail of the dream.

"All right, then," she says, "I have an idea. Will you wait here while I get you something?"

Within moments, she returns with the spare set of her special pink bedding. Together, we strip my mattress of its usual white cotton and remake it with my grandmother's sheets, ordered just for her from Chicago's Carter-Ferris-Mott. Slipping between them, I relish the silky pink softness, the scent of Ivory Snow, and I thank her with all my heart.

"I'm sure I'll sleep perfectly fine now."

She nods, cat-eye glasses winking in the light; then, lifting my chin between her fingers, she asks, "How come I never heard about this bad dream before?"

"Kept it to myself," I say.

"Because?" she wants to know.

"Because Daddy's got enough to worry about without taking me on, too."

"And you figure you can fend for yourself?"

"Yes!" I shoot back, then, meeting her gaze, tack on a respectful "ma'am."

"Oh, Reesa," Doto says, "you, your father and me . . . we are cut from the same quarry, rock-hard and marble-headed."

"Not at all like Mother," I say.

Doto doesn't like my tone and leans in so she can eye me more directly. "Your mother's a different kind of strong than we are, young lady."

"What do you mean?"

"I mean," she says, "we McMahons are the stuff that mountains are made of. But your mother . . . well, your mother's more like a river, which is stronger still. Do you understand?"

I don't and tell her so.

"No, of course you don't. You live in a state without a decent-sized mountain or river in sight. I'll tell you what: Next spring, I'll take you west with me to your uncle Harry's. We'll go to the Grand Canyon, and when you stand on the rim and see that sight carved out of solid rock by water and ice, you'll know exactly what I mean. We'll follow the Colorado River north. You'll see how fresh water makes the difference between a livable valley and an impossible desert. Maybe then you'll understand the kind of strength your mother has."

"Yes, ma'am," I say, needing to think about it.

"You're lucky to have the parents you have, Reesa. Don't you forget that," she says, squeezing my hand in goodnight. "Do you want this light on or out?"

"Out," I say. "I'll be all right."

"Of course you will," my grandmother chuckles. "Sleep tight."

T wo days later, Mr. Jim Jameson of Ohio parks his brown Dodge on the side driveway, away from the prying eyes across the Trail, and spends an hour or so talking to Daddy in the back. At one point, Daddy leads him into the showroom to point up and out the side door, at the spot that can only be Emmett Casselton's eagle's nest, the windowed office high above the tanks of Mayflower Citrus on the other side of the road. When they're finished, the two of them amble up to Mother and me at the front counter.

Mr. Jameson makes cheerful small talk, about the weather, the upcoming primary elections. Mother tells him she's on the fence between Stevenson and Kefauver, if, of course, Stevenson ever gets off the fence to run.

Daddy's a Kefauver man all the way. He relished the newspaper accounts of Kefauver's Senate Crime Investigating Committee hearings in Miami. Just last year, Kefauver's committee had a field day with Dade County Sheriff "Smiling Jimmy" Sullivan, who couldn't quite explain how, during five years in office, his personal assets jumped $65,000 while his sheriff's salary was never more than $12,000 a year!

"Believe me," Mr. Jameson laughs, "I've a stack of files six feet high on that one."

Kefauver's committee also uncovered that William H. Johnston, one of the Governor's cronies and a major state contractor, was a close associate of the Capone gang.

"You know," Daddy says, "Governor Warren was furious over that. He's vowed he'll never let Kefauver set foot in this state again."

"Won't that be interesting come primary time in May?" Mr. Jameson grins. "Though I should be *long* gone by then."

"Are you really that close?"

"Oh, there's some very interesting irons in the fire," Mr. Jameson replies. "Things are heating up. People are getting nervous. I anticipate a fair amount of action in the next couple weeks."

# Chapter 28

That Friday, Ren goes home after school with his friend, Petey Smith, who lives out in the country, a few miles east of Mayflower.

Daddy and I are set to pick him up before supper, around five.

Since the County Dump is just a mile or so past Petey's house, Daddy asks Robert to load up the truck with a bunch of stumps that've been cluttering our grove road for weeks. Daddy and I head out around four. At the Dump, the old Negro caretaker named Horatio Sykes ambles over and helps us unload. The dump *stinks*. Everywhere's that sweet sickening stink of things rotting, dying or in full, dark earth decay. Daddy tells me to breathe through my mouth, but I still feel the sting of it in my throat.

Afterwards, we double back to pick up Ren. Petey's house is deep in a grapefruit grove that belongs to Emmett Casselton. The blue and gold Casbah Groves signs glint at us from mile markers beside the road.

"Looks like old Emmett forgot to spray for leaf curl," Daddy says, noting the brown-tipped leaves as our truck weaves and bumps down the narrow dirt road toward Petey's house.

As we enter the clearing, Ren bolts out the screen door and into the yard. He's waving his arms frantically for us to stop. He's got a bandage around his head and Petey and his father hot on his heels.

"*Now* what?" my father says, heaving himself out of the truck.

"Daddy, Daddy, the Klan, a man . . . *shot* at us, shot *me*, just playing, '*gators*! He—"

I've never, in my life, seen Ren so flustered.

"Hold on, now, what's this all about?" Daddy's looking over Ren's head to lock eyes with Petey's father.

"Warren, you would not b'lieve it!" Mr. Smith, who everyone calls Smitty, says. "These two boys been playin' fine 'round here all afternoon. 'Bout a hour ago, they asked if they could run over to that ol' sinkhole lake in the grove, you know the one with Mr. Casselton's fishing camp on the landing in the middle? Well, they jus' wanted to see if they could spot a 'gator or two. Climbed up the water tower to get a better look. Ren, tell your daddy what happened next."

"We got up there, Daddy, and saw a whole bunch of men in white robes." Ren's face beneath the bandage is beet red, shiny with sweat. His voice has risen to a pitch like a girl's.

"It was the Klan!" big-eyed Petey puts in.

"They were marching, three across," Ren says, "down the big ramp and into the camp. They looked stupid in their pointy hats and all . . ."

"Like a bunch of fat ol' ghosts," Petey adds.

"Well, Petey and me . . ." Ren pauses to catch his breath. "We had us a couple pieces of irrigation pipe. We were just poking fun, making noises through the pipes. You know, like *Woooooo!*, like ghosts. Well, one of them started waving at us to stop."

"Big white sleeves flappin' like a crane." Petey demonstrates.

"We should've stopped, Daddy, I *know* that, but he just looked so funny waving his arms at us . . . we started laughing."

"And we just couldn't stop!" Petey says earnestly.

"Another man came out and started *shooting* at us! I mean pointed both barrels right at us and *shot*! When something bounced off the water tower and hit me in the head, I thought I was going to *die* up there!" Ren's hand flies to his heart, his chest heaves beneath his dirty T-shirt.

Petey's father Smitty shakes his head. "I heard it from the house and went runnin'. I was so *damn* mad, Warren, I ran straight through the saw grass to get there." He shows the slashes on his hands and arms from the razor-sharp grass. "Would've gone right in the middle of those guys if a big guard hadn't stopped me with a sawed-off shotgun. 'What the *hell* do you think you're doin'?' I yell at him. 'Since when does the Klan take to shootin' at a couple of kids?' I was mad, I tell you! The guard . . . he says he's sorry, says 'There's big stuff goin' on and the Grand Dragon from Jacksonville's in town. The boys are a little edgy,' he says, 'but they had no business shootin' at children. Those kids were lucky,' he tells me, 'the guy who shot at 'em was loaded with bird shot, coulda been a whole lot worse with *buck*shot.' "

Daddy is silent. Then, gently lifting the edge of Ren's

bandage to inspect his head, he says, "Let me see, son."
Bloody red scrapes begin a hair outside my brother's left eye.
They run across his temple to just above the top of his ear.

"Smitty says if it'd been a little to the right, I might've
lost an eye. I thought I was dead for *sure*," Ren says gravely.

Daddy pulls him close, but says nothing.

"You're telling me that fishing camp is the Klan's *headquarters*?" he asks Smitty.

"Can you b'lieve it? Lived here a year and a half and never
seen a thing. Usually meet at night, I guess. Today was somethin' special, 'cause of the Grand Dragon and all."

"Old Emmett's going to be hearing from me on this."
Daddy's voice tells me he is more than *mad*. He is *furious*.

When we get him home, Ren explains everything all
over again to Mother and Doto. Mother's eyes flit between Ren and Daddy. After Ren's done telling his story,
Mother wraps him in her arms and herds him off to the bathroom to clean and Mercurochrome his head. Mitchell, fasci-
nated by Ren's wounds, tags along after them. We can hear him
pestering everyone with questions, punctuated by Mother's
"Hush now, Mitchell," and Ren's loud "Ooow, that hurts!"

In the kitchen, Doto is fuming in Daddy's face. "Jesus H.
Christ, Warren!" *Doto never swears; Daddy's clearly as shocked by
it as I am.* "First these maniacs get away with *murdering* Marvin; then they run off Sal and Sophia. No doubt they had
*something* to do with blowing up the poor Moores. And now,
*now*, they're taking potshots at our own flesh and blood? This
is outrageous! Beyond barbaric! Are you going to *do something*
about this? Because if *you're* not, *I AM!!!*" Behind her cat-eye
glasses, Doto's ready to explode.

Mother appears in the kitchen doorway. "Now what?" she asks wearily.

Daddy's become a boulder. Everything about him, his neck, his voice, is solid rock.

"Now, I tell Emmett Casselton what I think of men dressed in sheets shooting at children," he says, stone-faced. "I also tell Mr. Jim Jameson that there's going to be a little fireworks at the Opalakee Klan headquarters."

"Warren, can we talk about this?" Mother pleads.

"We'll talk *later*, Lizbeth," he grits between his teeth. "Right now, I have a couple calls to make." My father, the human mountain, strides toward his office off the living room. I hear him firmly, deliberately close the door behind him.

"What's he going to *do?*" I ask Mother. My heart is pounding so hard I'm afraid she'll hear it.

"Lizbeth," Doto says, "the Klan has pushed Warren one step too far today. He's *got* to push back."

"But *how?*" I want to know, wishing I could stop the trembling in Mother's hands, wanting the flutter in my stomach to fly away.

"I guess we have to wait and see," Mother says, turning her face away from me. Doto motions for me to leave them alone.

In the living room, I find Ren where Mother left him, watching cartoons on the couch with Mitchell.

Mitchell jumps up when he sees me and, clutching his tummy, asks, "We going to eat soon, Reesa?"

Poor thing. In all the commotion over Ren, we've forgotten supper. "Run into the kitchen," I tell him, "Doto will feed you."

Ren remains slumped on the couch, his eyes glued to the

TV screen. The bright orange streak of Mercurochrome on his head reminds me I should probably feel sorry for him. But what I really feel is *mad*.

"What in the Sam Hill were you thinking, Ren?" I hiss at him, deliberately standing between him and his show.

"Don't want to talk about it."

"Of course you don't! Because it's probably the dumbest damn thing you've ever done in your life! Standing on a water tower, yelling at the Klan. You heard what they did to Marvin, you know they killed the Moores. What did you think they'd do to you?"

"Nothing," he mumbles. He's refusing to look at me.

"Nothing? You mean you *thought* nothing, or they'd *do* nothing?"

"I thought we were safe." He's pouting.

"And where in tarnation did you get that idea?"

"I thought we were safe," he says, meeting my eyes for the first time. "Because we're *white!*" He hurls the words at my chest.

There it is. The ugly truth that had been circling 'round my stomach, creeping up my spine, sneaking around the edges of my mind. The bald fact that skin color—the paper-thin veil that made Marvin an easy target and gave Ren his air of invincibility—no longer matters. With the Klan's attack on two white boys, the rules have abruptly changed; their evil is no longer limited to Negroes, Jews and Catholics. The Klan's crossed its own hate line. Now, *any* of us, even *children*, can be targeted. It's a dreadful thought. And I hold my brother completely responsible.

"This is all your fault!" I lash. "You've got Doto about to have a *heart attack*, Daddy on the phone saying *God-knows-what* to Mr. Casselton, and Mother worried out of her head! I hope you had your fun, Ren, because you've most certainly ruined *everything* for the *rest* of us!"

It was a mean and hateful thing to say. I aimed for his heart, and I could see by his face, I hit dead center. I'm glad and sorry at the same time. And, for the first time in my life, I am quite afraid.

## Chapter 29

Nobody's talking this morning. When Ren got up and Mother saw his head, its cluster of cuts round and ripe like a bunch of table grapes, his eye socket swollen like a small plum, she packed him in the car without a word and headed, we assume, to Doc Johnny's. Doto's carted Mitchell off to who-knows-where. And I'm left to help Daddy open up the showroom. *Divide and conquer—it's a sure sign the adults are upset with each other.*

Daddy and I make the short drive to the packinghouse without talking. As we enter from the back, I'm the first one to see it—the brown Dodge parked outside.

"Somebody wants their orange juice awful early," I say.

"Oh, I think he wants more than orange juice," Daddy says as he unlocks and slides open the big front doors. "Agent Jameson, I presume?"

"Mr. McMahon," Mr. Jameson says, reaching out his open window to shake Daddy's hand. "Do I need to present my badge again?" he asks me as he enters the showroom.

"No, sir," I say. It's obvious he's trying to keep things friendly.

"Mr. McMahon . . . may I call you Warren?"

Daddy nods, but says nothing. He's a stone wall.

"I got your message very late last night, drove over from the coast first thing this morning. What's all this about fireworks?"

"I thought you should know that the Opalakee Klan is about to get a taste of its own medicine," Daddy says flat-out.

"What do you mean . . . medicine?" Mr. Jameson asks.

"The very same substance they administered to the Moores."

"Dynamite? You're going to dynamite the fishing camp?"

"Yes, I am," Daddy says, locking his jaw.

"Hold on, Warren, our agents have appropriated pretty much all the dynamite in the county." Mr. Jameson's smile's gone a little wobbly.

"Nobody's appropriated mine!" Daddy tells him.

A noise in the back room startles the three of us. Mr. Jameson wheels around, as Daddy and I realize it's only Robert, come as usual to sweep the floors and rake the gravel.

"Our employee, Robert Carmichael," Daddy tells Mr. Jameson, nodding toward the back.

"Warren . . ." Mr. Jameson's voice has totally dropped his friendly-fellow routine. "I have no business telling you this, but I'm going to . . . The U.S. Attorney General has agreed to convene a Grand Jury in Miami the first week of April. We'll be presenting everything we have on the Opalakee Klan, its involvement in the deaths of the Moores, as well as the Gordon Klavern's bombings in Miami."

*What about Marvin?* I want to scream, my hands fisting so hard my fingers hurt.

"If you take *any* aggressive action now," Mr. Jameson tells Daddy, "you could destroy our hopes of ever bringing these Crackers to justice. The subpoenas are already typed, and we're set to deliver them on Monday."

"They shot at my son, nearly took his eye out," my father says, flint-faced.

"They're fools, Warren. You want to know why the Grand Dragon's in town? To try to calm them down. We've been all over these guys like stink on"—he glances in my direction— "*feces.* Some of them are worried about having their precious family names dragged into court, so they've quit, surrendered their robes and their dynamite and quit. The Opalakee Klan is going *down.* You can't ruin this for us."

"Nobody shoots at my children without retaliation."

"You want to *retaliate*, Warren? I've got just the job for you."

"What?" Daddy asks, eyeing Mr. Jameson.

"Since last time we talked, we've found an insider, an older gentleman who says there's a hidden compartment inside the fishing camp building which could put nails in a whole lot of coffins. Membership records, treasurer's books, things like that. That's *legal* dynamite, Warren, a whole lot more powerful than the stuff you want to plant."

"So why don't you just go in and get it?"

"No judge in this county would give us a warrant. What we're talking about here . . ." Mr. Jameson looks down at his shoe, then up. "Well, to be honest, what we're talking about is illegal break-in and entry."

"I'll do it."

Mr. Jameson doesn't seem to understand.

"I was going in to plant some dynamite," Daddy says

quietly. "If you're telling me I can't do that, I have to do something."

"Well, uh, we sort of see this as a two-man job. One to go in and find the stuff and one to stand watch."

"I'll go with you." Robert emerges from the back. He's carrying the push broom diagonally, like a rifle, in front of him.

"This is a *man's* job, son," Mr. Jameson tells him.

" 'Scuse me, *sir*," Robert says, blue eyes blazing. After all, he *is* seventeen. "The reason we moved here was to get away from the Klan in South Carolina. They practically *killed* my father because somebody confused him with some man dating a Klanner's ex-wife. They beat him with a cat-o'-nine-tails and left him for dead right on our doorstep. I *hate* the Klan. If Mr. Mac needs me, I'm *in*."

Mr. Jameson stares at Robert for a long second, we all do, then turns back to Daddy and lifts both hands, palms forward, in a way that I know means *your call*.

"How much time do we have?" Daddy asks him.

"Why?" Mr. Jameson asks.

"Well, I'd planned to go the next moonless night, which, according to the calendar, is eight days from now."

"You've got *that*, but not much more. We need to have all the evidence in hand as soon as possible."

"Do I call you when I have it?" Daddy wants to know.

"No. No calls. Let me get you something from the car."

Mr. Jameson strides to the Dodge and pulls out a stiff flat canvas bag, about the size of a TV tray. When he hands it to Daddy, I see the mailing label is addressed to the P.O. box in Orlando.

"I don't know how much postage you'll need, but there's a twenty inside to cover it. Send it first class, okay?"

"Right, as if I'm going to break into Klan headquarters and send whatever I find by parcel post?" Daddy shoots back.

"I am, uh, authorized to pay you two hundred fifty dollars for your trouble," Mr. Jameson says.

"I don't want your money," Daddy tells him right away. "The only thing I do want is your word that you'll strike any mention of my name, or Luther's, or young Robert's here, from your files."

Mr. Jameson nods. "Warren . . . if you get caught, I never heard of you. If you live, make sure your attorney packs the jury with tenderhearted parents of boys your son's age."

"I'm way ahead of you." Daddy's extending his hand. "Will we see you again?"

"Only in the funny papers," Mr. Jameson says, returning his grip. Then, "You're doing us a tremendous service, you know."

"Let's hope so," Daddy answers.

"Pleasure to see *you* again, young lady," Mr. Jameson tells me. "Stay out of trouble, young man." He cocks and points his fingers like a gun at Robert, then walks out into the sun.

The months of hand-holding and head-ducking are over. The weeks of waiting for *some*one to do *some*thing are done. My father has finally found his way into the fight.

He turns, signaling to Robert to follow him up the stairs and onto the platform. I'm left in the still-dark showroom to turn on the lights, unlock the cash register, and deal with the tornado of feelings—pride, relief, terror—whirling around me.

Outside, off one of the big specimen trees planted by the drive to impress the tourists, an overripe grapefruit falls to the sand. The sound's like a heavy fist hitting flesh.

# Chapter 30

Daddy's decision to help the F.B.I. sparks off a slew of other choices: He, Mother and Doto choose not to demand a police investigation of Ren's shooting ("The Constable was probably standing there in his sheets when it happened, anyway," Doto sneers); not to discuss the details of the shooting outside our family ("I've told Petey the same thing," Smitty says, "after I spoke my piece with Mr. Casselton." "Who is, after all, his landlord," Daddy reminds Mother); not to disclose his F.B.I. plans to Ren and Mitchell ("They're too young," Mother says, "and they know way too much already"); and, finally, to ask Armetta and the maids for help.

The decision to keep the source of Ren's injury a family secret hits the boys hardest. Ren was hoping for some center-of-town showdown between Daddy and the Klan, like in *High Noon* with Gary

Cooper, Ren's favorite actor. And Mitchell remains mesmerized by the mechanics of the "bad guy's bird shot" bouncing off the metal water tower to hit Ren in the head.

"I saw the very same thing on *Hopalong Cassidy!*" he insists, till I want to throttle him.

The day after Daddy agreed to help Mr. Jameson is a Sunday.

I've got Mitchell by the hand on our way into Sunday school when eagle-eyed Miss Maybelle intercepts us with "Where's my hero this morning?" (That's what she calls Ren ever since he rescued her from the rattler.)

"He got shot!" Mitchell blurts out.

"No, no, *caught,* Mitchell, Ren got *caught* by a branch climbing up the big live oak out back. Scraped his head from here to here," I show her, all the while squeezing Mitchell's hand, *hard.*

"Swoll up like a balloon," Mitchell says, finally getting into it.

"Purple as a plum," I say as Miss Maybelle continues to give me the eye.

"Goin' to miss school tomorrow?" she wants to know.

"Maybe a day or two," I tell her. "But Doc Johnny says he'll be good as new by next weekend."

Later that afternoon, it's Mother who has to run interference with a concerned Miss Maybelle. "He's sound asleep," Mother tells her at our front door, accepting a plate piled high with "feel-better brownies."

Now, about the maids: It was a lifetime ago that Daddy joked to Luther about his personal spy ring, the circle of choir members who work as maids in the homes of area Klansmen. Before Marvin's murder, the circle was mostly social. Afterwards, it turned political, seeking and sending information to Armetta, who in turn fed it to Mr. Harry Moore.

Along the way, Armetta and Mr. Harry and his wife, Harriette, became friends. It was Armetta who invited the Moores into The Quarters and helped them register eligible adults to vote.

Fueled by the Moores' murder, it's Armetta who convinced the ladies of the choir to fill in the blanks on the F.B.I.'s list of Klan members. It's Armetta who expanded the circle to include several other maids from the Colored Town in Opalakee. "It's Armetta," Daddy assures Doto, "who'll find out if Monday, March twenty-fourth is a Klan meeting night or not."

Luther argues strongly that he should be the one to go with Daddy. "Robert's jus' a boy. Ah know those groves like the back of mah hand."

"No, Luther," Daddy argues back. "If you and I got caught, a Negro and a Yankee in Klan headquarters, neither of us would live to tell about it. With Robert, I can play the upset father and probably talk my way out of any trouble."

"Ah'm driving y'all then," Luther insists. "Ah know jus' where to let y' off and the safest place to pick y'all up."

"And what if they run into you, alone in the middle of a white area in the dead of night? You'd never see daylight. This is a two-man job and you can't be one of them. All I need is for you and Armetta to confirm that the twenty-fourth is clear."

Whatever objections my mother has to Daddy's plan—I can tell she's not the least bit happy about it—have been raised outside my hearing. Daddy's resolved, a man on a mission. And Mother is real quiet, more Poker Faced than ever.

It's two days before Buddy's tail wagging and the familiar

*tappety-tap-TAP* on the back door tell us Luther has Daddy's answer.

The boys have left the table already and are plopped in front of the television laughing at Allen Funt's *Candid Camera* show. I'm at the fridge, refilling our tea glasses, so I let Luther in.

"Evenin', Rootin'-Tootin'!"

"Hey, Luther, pour you some tea?"

"That'd be fine, real fine, thank you. Evenin', MizLizbeth, Miz Doto. How y'all tonight?"

"You're in high spirits," Daddy says and invites him to "have a seat" in Ren's empty chair.

"You bet Ah *am*! There are Grand Jury subpoenas showin' up all over the place, at some of the finest homes and oldest names in Opalakee. The ladies say they ain't never heard the blues sung so bad; the folks with the white robes hangin' in their closets are whinin' to beat the band. People callin' each other back and forth, wantin' to know what they s'posed to say, where they g'wan to stay, how long they g'wan to be gone, and how the hang did the Governor let this happen. Well, of course, they not sayin' 'hang,' but Ah won't repeat what they really sayin' in front of the ladies."

Daddy nods. "Jim Jameson said the subpoenas'd be there."

"That he did and that they are," Luther agrees. "And as long as we're talkin' 'bout what's happenin' where, looky here what *Ah* got."

Luther unbuttons his shirt pocket and pulls out a small, folded piece of paper. Carefully, he opens it to full letter size, laying it on the table in front of Daddy, smoothing out the creases with the flat of his hand. I peer over Daddy's shoulder to see.

It's a flyer announcing a "Kounty-wide Klonverse," inviting "all members of the Orange Kounty Klaverns of the Invisible Empire" to gather on the north shore of Lake Eola in Orlando, Friday night, March twenty-first—three nights from now!

"Where in the world did you get this?"

Luther looks at Daddy sideways. "You know, Mist'Warren, any laundress worth her salt checks the pockets of the dirty clothes before puttin' things in the washer. Ah got four more just like it if you want extras."

"So, instead of the twenty-fourth, we'll go in on the twenty-first. Luther, tell Armetta this is a Godsend!"

"You got *that* right, Mist'Warren." Luther's smile is wide and golden. "Could be the first time the good Lawd sent word by way of a laundry chute!"

The seventy-two hours between Luther's arrival with the flyer and Daddy and Robert's March twenty-first "invasion" of the fishing camp pass me in a blur. The days at school roller-coaster in and out of crazy. Although our teacher, Mrs. Loreen Finney, promised last September, "I won't put up with any foolishness," she's still having trouble controlling the boys in our class. Most seem bent on seeing who can get sent to the principal's office first, ahead of the others. The nights make my stomach churn, as Daddy, Luther and Robert sit on the front porch suggesting, rejecting and arguing over details of The Plan.

At *last*, late Thursday, March twentieth, everything finally seems set. The ladies of the C.I.A. have confirmed that most all the Opalakee Klan members are committed to attending "the Rally in Orlando" the next night. The flyer outlines the meeting time "from eight o'clock until midnight," so The Plan is this:

At nine P.M., Luther will stop by the Dump to see his old friend Horatio Sykes, Negro caretaker there. Together, they'll unlock the Dump's little-used back gate. At nine-thirty Daddy and Robert will enter the back gate, park Daddy's truck behind the shed, and climb through the barbed-wire fence into the grove closest to the camp.

As Daddy and Robert approach the fishing camp from the south side, Luther and his friend, driving Horatio's truck, will cruise into the driveway on the north side of the camp and make sure there are no vehicles parked on the property. (Horatio often picks up trash at the camp and is certain they'll be safe.) If everything looks good, at ten o'clock, Luther will flash a single "go" sign with a flashlight across the lake toward the ridge where Daddy and Robert will be waiting.

Daddy and Robert will wade across the small lake which, Horatio swears, is no more than four feet deep in the center. The wide rim of razor-sharp saw grass on each side prohibits any kind of hike-in entry. They'll enter the camp's main building from its blind side.

Once there, Robert will stand guard by the front door while Daddy looks for the hidden compartment. The Plan allows for twenty minutes of search time; they must be out of the camp no later than ten-thirty, wade back across the lake, get through the grove, return to the truck and be home by eleven, at the latest.

On the face of it, everything makes sense to me except one part. For thirteen years, I've begged my father to swim with us in any number of lakes around here. Not *once*, not *ever*, has he done it.

"Swimming pools and oceans are fine, Roo," he's always

said, "but ever since the polio I just can't bring myself to get wet in a Florida lake."

"So why are you willing to wade through this one?" I want to know.

"This is different, Roo," he tells me, calm as calm can be. "*This* is war."

# Chapter 31

arly Friday night, Doto herds the boys out of the house for dinner and a movie, a new Gene Autry, The Singing Cowboy, Western. As planned, I stay home to keep Mother company.

At 8:14, Daddy and Robert sit at the table, dressed in old dark-colored clothes and shoes, ready to go. Mother's silent. I'm tightrope anxious and trying hard not to show it.

Mother and I jump at the sound of Luther's knock. Letting him in, I'm surprised to see him dressed in a white shirt, dark tie and suit, as if for church. Behind him, Armetta in a navy blue dress carries a fat canvas bag by its cloth handles.

"Brother Luther, welcome," Daddy hails him. "You, too, Armetta?"

"Luther and I thought y'all could use a

little company while the men are out gallivantin'." Armetta's eyes are on Mother. "Were we wrong?"

"Not at all. Thank you," Mother tells her and I can see she's grateful. "I appreciate you thinking of us."

"Thinkin' of myself, too. Waitin's hard work, unless you have comp'ny to distract you." Her comment conjures up something Luther told Daddy the night Marvin was missing. "Armetta's about worried herself to *death*," he'd said. I want to hug her for being here.

"Luther, how come you're dressed like that?" I have to ask.

"Well, y'see, Roo," he says, enjoying himself, "mah friend Horatio at the Dump has a sort of bad reputation, mainly 'cause he likes to cook up a li'l moonshine now and then. A lot of people might find it hard to b'lieve a churchgoin' man like mahself would visit a man like Horatio, unless, of course, it was to witness to him about his terrible evil ways. Horatio and Ah decided it'd be best, for *his* reputation and for *mine*, if Ah played the part of Brother Luther tonight. Got mah Bible in the car and everythin'. If we get caught at the lake or if anybody asks any questions, Ah might have to claim that Brother Horatio has *seen the light* and wants t' be baptized there and then!"

Somewhere during Luther's explanation, I realize everybody at the table's grinning but Mother and me. Armetta reaches over and pats my hand. "It's okay, honey, the Lord's got a sense of humor jus' like anybody else. Even King Solomon did a li'l play-actin' . . . for a good cause."

Luther looks down at his watch. "Y'all got 8:25?" he asks. As Daddy and Robert check their wrists, I eye the time on the kitchen clock above the stove.

"Ah b'lieve," Luther says, "we could do with a word of prayer b'fore we go."

"I think so, too, Luther," Daddy agrees. "Please."

"All right, then." Luther spreads his palms out to me on his right and Daddy on his left. Wordlessly, we join hands around the table and bow our heads. Luther's hand on my left is strong and calloused, his grip firm. Armetta's hand, on my right, is velvety, smooth and comforting.

*"Lawd,"* Luther says, low and respectful,
*"You been watchin' over us for a* **long** *time,*
*from our first breath to this one.*
*You know our* **hearts**, *Lawd.*
*And, You know we have* **no hope**
*of accomplishin' our task tonight*
*without Your help.*
*We* **feel**, *Lawd, like old Joshua, when You took him*
*to the great walls of Jericho and told him*
*to let Your trumpets* **blow**.
*Blow those trumpets, You said,*
*and the great walls of Jericho will come tumblin'* **down**.
*Old Joshua b'lieved You, Lawd, and so do we.*
*We ask You tonight:*
*Lay that trumpet in our hands.*
*We all know our part, Lawd, and we gonna do the best we can,*
*But it's Mist' Warren and young Robert here*
*who need Your help the* **most**.
*Guide they steps, Lawd.*
*Protect they path.*
*Show them the way to the secret hidin' place and,* **Lawd**,
*Lay that trumpet in they hands.*
*Give it to 'em, Lawd, then bring 'em* **home**, *safe and sound.*
*We* **thank** *You for the help*
*and for the hope that fills our hearts tonight.*

*We bless You for the privilege of doin' this in Your name.*
*And we praise You, Lawd, tonight and forever.*
*Amen and thank God."*

I hear my parents and Armetta echo Luther's "Amen," and
both Luther and Armetta squeeze my hands before letting go.
"Well," Luther says, standing, "Ah best be goin'. Watch
for the light on the lake at ten. Lord willin' and the Klan
don't rise, Ah'll see y'all back here at 'leven o'clock."

Beside me, I hear Armetta suck in a soft breath as Luther
leaves. Daddy and Robert, with thirty minutes to kill, decide
to walk out and see him off, check the gear on the truck one
last time.

Just before nine, they come back inside. Their goodbyes
seem ordinary—Robert's, a shy wave around the table,
Daddy's, a quick kiss for Mother and a confident "be right
back" for Armetta and me—as if they were headed to the
hardware store instead of into the very heart of the Klan's secret headquarters. As if life, as we know it, doesn't hang in
the balance of what happens out there tonight. My chest feels
clenched like a fist, like I'm sucking breath through a straw.

As the screen door slams shut behind them, Armetta
lifts her canvas bag up onto the table.

"Reesa, Ah got somethin' you might be interested in.
Know what this is?" She's holding a plastic container with a
large brown glob inside.

"No'm," I tell her, straining to hear Daddy's pickup drive
away.

"Well, with a little baking, *this* is a batch of my world-
famous snicker doodles. You think you could find us a

cookie sheet, maybe set the oven to three hundred an' fifty degrees?"

As I search for and set out the cookie sheets, I feel suddenly chilled. In all the debates over tonight's plan, nobody's dared mention the real danger Daddy's walking into. *What if the fishing camp isn't empty? What if somebody sees Daddy's truck driving into the Dump? What if they recognize Luther's car, too, and put two and two together? Everybody knows Daddy and Luther are friends.*

My hands, fiddling with the cover on the cookie dough, feel thick and stupid, like I've forgotten how to move. Armetta reaches over and covers them, warming me like a fire.

"MizLizbeth, I brought my sewing box along. I know with all these chil'ren, you *must* have some clothes that need mendin', socks that need darnin'. If you'd like to help Reesa with the snicker doodles, I'll be happy to sit right here and do a little mendin' for you."

Mother looks at Armetta's face, searching, I think, for the words she'd like to say. Her hazel eyes are wet-rimmed with feelings.

"It's all right, MizLizbeth. I'm an old hand at passin' time. Could you bring me that mendin' please?" Armetta says softly, opening her sewing box.

Just after ten, the cookies are done. Mother pours cold milk all around. As we sit down to sample our still-warm efforts, Armetta tells me she was my age when her Mississippi grandmother taught her the recipe.

"Have you always lived in Mayflower?" I ask her.

"Oh, no, chil', I was born and raised in Ocoee."

"Ocoee! There aren't any Negroes in Ocoee."

"Not *now*, but there used to be a whole community, like The Quarters here in Mayflower, only bigger."

"What happened to it, Armetta?" Mother asks.

"Election Day 1920 happened, and a man named Mose Norman, our neighbor, drove downtown to vote," she says, leaning forward, her eyes and voice calling us into careful attention. "The local Klan was mostly Dixiecrat and they were worried that day because *most* Negroes were votin' Republican.

"The Klan showed up at the polls and started pushin' and shovin' our people away. Well, Mose Norman got hit and that made him mad. Mose drove over to O'landah to complain to a lawyer man, Mr. Cheney.

"Mr. Cheney told him to drive back and write down the names of *anyone* interferin' with the vote, and anyone else who got turned away. Long story short, it turned into a mob scene and that night, the Klan showed up and set fire to our houses."

"I remember hearing about this," Mother says. "Didn't the locals call it the Ocoee Riot?"

"Oh, they called it a lot of things, not much of it true." Armetta eyes her mending.

"Late that night," she continues, "there was a big gun battle at the home of July Perry, who lived in the middle of his own orange grove. At the time, he was the most influential Negro in town. Now, July Perry hadn't done a *thing* but the Klan came after him jus' the same, said he was hidin' Mose Norman in the house. 'Course, by that time, old Mose was *long* gone.

"When July Perry asked to see a search warrant, the Klan opened fire. July Perry tried to scare 'em off by showin' 'em his high-powered rifle, but it didn't help. When two white men attacked his daughter, he shot 'em. Sheriff tried to haul him into jail, but the mob lynched July Perry, on the big oak tree outside his house."

"Armetta!" Mother exclaims. I hear the tremble in her voice and know she's thinking of Daddy.

"The rest of us jus' scattered, scared outta our wits by burnin' crosses and flamin' houses. For a couple hours, my family—Mamma, Daddy and the six of us kids—hid out in a orange grove, listenin' to the sound of gunfire and people yellin' and cryin' in the streets. Then my daddy decided it was safe to move and we started walking. It was *pitch-dark* that night. Most of us had been asleep in our beds when the trouble came, so we were barefoot. We walked all night, through the palmetto flats outside Ocoee, through the piney woods around Lake Opalakee, then *finally*, just before sunrise, we made it to Mayflower, where our cousins took us in."

"How old were you?" I ask.

"A year less than you, honey." Armetta's eyes glow like embers. She seems at once both here and back there walking barefoot through the pitch-dark wood. "You remember Selma, works at the Garnet house now?" she asks me.

"Yes," I say, nodding her on.

"*Her* people were in Ocoee, and they went to Opalakee. Others went to Kissimmee or to Eatonville outside O'landah, wherever they had fam'ly or friends. All in all, 'bout fifty people died that night, includin' my best friend, Jolily Johnson." She stops, then says, "But *no*body never did anythin' about it. The F.B.I. came into town later, took statements from all the *white* men involved, didn't even *bother* talkin' to a single Negro."

"But what about your things, your property?" Mother asks.

"*No*body ever went back. At first, we were scared to. Later on, we just didn't want to." Armetta picks up her needle, pulling thoughtfully at the thread. "We keep in touch, though," she says, her face softening as if she'd remembered something pleasant. "Matter of fact, a bunch of us get together fairly reg'lar, not to dwell on what we *lost*, mind you. But to remember they's *some* things can't nobody take away, no matter *what*."

My eyes stray up to check the clock. Mother sits staring at the plate of fresh-baked cookies, untouched between us.

## Chapter 32

At 10:33, we hear the purr of the DeSoto coming down the driveway. Mother and I hurry out to help Doto with the boys, who are both asleep in the deep leather seats. I carry Mitchell, Mother half carries, half walks Ren up the stairs to their beds.

The kitchen clock shows nine 'til eleven when we hear Luther's truck, followed by his careful tap at the back door. Mother gets up quickly, stiffly, to open it.

"Should be right behind me, MizLizbeth," Luther tells her quietly. He's loosened his tie, left his jacket in the car. Walking in, he pauses beside Armetta to place a hand on her shoulder. She covers it with one of her own.

"Be here any minute now," he says and the five of us—Mother, Doto, Luther, Armetta and me—sit silent, listening for the truck. I watch the second hand hop around the clock, nudging the minutes from 10:57 to 11:03 to a full ten after.

Luther checks his watch and shakes his head. "I *saw* 'em," he says, "walkin' outta the lake and into the grove. Shouldn't've taken but another *five* to reach the truck."

Mother stands and leaves the room. I hear her walking back and forth on the porch. Luther and Armetta follow her. As I get up to join them, Doto stops me, tells me to "sit down and stay put." *What's wrong? Where are they?* I want to scream.

Doto remains confident. "Calm down. Your daddy's smarter than any ten of those men put together. He'll be here."

Like a wave, fear rises up to choke me. *What if you're wrong?* I wonder. As if she's read my mind, Doto glares at me to keep the faith.

At 11:30, worry, like a magnet, pulls Doto and me out of the kitchen and onto the porch. Nobody's talking. Out in the yard, the crickets rub their wings and my nerves together, a pair of bullfrogs croak our concern, and a lone night bird cries for its mate.

I stand beside Doto, willing Daddy home. *It's a ten-minute drive; you should be here NOW!* My heart bangs inside my chest. For another lifetime, we stand and wait, watching the dark, not wanting to acknowledge the possibilities that swirl like demons around us.

And then, we hear it . . . the roar of the truck entering the driveway, its headlights arcing into view. Mother flies down the steps. Daddy brakes, leaps out and grabs her tightly. I wait my turn to hug him.

"Tire!" he says. "Goddamn *flat*. Picked up a nail on the way in . . . flat as a pancake when we got back."

"They're *fine*," Doto announces, queen to her court.

"Right as rain," Luther says, shaking off dark thoughts.

"And just about as wet," Daddy says, tossing Robert a towel and swinging his waterproof ditty bag onto the table. "Sorry for scaring you all. Everything was fine until that tire. Never changed a flat so fast in my life."

"We made it through the grove in *no* time, saw Luther's light and headed down the beach," Robert tells us.

"Didn't see a soul," Luther tells him. "Ev'ry one of them Klanners musta been at that big rally downtown."

"The lake wasn't any more than three and half feet deep," Daddy says. "We waded right across it, holding the bag and the shotgun over our heads. Only thing was, in the middle, Robert looks at me and, quiet as can be, asks, 'Did Ren ever say whether or not there's *'gators* in this lake?' "

As Mother gasps, Daddy smirks, "Let's just say it's a good thing my pants were already wet. We picked up the pace after that. Made it to the fishing camp fine, but as we walked up onto the beach, Robert nearly stepped on a *water moccasin*."

A shiver snakes up my spine. Unlike a rattler, a deadly water moccasin will strike without warning, just as soon kill you as look at you.

"Scared me half to death," Robert says. "Didn't dare shoot it, though. Mr. Mac's next to me whispering, 'Stand *still*, stand *real still*.' Now how am I s'posed to stand still when I'm shakin' like a leaf?"

"Snake was as scared as we were," Daddy says. "After a while—"

"He means *forever*," Robert interrupts.

"—it slithered off. After that, we expected just about anything. Crept up to the door of the building and started searching for a padlock. Robert tries the handle and the door *opens*—we walked right in!"

"Tell 'em about *that*," Robert says, nodding Daddy on.

"Damnedest thing I've ever seen. On the outside, that building's just plain pine clapboard, badly in need of paint. Inside, we switched on our flashlights and it's varnished tongue-and-groove cypress, paneled like a high church or a courtroom. There's a small anteroom, like a vestibule, in front and a big paneled door; beyond that, a fairly large meeting hall."

"You wouldn't *believe* it," Robert tells us.

"Black, red and gold everywhere," Daddy says. "Like a House of Horrors, with a big square painted on the floor. In the middle of that, some kind of altar."

"Gave me the *creeps*." Robert mock-shivers.

Daddy nods. "On three sides of the square there are chairs, some kind of ceremonial seats. And on the far side, opposite from where we came in, there's a throne on a raised dais, big as a church pulpit but painted blood-red and black."

"With a *huge* Florida longhorn cow's skull above it." Robert holds his hands wide apart to show us the size of the skull and horns. "I told Mr. Mac, 'Wouldn't surprise me to see the Devil himself sittin' up there.' "

"Made my skin crawl," Daddy agrees. "I went one way, Robert went the other, tapping the paneling with our ballpeen hammers, looking for a hollow spot. Took us about ten minutes, but just behind a small table on a side wall, we found it—hollow panel, about waist high, with a sliding door concealed in the woodwork. We got that open, and inside, there was a shelf and a good-sized tin tackle box. We opened that and found three books and a zippered bank pouch. The top book was a Bible."

"Presented to Mr. Reed Garnet, on the occasion of his confirmation into Opalakee Presbyterian Church," Robert tells us.

"Age twelve, by his loving mother." Daddy grins.

"Oh, Lord," Mother moans, "wouldn't Hannah Garnet just die if she knew where that Bible ended up?"

"Maybe, maybe not." Armetta purses her lips.

"We left it there, along with the pouch, which had a little bit of cash in it, and took the other two books with us," Daddy says.

"What were they?" I ask, hardly able to breathe.

"Not much." Daddy shrugs. "Just the Membership and Attendance Records. And the Treasurer's Log."

"Ohhh, if that don't beat *all!*" Luther is grinning, slapping his thigh.

"*Then* what happened?" Doto demands.

"We put the hammers and the books in our bag, slid that tin box back inside the secret panel, closed the door, waded back across the lake, crossing our fingers that if there *were* any gators they *weren't* hungry, ran through the grove, changed the flat and hightailed it home!"

"Were you scared?"

Daddy turns to face me. "Terrified," he tells me softly.

"Can we see what y' got?" Luther asks.

"You bet!" Daddy empties his bag in front of us.

Maybe because I was expecting big leather-bound volumes, like Doto's ledger books, the black-and-white cardboard composition books, like Ren and I use in school, surprise me.

Daddy opens the Membership Book first. There, in someone's tidy handwriting, is the list of names far longer than the F.B.I.'s list I saw last month. This one has columns with years of dates across the top and checkmarks showing who attended which monthly meeting. Apparently, the last meeting was just five nights ago, with all but a few members present and accounted for. After that, there's a section listing Klan Officers. Emmett Casselton's at the very top, as Exalted Cyklops, above a list of strange-sounding titles like Klaliff, Kludd, Klokard, and others with the letters KL.

The second book, the Treasurer's Log, has neat, numbered entries for dues paid and fines collected. Armetta is the first to notice that in the back of the Treasurer's Log, there are a few odd enclosures. All of a sudden, she freezes, eyes wide, nostrils flaring, hand flying to her throat.

"What is it, Armetta?" Mother asks her.

Slowly, carefully, without removing it from its place, Armetta points out the newspaper clipping. "I have a copy of this at home. It's the story about the Moores registering voters in The Quarters. My name's in it, too." Turning the page like it will tear if she touches it, she uncovers another sheet taped into the book. A rough pencil drawing. "Good God Almighty! You realize what *this* is?"

Daddy leans forward, studying the bunch of squares and rectangles with letters inside. I see "P," "K," "LR," and, in one, a "BR" with a circle around it.

"Luther! Don't you recognize it?"

"Recognize what?" Luther says, his eyes darting from the drawing to Armetta's face and back again.

"It's the Moores' house!" Armetta says, pointing. "See here, 'P' is for porch, 'K' for kitchen. This 'LR' right here is the livin' room. You and I sat right there last October visitin'. This 'BR' over here, the one with the circle, is the bedroom where the dynamite went off."

"Are you *sure* about this?" Daddy asks, his blue eyes boring into her brown ones.

"Dead sure," she says, returning his gaze steadily.

Daddy sits back in his chair. I find myself staring at the open window over the sink, wishing it was closed.

After a few long seconds, Daddy leans back in. "Anything else?"

"These last two sheets aren't taped . . . let's look." Armetta unfolds the two sheets and places them in the middle of the table. The first one is a duplicate of the flyer inviting Klansmen to tonight's Kounty-wide Klonverse in Orlando. The second one is titled *Why the K̲lan li̲K̲es IK̲e!* It calls on "Good Democrats and Real Southerners" to support Eisenhower for President. The flyer cites Ike's record as "an enforcer of racial segregation in the U.S. armed forces," his "opposition to civil rights legislation," and his "support of immigration laws which bar Colored Races from entering the country."

"Jim Jameson was right, this stuff *is* dynamite," Daddy says. "Lizbeth, where's the pouch?"

As Mother retrieves the mailing pouch Mr. Jameson gave Daddy, Armetta folds and replaces the flyers in the book. Daddy brings Armetta a plain sheet of paper and asks her to write a note to Jim Jameson stating that the drawing in the Treasurer's Log appears to be the floor plan of the Moores' home which she visited last fall. After she writes the note and signs it, Mother and Daddy sign it, too, as witnesses. Daddy puts the note on top of the two composition books, slips them inside the mailing pouch. He seals it and hands it, along with Mr. Jameson's twenty-dollar bill, to Luther, who's agreed to mail it from the Wellwood post office first thing tomorrow morning.

"Once you put that pouch in the mail, we've done our part. Now, we just have to hope that the Good Lord and the Grand Jury do theirs," Daddy tells him.

"Amen to that," Luther echoes.

"I still wish we could've blown that place up tonight," Robert says on his way out the door.

"Back to hell where it came from?" Daddy asks. "Me, too."

Robert grins and waves goodnight.

"We'll see y'all later," Luther and Armetta call quietly as they disappear into the night.

In the kitchen light, my parents' faces seem drained of the excitement that filled the room just minutes ago. I'm dead-tired myself, not wanting to think.

"And now we wait," Doto says, so softly I almost don't hear her. I've never seen her look so old.

"Now," Daddy says, helping her up, herding me out of the room, "we try to get some sleep."

The Saturday morning after Daddy and Robert went into the Klan fishing camp, Ren (who knew nothing about their efforts) did the second most foolhardy thing of his life.

Privately, he and I had decided that the man who shot at him was most probably J. D. Bowman, the same trigger-happy Klansman who murdered Marvin. "But, of course, we'll never know for sure," I told him, trying to let that particular sleeping dog lie.

Well, Ren, applying the kind of cockeyed logic that only a boy is capable of, got up and took himself off to Carney's Coffee Shop, the flat-topped fried-food restaurant across from Voight's Grocery Store. Everybody knows Carney's is where Mr. Emmett Casselton, King of the Klan, regularly holds court with two or three other men in the big corner booth facing the street.

Ren walked in, sat himself at the counter, ordered a hot apple fritter and a glass of milk, and settled in to eavesdrop on Emmett Casselton's conversation!

"I was hoping they'd talk about the shooting and who did it and all," he brags to me later, cocky as can be.

"Are you *crazy?*" I yell, dumbstruck by his brashness. "The Klan almost blows your head off and, first chance you get, you're off to Carney's pestering Emmett Casselton?"

"I wasn't pestering him, I was just listening. But all he talked about was money, price of fruit, price of juice, price of land. Hardly worth the trip."

"And that's *all* that happened?"

"Well, yeah, until they got up to pay and Mr. Casselton noticed my Dodger cap. I had it pulled way down so he couldn't see my head." Ren's scrapes have healed into beet-red welts.

"*And?*" I'm ready to strangle him.

"And he asks me, 'You a Brooklyn fan, boy?' "

"And you said . . ."

"Well, nothing at first. He's kinda scary-looking. Got these pale alligator eyes with no lashes, big old nose with gray hairs sticking out the holes, and skin like leather with sun spots all over him."

"So, you didn't answer him?"

"Yes, I did, too. I said 'yes, sir.' And, he said, 'The Brooklyns are bums. Goddamn nigger lovers never won a Series, never will.' "

"Oh, *God!* And you said . . ."

Ren grins. "I gave him Marvin's V-sign and said, 'Maybe this year, sir.' "

I *groan.*

"And he didn't say nothing, just looked at me like I was an idiot."

"You *are* an idiot!" I rail, shaking him. "If you don't swear this *minute*, Ren McMahon, on the Holy Bible, that you will *never* go near Carney's again, I'm going to tell Daddy *and* Doto, and you know they'll make *mincemeat* out of you!"

"Leave me alone. Lemme go!"

Because our family seems so different from other people's in Mayflower, Daddy's always joked that we are strangers in a strange land. Somehow, Ren twisted that into believing he was anonymous or, worse yet, invisible. I have no idea whether Emmett Casselton recognized him as "the McMahon boy" or not. But I'm worried that Ren's visit to the coffee shop draws attention to our family at a time when, Daddy says, "we need to be laying low."

# *Chapter 33*

Monday, April first, Fool's Day, the Federal Grand Jury convenes its investigations into Ku Klux Klan activities in the state of Florida.

By Tuesday morning, the news from Miami crackles through the school hallways like an electric current. Fourteen Klansmen have been subpoenaed statewide, twelve of them from Orange County, nine of them from Opalakee.

Before the first bell rings, Joan Ellen Marks broadcasts the morning report to a group of us lined up outside our classroom.

"Miz Lucy came over last night, mad as hell and wailin' like a banshee," Joan Ellen says. "I guess Mr. Reed thought there'd be a bunch more people from a bunch more Klans. But there aren't but a few who aren't from Opalakee. Miz Lucy's 'bout gone 'round the bend ravin' that Mr. Reed's gonna wind up in *jail*! If *that* happens, Miz

Lucy swears, she'll never be able to hold her head up in this town again; she and May Carol'll wind up in the *poorhouse*, or else livin' with Mr. Reed's mother, which Miz Lucy says would be a *fate worse than death*. It took Mamma most of the night to calm her down."

"What about May Carol?" I ask, remembering her mother's stinging slap at the Garnets' pool party.

"She spent the night with me but went home to Miz Lucy this mornin'. Don't think she'll be in school today."

In class, everybody wants to talk about the same thing, peppering our teacher with questions about Grand Juries and U.S. Prosecutors. Mrs. Finney, smelling an opportunity for some real-life Social Studies, puts aside Americanism versus Communism and begins a comparison of States' versus Federal Rights.

"At the heart of this week's events in Miami is the question of *jurisdiction*," Mrs. Finney says, writing the word on the board. "Who can tell me what that means?"

My classmates, several of them related to the Klansmen now in Miami, appear well versed in the differences between state crimes (robbery, assault and battery, murder) and federal ones (the infringement of someone's Constitutional rights).

"The jurisdiction of a Federal Grand Jury applies only to areas governed by *federal* law," Mrs. Finney tells us. "Unless the Federal Prosecutor can prove that a federal crime has been committed, the people subpoenaed to Miami will have a nice vacation and come home in a few weeks, okay? May we move on to mathematics now?"

T he news passed on from the maids to Armetta to us is pretty much the same. The nine members of the Opala-kee Klan as well as the five others from the Orlando, Ocoee and Miami Klans were expecting many more Klansmen to be subpoenaed. Safety, so to speak, in numbers. They remain confident, however, and have been advised by no less than the state's Grand Dragon himself that no federal jurisdiction applies.

Apparently, the Klansmen are free to discuss their testimony outside the courtroom and, according to the maids, call their nervous wives at home almost every day. "Loose lips sink ships," the saying goes. They certainly destroyed Miz Lucy Garnet.

We hear the story from Armetta, who got it from Selma, who was *there*. "It's pure pitiful," Armetta tells us, "hurt my heart to hear it." Mine, too.

After ten days of cooling his heels in a Miami motel room, Mr. Reed Garnet finally got his turn to testify.

Miz Lucy was a nervous wreck waiting to hear from him, smoked a pack of cigarettes nonstop before Selma even had time to clear the breakfast dishes.

After taking the oath and his seat, Mr. Reed answered the first question put to him by the Federal Prosecutor ("Are you a member of an organization known as the Ku Klux Klan?") with a confident "No."

Then the prosecutor, open file folder in hand, asked his second question. "Are you not presently a member in good standing of the Opalakee Klavern of the Ku Klux Klan?"

Again Mr. Reed said "No."

After that, the prosecutor turned to shuffle through the stack of file folders on his table. That's when Mr. Reed saw it, the briefest flash of a familiar black-and-white pattern. At first, he told Miz Lucy, it reminded him of a schoolboy's composition book. But as the prosecutor turned to ask his third question ("Are you not a former Exalted Cyklops of the Opalakee Klavern of the Ku Klux Klan?"), it reminded him of something else.

An hour later, during the morning recess, Mr. Reed called home, fuming to beat the band. Miz Lucy took the call in the kitchen, a scant five feet from where Selma stood cleaning out the oven.

"Lucy, listen to me carefully," he said in a tone Selma said was way beyond upset. Mr. Reed was *riled*. "Call Emmett. Tell him to check the fishing camp. I think they've got our record books! How the hell could they have our record books?"

"What record books?" Miz Lucy asked him.

"Membership, attendance, the goddamn list of officers. We keep them at the camp, but I swear I saw them here in the prosecutor's files!"

"Oh, Reed, what does this mean?" Miz Lucy wailed, sinking like an empty sack into the kitchen chair.

His answer was loud enough for Selma, scrubbing the oven, to hear every word. "It means I just fucking *perjured* myself in front of the goddamn Grand Jury! Hang up the phone and call Emmett *now!*"

Miz Lucy did as she was told. Her call to Emmett Casselton included a strident retelling of every word Mr. Reed had said, followed by fifteen minutes of frantic pacing and chain-smoking, waiting for the return call.

Emmett Casselton's confirmation ("They're gone") sent Miz Lucy into orbit. Two more calls—one to her brother, an attorney in Macon, and a second to Miz LouAnn Marks, her best friend next door—pushed her spread-eagled, sobbing hysterically, onto the sofa.

"If I'd been there, I'd have known what to do," Armetta tells us sadly. "Poor Selma'd never seen her that way, hadn't the slightest idee how to handle things."

Miz LouAnn arrived shortly, grabbed a bottle of bourbon and hauled her friend back into the bedroom. An hour later, Miz LouAnn emerged, told Selma, "Miz Lucy's resting. Under no circumstances, is she to be disturbed."

Mid-afternoon, Miz Lucy stumbled into the kitchen in search of some ice. She found Selma serving May Carol an after-school snack and told May Carol that when she's finished she's to run next door and play with Joan Ellen. Then she asked Selma to leave early, she needed peace and quiet "to rest," she said. Both Selma and May Carol did as they were told.

That evening, Miz LouAnn brought her friend supper on a tray. When her knock on the door went unanswered, she let herself in and found, to her horror, that Miz Lucy, aided by the bourbon and her barbiturates, had rested herself into peace and quiet of the most permanent kind.

T he news of Miz Lucy's suicide casts a pall over Opalakee, and puts thoughts in my head that I'd rather not think about.

Armetta's worried sick about May Carol. "That chil's gonna need all our prayers to survive life as a Garnet without her mother," she says, shaking her head.

I remember last March, how fragile and upset May Carol looked when Armetta, her other mother, left. Now she's lost her real mother, too. What's to become of her if Mr. Reed goes to jail? Why is it, in this whole mess, ever since Marvin, innocent people are the only ones suffering?

M r. Reed Garnet, granted temporary leave by the Grand Jury, returns home to bury his wife. My parents, knowing the small Opalakee Presbyterian Church will be packed with wary Klansmen and their heartsick wives, send flowers but elect not to attend.

After the funeral and the paying of respects at the Garnet home, Joan Ellen and May Carol sit quietly on the patio just off the living room while Miz LouAnn suggests to Mr. Reed that May Carol move in next door.

In the girls' locker room, Joan Ellen shares what happened next:

"So Mamma says to May Carol's Daddy, 'Reed, that child's been through so damn much. Why don't you let her stay with us for a while, at least 'til this business in Miami's cleared up?'

" 'Might be longer than you think,' Mr. Reed says with a smirk. '*Besides*, she's goin' to Mother's,' he says, meaning May Carol's grandmother, Miz Hannah Garnet. Y'all know what Miz Lucy used to call Miz Hannah, don't ya? H-R-H, which Miz Hannah always thought stood for *Her Royal Highness*, you know, like the Queen? But Miz Lucy told Mamma it really meant *Hannah Right outta Hell!* They did *not* get along!

"Anyway, my mamma says, 'Reed, you can't let that old hellcat have that child!'

" 'It's a done deal, LouAnn,' he says. 'And Mother's already arranged May Carol's transfer to Mount Laura Academy.'

" 'Dammit, Reed, *no!*' Mamma tells him. 'You know every time Miz Hannah brought up that prissy-ass boarding school, it made Lucy crazy. You know how *set* she was on keepin' May Carol home!'

" 'Well, Lou,' Mr. Reed says, just as *mean* as could be, 'if she was *that* set, she should've stuck around instead of climbin' into the booze and her little pill bottles!'

"*Well*," Joan Ellen reports to us, rolling big eyes around our circle, "when he said *that*, I thought my mamma was gonna strangle him. And poor May Carol, sitting right next to me, heard every word!

" 'Reed Garnet,' my mamma says, 'you *knew* Lucy was havin' a hard time of it. If you'd spent *one damn minute* thinkin' about *her* instead of yourself . . .'

" 'Ain't a problem anymore, is it, Lou?' Mr. Reed says.

" 'You are every bit the *animal* she always said you were!' my mamma told him.

" 'Well, then,' he says, in a real *ugly* voice, 'you'll excuse me, but I have a plane to catch. The Miami *zoo*keeper's waiting for me to crawl back into my *cage*.' And with that, he opened the door and told Mamma to '*Go home!*'

"Last time we saw May Carol, he had her all packed up and on her way to Miz Hannah's house. Damn jackass didn't even give us a chance to say goodbye."

*Chapter 34*

In the gray days after Miz Lucy's suicide, there are no further updates out of Miami. Reporters camped outside the Federal Courthouse pester the Federal Proscecutor for news. "Patience," he chides them. "This process will not be rushed." The papers are guessing another two to three weeks before "justice is served."

The big question I have is "Who's saying how much, about what?" Backed into the corner of perjury versus self-preservation, how long before these human snakes bare their fangs at each other? *It has to happen, doesn't it? They can shed their skin, but not their nature, right?*

Mother believes the longer the proceedings run, the better. "It takes time," she tells me, "to draw everyone's cards out on the table."

Hope has begun to glimmer at our house like the flame of a small candle. I see it first in Mother. Or, rather, when the woman who looks like my mother but hasn't acted like her real self for months invites me to play a game of Gin Rummy. The first hand is awkward, but, after the third, she catches my eye when I say "gin," and grins. My mother's lopsided, dimpled grin.

I don't dare acknowledge it, for fear of somehow scaring her away again. But as I gather and sweep the cards in her direction, with a quiet "your deal," I feel the pieces of myself fall back into place, and my heart welcomes her home.

While the small towns surrounding Orlando wait for the results of the Grand Jury face-off in South Miami, another confrontation draws our attention north to Tallahassee. Presidential candidate Estes Kefauver is on his way, back onto Governor Fuller Warren's forbidden ground.

Everyone's anticipating the fray, including the ladies at Miz Lillian's Beauty Parlor:

"They say Governor Warren's goin' to meet him at the border with the state troopers," claims Miz Ethel May Burch, cut and curling. "Goin' t' tell Kefauver to turn around and take his coonskin cap and his redheaded wife back to Tennessee."

"I hear he's flyin' into Miami," Miz Lillian says. "Goin' t' cavalcade right up the Trail, all the way to Jacksonville."

"What color red is his wife's hair?" Miss Iris asks.

" 'Bout the same as mine," Miz Lillian tells her.

"Outta the same *bottle?*" Miz Ethel May asks wickedly.

"Now, now, Ethel May, only my hairdresser knows for sure," Miz Lillian shoots back, patting her copper-red French twist.

"I personally think it's *foolish* of Governor Warren to make such a big *deal* outta this," Miz Agnes Langford, my old Sunday school teacher, says. "Any of y'all see Senator Kefauver on television during the hearings in New York? That man tore that thug Costello to pieces. If Governor Warren thinks Kefauver'll be a pushover, he's likely to be surprised."

"You for Kefauver, Aggie?" Miss Iris asks.

"Well, I'm just not sure I'd be comfortable with a Cracker like Russell in the White House, or if the rest of the country would be, either. Personally, I think Kefauver's got a better chance of beatin' that warmonger Eisenhower in the fall."

Everyone at Miz Lillian's knows Miz Agnes has a son in Korea and is anxious to get him home.

The following week, both Democratic candidates, Senator Kefauver of Tennessee and Senator Russell of Georgia, come calling on the voters of Florida. Not long after Kefauver's arrival, Governor Warren openly challenges him to a twenty-one-question debate.

"I'd be happy to talk to the Governor," Kefauver replies, "but a debate's sort of a *candidate* thing. Last time I looked, I didn't see the Governor's name on the ballot. Is it there? Did I miss it?" Kefauver asks the press.

Both Senators tour the state, shaking hands, making speeches up and down the Orange Blossom Trail. I'm at the packinghouse when Senator Russell's parade passes through Mayflower. A dozen state trooper cars, lights flashing, sirens blaring, announce their arrival and departure at both ends of town. In the middle, the Georgia Senator and the Governor wave like kings from the air-conditioned comfort of their shiny gold Mercury.

Kefauver's pass-through was much smaller, Daddy tells us, riding in an open convertible with him and his pretty wife smiling and waving at the people beside the Trail. Mother confirms that Nancy Kefauver's hair is very much the same color as Miz Lillian's. Whether or not Miz Kefauver's a natural redhead, she couldn't say.

O n May fifth, the day before the Presidential primary, Luther stops by with questions about the voting process. This will be his very first time at the polls. He wants to make sure he knows *exactly* what to do.

Daddy says he's not surprised that Luther and most of the folks in The Quarters are backing Kefauver.

"Ah like the way he talks about cleanin' up the gov'-ment," Luther says. "Wish he'd start right here with Gov'nor Warren. That man has deviled poor Mistuh Kefauver up and down this state with his 'Twenty-one Questions,' like it was Mistuh Kefauver caught buyin' concrete from Al Capone! Ah hope he gets his chance to clean house in Washin'ton. God knows Ah'd be willin' to lend him a hand with a broom!"

The next night, I stay up late with the adults to watch the results roll in on the television. As expected, the larger cities and the eight counties around them go for Kefauver. The country counties, especially those in the panhandle, tip heavily toward Russell.

In the end, Russell wins, nearly 360,000 votes to Kefauver's 285,000. Despite the fact that their man lost, Daddy and Luther are jubilant. "Governor Warren promised Kefauver a humiliating defeat," Daddy explains. "But thanks to th' *Negro* vote, he didn't get it!" Luther boasts. "We kep' things fair an' square." *Like a democracy should be*, I decide. *Wouldn't Mr. Harry've been proud to see that?*

As both candidates head north with less success than either had hoped for, attention turns south, back to Miami.

T he headline on the front page of *The Miami Herald* says it all:

## TRAIL OF VIOLENCE LAID TO KLANSMEN

Daddy reads the lead story aloud:

A federal grand jury Wednesday submitted "a catalog of terror that seems incredible" in a report of Ku Klux Klan activities that ran the gamut from murder and arson to beatings and bombings.

Two White girls were severely beaten for bathing in the nude; a Negro man was shot in the back; the home of a Negro woman in Miami was burned; a Negro man and his wife were killed when their home was bombed;

"Mr. Harry and his wife!" I cry.

"Yes," Daddy nods. "Let me finish . . ."

a White man was beaten for neglecting his family; a Negro worker was thrashed for union activities.

"Nothing about Marvin?" I'm fuming. Daddy gives me the eye and continues.

These are only some of the acts attributed to the KKK by the jury in its roundup of terrorism dating from 1943.

Only those acts to which one or more Klansmen admitted participation were attributed to the KKK by the jury as it recited a long list of unbridled acts of violence in Greater Miami and central Florida . . .

The jury said the list it submitted to Federal Judge John W. Holland in its partial report is far from complete. "Details grow monotonous through sheer repetition," it explained.

The story Daddy reads says that, after a brief recess, the Grand Jury will hear more witnesses and *"consider criminal aspects over which there may be federal jurisdiction." Their statement indicated that the jury expects to return indictments when it reconvenes.*

After seventeen paragraphs outlining the gruesome list of confirmed Klan activities, the Grand Jury has this to say about the KKK:

> It is founded on the worst instincts of mankind. At its best, it is intolerant and bigoted. At its worst, it is sadistic and brutal. Between these two poles it has its existence.
>
> Out of the wells of prejudice, it draws its inspiration. It is a foul pollution in the body politic. It is a cancerous growth that will not be cured until the hand of every decent man is raised against it and the whole power of the law is marshaled to stamp it out.

At the tail end of the story, buried at the bottom of page 10, are the three sentences that quickly become the talk of Mayflower:

> The jury revealed for the first time that two years before the Moore murders, a floor plan of the Moore house was exhibited at a meeting of a Central Florida klavern. The report stated, too, that newspaper clippings of Moore's activities were read at klavern meetings and that mention of him was made on other occasions and in other places. The jury said the Central Florida klaverns were "known to have a malevolent interest in Moore."

# Chapter 35

Doto stands on the back porch, inhaling the warm May air.

"What a beautiful day!" she calls into the kitchen. "Why not have Sunday dinner out here?"

"Why not?" Mother calls back. "Reesa, will you set the picnic table, please?"

Doto and I wipe down the backyard table and chairs. She helps me spread the cloth and place the plates, glasses, napkins and flatware. While Mother calls Daddy and the boys to dinner, Doto and I carry the platters and bowls outside to the shaded backyard: pork chops fragrant with rosemary, mashed potatoes and brown gravy, fresh green beans and applesauce.

"It's dinner-on-the-grounds just for us!" Mitchell crows, his blond buzzed head aglow in the sunlight.

We gobble up our food, gab about the Sunday service. Ren reports that the Dodgers' best pitcher, big Don Newcombe, has been drafted into the army and is on his way to Korea. Doto praises Mitchell for his much-improved table manners. As we sit sipping the last of our tea, we hear, then see, Luther's old Dodge at the head of the driveway.

He and Armetta get out of the car, still in their church clothes.

"Well, ain't y'all a picture?" he calls, smiling. "Enjoyin' this pretty Sunday?"

"Sure are," Daddy calls back. "Ren, pull those lawn chairs over here for Luther and Armetta. You two eaten?"

"Jus' finished." Luther patts his belt buckle.

"Had a potluck with the choir," Armetta says, sitting down in the shade. "Lord, was it good!"

"The choir?" Daddy asks, looking curious. "Any gossip from the good ladies of the C.I.A.?"

"Actually, that's why we've come." Luther accepts the glass of tea that Mother's poured for him. "Somethin' pretty important," he says, leaning forward. "Y'all know the Gran' Jury's out on recess, which means the Klanners have come home for a few days. There's been a bunch of little parties and barbecues for 'em which, of course, the ladies have prepared."

Armetta looks around and tugs her chair closer to the table. "Mist'Warren, the question everyone's been chewin' on is 'Who stole the record books with the clippin's and the floor plan and gave 'em to the F.B.I.?' They've been 'round and 'round, tryin' to figure it out. Middle of last week, one of the men remembered somethin'. Somethin' about the men shootin' at some chil'ren and the fathers bein' fit to be tied about it. The talk's been all over Mistuh Emmett about who that was and could they be the one?"

Daddy leans forward, elbows on the table, resting his chin on his upright, folded hands. His jaw's gone concrete.

"The Klan's been chewin' on it all weekend, talkin'

amongst theyselves. They've ruled out the other boy's father; Mistuh Emmett says Mistuh Smitty'd never have the *nerve.* They've decided, well, what they're *sayin'* is, since you're a Yankee, and mad and smart enough to pull it off, they thinkin' it was *you.* . . ."

"What's that mean?" The sun glints off Doto's cat-eye glasses.

"Well, not much, we thought," Luther says. "With as much trouble as they in already, we figured they wouldn't dare try anythin' else . . ."

"But?" Daddy, his face still expressionless, eyes Armetta.

Inside, I feel a trapdoor open and my stomach fall through it.

"But," she says, "last night, Polly—she works for Miz Hannah Garnet, Mistuh Reed's mamma—Polly heard Mistuh Reed talkin' to Mistuh Emmett about 'callin' out the Klavaliers.' "

"What are the Klavaliers?" Mother's hand reaches over to curl under Daddy's arm.

"That's a Klan term for the men who jump you with axe handles and ball bats," Luther says quietly. Daddy draws a breath.

"Mistuh Emmett said *no,* it was time to *lay low,* but Mistuh Reed said he'd already called 'a couple of the O'landah boys, just a little walk and talk.' "

"Which *means,*" Luther says, "a little rough stuff but no killing."

"Are you saying the Klan's coming after Warren?" Doto blazes.

"I'm sayin' there's *talk,*" Luther tells her.

"What can we do?" Mother's face is drained of color.

"You can pack up and leave *right now,*" Doto replies

firmly. "Take a vacation, a *long* one. You said you had a pretty good winter, you can afford it. If you can't, *I'll* pay!"

"It's not that, Doto," Daddy says calmly. He squeezes Mother's hand. "If we turn tail and run, the Klan'll make sure we have nothing to come back for. We can't afford to lose *everything*."

I hold my breath.

After a moment, Mother straightens, squaring her shoulders. "Luther, Armetta, you know these men better than we do. What do you suggest?"

Luther leans in, hands on his thighs. "Well, Ah'll *tell* you: Ah know you have a scatter gun," he says to Daddy. "Load it and take it with you wherever you go. Take the dog, too," he says, pointing at Buddy. "These things tend to happen at night, so don't go out unless you absolutely have to. If you do go out, go as a fam'ly, never alone. The Klanners think of theyselves as Southern gentlemen. They don't usually attack a white man in front of his wife or chil'ren."

"This is *abominable*!" Doto fumes, fire in her eyes. "I'm hiring some security guards. If we can't find them local, I'll get some Pinkertons down here from Chicago, armed to the *teeth*!"

"No, Doto, no," Daddy tells her quietly. "It's probably just talk. And, if it isn't, we'll deal with it ourselves."

"Mist'Warren, MizLizbeth, Ah'm sorry to spoil your Sunday dinner like this," Luther says gently, "but Ah told Armetta you'd want to know right away."

"You were absolutely right," Daddy tells them both. "Thank you, and *please* thank the ladies for their help."

So begins my family's final nightmare.

ince the first of the year, my friend
Vaylie's postcards reveal that her
father's "spells" have gotten more
frequent. She's been "on tour" more
often than not—to Savannah, Plymouth
Rock and Cape Cod, Charleston, South Carolina, and last month, Quebec, Canada. I'm
delighted when, at last, an envelope containing a real letter arrives:

> *Dear Reesa,*
>
> *I'm sorry it's been so long since I wrote
> you. As you can tell from my postcards,
> Mamma and I have been away, a lot!
> The bad news is, no matter how hard
> I've tried to keep up, I've already
> flunked seventh grade and will have
> to repeat it. The good news is Daddy's
> gone to live in a sanatorium and we get
> to stay home.*
>
> *How this came about is a very long*

*story. I'll give you the short version: With Mamma and me out of town so much, Daddy's mamma had to deal with him a whole lot more than usual. After he wrecked her car, stumbled into church drunk, and got mad enough one day to shoot my horse, his mamma decided he might have a problem after all. She got the best doctors in Richmond and Washington, D.C., to examine him. All of them said the same thing: Daddy's a "manic depressive," which means when he has a bad spell, he's completely out of control. (Somehow, my daddy's mamma believed the doctors over what Mamma and me have been trying to tell her for years.)*

*The sanatorium is just as nice as can be. You'd never know it was a nut house for rich people. Mamma and I visit him every Saturday, and Whit and Claudette go three times a week. With his medicine and the "treatments" (I think they shoot electricity into his head, but nobody will tell me for sure), Daddy seems to be pretty happy. Once a week, on Sundays, if the doctors say he's been good, his mamma takes him out to her horse farm. He loves to watch the horses run, seems to have forgotten what he did to mine.*

*Mamma seems much happier, too. She's stopped taking her nerve pills and is starting to look and act like her old self again.*

*As for me, I have to thank you for that letter you wrote me, sitting in your tree. I carry it with me wherever we go, and read it whenever I feel really bad. Thanks to you, I never gave up hope. Because you believed in me, I figured I was honor-bound to believe in myself. My new tutor, Mrs. Bradford, says that if I work extra hard, there's a slight chance I might catch up with my old classmates. I KNOW I can do it, Reesa. My luck, like the tide, has turned!*

*Love,* VAYLIE

*Dear Vaylie,*

 *I was so glad to get your letter and to hear you're home for good! I'm sorry about your daddy, though, and about what he did to your horse. It must have been awful for you.*

 *Do you like your surprise? It's a rattler skin, of course. One of your "cousins" shed it in the scrub behind the old sinkhole. It means he's grown a brand new skin, with one more rattle on his tail to boot. When I found it, it reminded me of you, of all you've been through, and how you've made it through without losing your way.*

 *Oh, Vaylie, I wish I could say the same for me.*

 *Things are as bad as they can be here, and getting worse. And, I can't begin to see a way to wiggle our way out.*

 *What's happened is this: My father got involved with the Federal Bureau of Investigation, helping them find out who killed the colored couple, Mr. and Mrs. Harry Moore. It was the Klan, of course. Everybody knew it. But not a single white person was willing to do anything about it—except Daddy. What he did was a good thing, the absolute right thing to do. But now the Klan's found out about it. And we hear they're sending some men after him to get even.*

 *Vaylie, there's not another person in the world I can tell this to: I'm as scared as I can be. My parents try to act as if everything's okay, but I know it's not. I can see in their eyes that they're scared, too. Worse yet, so's my grandmother, Doto, and she's never been afraid of anything in her life!*

 *The worst thing, Vaylie, is the upside-downness, the inside-outness of things. Like the crazy people rule the world and they're after us because we're <u>not</u> nuts. For the first time, I understand why your mother took you on tour so much. I wish somebody would take us out of here until everything's over.*

 *But that's not my parents' way. "We'll get through this,"*

*they say, and I wish I could believe them. But the truth is, I'm not sure who, or what, to believe right now.*

*I don't know if you're a praying person, Vaylie. We've never really talked about it. But if you are, please, please, please, put an extra word in for my family, and for me.*

*Your tried and true friend, Reesa*

# Chapter 37

There's just no describing the infinite difference between everyday life lived unawares and the agony of keeping watch for strange men who want to hunt and hurt your father.

It's the little things that loom largest: the lock on the back door that hasn't worked for years and *who knows* where the key is anyway; the after-dark carton of milk that normally Daddy would run and get, turned into an awkward family outing; the two-minute drive between church and home, after Wednesday night's choir practice, now too risky to be taken alone; the swishing sound outside, maybe not the wind rustling the palmettos.

Nights especially last an eternity. Somehow, my family gets through them, avoiding the obvious with small, coded conversations and polite I-don't-mind alterations in long-established routines:

Doto, the queen of hot fudge sundaes, gives up her favorite dessert rather than have Daddy risk an after-supper run to Mr. Voight's freezer section. And she seems to have a huge amount of paperwork which keeps her at her post on the front porch whenever we're home.

Mother, who hasn't sung in the choir for years, rejoins the sopranos in the second row. She rides to and from practice with Daddy, and Buddy stands sentry, tied to the choir loft door.

Buddy, who's spent most of his life sleeping in my room, moves, at my suggestion, to the rug at the foot of my parents' bed.

Ren and I keep an eye out for anything, everything the least bit out of the ordinary. And Mitchell wears his cowboy six-shooters everywhere, "in case," he tells us, "the bad guys come."

Just before Memorial Day, the Grand Jury, having reconvened its proceedings in Miami, hands down its indictments.

Seven men from our area are ordered to surrender on June nineteenth for arraignment before the Federal District Court. Starved for resolution, I gobble up the details of the *Miami Herald* story:

> They were charged with lying under oath when they denied to the grand jury that they were members of the Ku Klux Klan, or that they took part in a series of violent acts in Central Florida from 1949 to 1952.

J. D. Bowman leads the list of those indicted! The charges against them range from denying membership in the Klan to denying involvement in a number of incidents, including the attempted abduction of two N.A.A.C.P. lawyers and two Negro reporters, the beating of a local Negro for union activities, the flogging of another and the burning of a shack occupied by a man accused of molesting small girls.

When Daddy reads the article, he tells me, "It's important to note that they're *not* being charged for actually *committing* the crimes, but for *lying* about them to the Grand Jury, Reesa. There's your lesson in the difference between state and federal jurisdiction."

Justice, by a thin thread called perjury, has been served. Even though the indictments carry no direct mention of Marvin or the Moores, it seems that, at least, *right* has won out. After weeks of self-enforced confinement, the need to celebrate pushes my family out of the house.

We pile into Mother's station wagon, Buddy in the back, and drive to Orlando and the new Ronnie's Restaurant for hamburgers and ice-cream sodas all around. The evening floats, light, optimistic, party-like, until Doto suggests that "now that this is over, I can think about heading home." The boys and I howl in protest.

On our way home, my brothers fall asleep against Doto in the back seat; Mother and I remain alert, out of habit, in the front. We enjoy the night, the familiar sights, as Daddy wheels north up the Trail, onto Old Dixie and into our driveway.

Halfway in, however, Mother hisses, "Warren, *stop the car!*"

$\mathscr{C}hapter\ 38$

Hands fly out in front of me as Daddy hits the brakes and Mother cries, *"There,* behind the palmetto."

From the floor of the back seat, the boys elbow their way up sleepily, asking, "Whuh? Whuh's that?"

"Shhhh!" Daddy flicks the headlights to bright. There, in the narrow space below the big palmetto beside our walkway, are two pairs of dark pantlegs with heavy boots.

Daddy slides his shotgun from under the seat, says softly, "Doto, on the count of three, open your door and lean to the right. Buddy's coming through."

"One, two, *three*!" As his door and Doto's fly open, front and back, Daddy yells, *"Get 'em,* Buddy, *get* 'em!"

Buddy bounds over the back seat, out Doto's door and tears up the driveway, barking like a banshee. Two men appear in the shadows, running, axe handles in hand. Daddy springs to the front of the car, carrying his shotgun, and rests an arm on the hood to steady his aim. I hear the clicks as he releases both safeties. Panic yanks me to the dash.

"Buddy," I cry. "Don't shoot Buddy!"

Suddenly, one of the men, shorter, gray-haired, stumbles on a tree root and falls. Grabbing his ankle, he turns and freezes in our headlights, a grizzly face pinched in pain.

Buddy closes in, snarling. I gasp as the other man slams Buddy's head with his axe handle and yanks his partner to his feet. Buddy collapses, yelping, on the drive.

Without a word, with both men clearly in his sights, Daddy slowly shifts his aim up, above their heads, and fires both barrels into the night.

We watch them run, three-legged, away from us and around the car barn in the back. Buddy staggers to his feet, still whimpering in pain, and runs after them.

In a blur, Daddy hurls himself back into his seat, dropping the shotgun onto the floorboard, and jabs the car into gear, engine racing, up to the house.

"Quick, quick, quick!" he hollers, yanking arms, elbows, and Mitchell's whole body up the walk, across the porch and into the living room, away from outside doors and windows.

Ren and Mitchell sit stunned on the sofa. I perch, numb, on the arm of Daddy's chair. The adults race around the house checking locks and latches, crimping curtains, tucking blinds to seal out the night.

"Warren," Doto blazes on the porch, "you had a clean shot! *Why* didn't you take it?"

"I had two thoughts . . ." Daddy tells her flatly. "If I took the shot, I'd've killed them. If I'd killed them, the Klan would kill me, probably before I made it to Orlando to report the crime. Where would that leave Lizbeth and the kids?"

"Oh, Warren, what *now?*" Mother whispers. I've never seen her so pale.

Outside, somewhere in the back grove, an engine roars to life and recedes. Buddy's hoarse bark turns into the howl that usually means whoever was here has left.

I shoot to my feet without thinking and run to the back door.

Daddy joins me and whistles for him from the porch. We hear his woof acknowledging the whistle. Then Buddy, tags jangling, tail wagging raggedly, limps out of the darkness.

"Good boy!" I say and drop down to pet and hug him. At my touch, Buddy yelps in pain.

Daddy moves in to inspect the bump on Buddy's head, the gash on his shoulder and his apparently tender rib cage. "He's bruised pretty bad," Daddy tells me, "but nothing appears to be broken."

*What kind of monster beats a dog with an axe handle?* I want to rage, but the truth hits me, Buddy was not their intended target. And an even more awful idea follows: *This is what they did to Marvin.*

"C'mon, honey," Daddy says softly as he leads Buddy and me back into the living room. "Those men are gone and there's nothing more to do about it tonight. How about you kids watch a little television before you go to bed?" He turns it on and switches channels to an old movie, James Cagney tap dancing in *Yankee Doodle Dandy.* "We'll be in the kitchen for a while," he says, as Mother and Doto trail him out of the room.

I fall back within a whirling chair, straining to hear them in the kitchen. They decide to leave the bright overhead light off "just in case." Their chairs scrape as they take their seats at the table. The talk is low-voiced, urgent. I know the topic is what do we do now. And, I can tell by their tones, they are *not* in agreement.

After half an hour or so, the boys have nodded off. My parents return to carry them upstairs, bidding Doto a strained goodnight. Without a word, my grandmother mounts the steps, heavily, to her room.

Mother comes down first to see me off to mine. Her face is still pale, her eyes overbright. Her fingers under my chin, as she tells me "Buddy will sleep with you tonight," are ice cold. When Daddy lets him in a few minutes later, calling softly "Goodnight, Rooster," Buddy curls with a heavy sigh in his old spot, beside my bed.

In their bedroom, I hear Mother and Daddy undress without a word. Then, for what seems like hours, I hear my parents argue in the night.

Daddy thinks Doto's right, Mother should take us home with her to Chicago. Nana's there, too, he says, she'll have plenty of help. Mother insists no, *that's* not her home, *this* is, and she won't leave him here alone. Back and forth, the argument goes: Daddy insisting, pleading, blazing, begging; Mother refusing, no matter *what* we will not go without him, she will not leave him or allow him, or Doto, or *anyone*, to split up our family. It would be like a death sentence. "These children need their father," she tells him and I hear in her voice, as he must, the pain of her own too-early loss.

My grandmother's pink sheets provide no refuge to me this night, as the very fabric of our lives stretches toward its breaking point. Everything I've ever known or valued seems to hang in the balance of my parents' argument.

Worry, like a vise, tightens my chest. *Please, God,* I think, unable even to whisper a prayer, *I've not been good at this faith thing, I don't even know the words. Please, please help us, help them, know what to do.*

Daddy's tried everything, every argument or approach he can think of; but the stronger-than-stone woman that is now my mother *is* not, *will* not be moved. Silence like a cavern sits between them until, at last, he gives into her. "All right," he tells her, "we'll get through this together."

"We survived the polio," she tells him, "we'll survive this. Somehow, you'll figure our way out."

I hear tears in their voices and, burying my head in the pillow, cry my own.

N ext morning, at Mother's insistence, in the face of Doto's poorly masked exasperation, any discussion of what happens next is "tabled until further notice."

"Daddy needs time to think," Mother tells us.

It takes him a week.

# Chapter 39

R en and I watch him from under our eyelashes, ears open wide for a clue, a sign, some kind of indication as to what he's thinking.

He shows us the piece of dark cloth he pulled from Buddy's mouth, and we tag along after him as he checks the dirt beside the old car barn. We see the tracks where Buddy caught up to the men the second time. There's blood in the dirt where someone was bitten. One of the men dragged one foot behind the other. Daddy points out the tire tracks where they parked, and more where they drove off through the grove onto Wellwood Road.

Later, we see Daddy enter the car barn. Ren races outside, pretending to look for Buddy, and passes the door, peering slyly in.

"He's unlocked the chest where he keeps the dynamite and he's counting the sticks," Ren reports to me, winded, having run all the way around the house, through the front rooms, then back to my bedroom.

We hear him whistling for Buddy and from my room's window watch him stride, carrying the shotgun, into the grove behind the house. We follow him, as quiet as we can, and find him standing at the outer edge of Dry Sink, staring into the hole's old, dried-up center as if there was something there to see. We try to sneak back before he sees us, but Buddy sniffs us out, tail wagging and barking. Daddy scowls when he sees us and tells us to "go home."

We ride with him in his truck, aware that he slows unnecessarily as we pass Carney's Coffee Shop, where Emmett Casselton and a few other Klansmen meet for breakfast.

In the morning, while we get ready for school, Daddy sits at the piano playing slow, quiet songs I've never heard before. He's playing them from memory, without sheet music.

At supper, he seems himself. But afterwards, instead of joining us in the living room, he sits in the dark on the porch, sometimes front, sometimes back, cradling the shotgun with one arm, scratching Buddy's ears with the other, staring off into the night.

Luther drops by twice, but not to see us. He and Daddy sit together on the pitch-dark porch, talking. We're not allowed to interrupt.

The waiting, the not-knowing grates on Ren. He argues about stupid, long-settled things: who sits where on the sofa, who clears the table, who bathes the dog. He picks on me and gets nowhere, then turns on Mitchell and makes him cry, which brings the wrath of Doto down instantly on both of them.

On her part, Mother's mostly quiet. I watch for the signs of her slipping away from us, but she's surprisingly peaceful and still present. Her belief that Daddy will "find our way out" shields us from Doto's darker doubts. My grandmother's not talking. But her face, when she thinks we're not looking, says volumes.

My habit over these days has been to escape to the shelter of the old tree beside the sinkhole, or, after supper, the privacy of my room. I have the oddest memory from the other night, after the men left and my parents argued and decided to stay together. I heard something inside my head. A sort of whisper—not by my parents, not by me. But clearly: *Be still and know*, the whisper said. These four words, half of a half-forgotten Bible verse, hum inside my head—not singsong, more like a circle—*Be still and know*, the circle says. And somehow, it helps.

Today, I've climbed the old tree higher than I've been in years, past my favorite limb shaped like a hammock, past the heart carved in the trunk, up into the newer, younger branches where the tree spreads out below me as if upended. The sky has flattened from a bright blue bowl into a pale gray plate. Charcoal thunderclouds crowd its rim. Rain falls in a smoky river from the sky onto the palmetto flats east of here. South toward Opalakee, patches of blue show through breaks in the cloud cover. And there in the west, sunlight pours through a great wide crack; slanting columns of light turning the grove tops glittering emerald.

This patchwork sky suddenly reminds me of my family: Doto's stormy doubts, Ren's rainy anxiety, and Mother's shining faith in Daddy's bright promise. All of us appear so different. Yet we're stitched together in a crazy quilt, draped across the blueness that shields us from the black beyond.

It's the blueness that gets me. Vast enough to create and sustain this bowl brimming with life, rimmed with death;

bright with sunlight, dark with rain. It's the blueness I feel, coursing like a river through this tree and me, from wherever I came from, to wherever Marvin went. Not a driving force. But a pull, like a magnet, that knows the way from here to that place where all things end, and begin again.

*Is this*, I wonder, sitting perfectly still, *is this what the whisper in the dark wanted me to know?*

O n Saturday morning, Daddy stops me on my way out the back door to the big oak. "Find Ren," he says, "and meet me in the truck."

# Chapter 40

I sit on the truck seat beside Ren, wondering what's next, watching my parents. Daddy walks Mother to the station wagon, opens the door for her, closes it after she slides in. He leans in and kisses her, not in the usual way, but longer. She starts her engine, backs out and drives away. Daddy walks toward us carrying his shotgun.

"This is it, boys and girls," Daddy says as he climbs into the truck, and lays the gun across our laps. "Reesa, Ren, I know this has been hard, not knowing what's going on, but your mother and I decided it was best. After today, hopefully, it'll all be over. We'll get our lives back on track."

"What are you going to do?" Ren asks him, quietly, man-to-man.

"What *we* are going to do is have a chat with the Exalted Cyklops. We all have a part in this. Let me tell you yours."

W hen Daddy, Ren and I drive by the coffee shop, we see them clearly, in the corner where they always sit. As our truck passes, one of them stands up with the check in his hand and walks to the cash register, pulling out his wallet.

"Good," Daddy murmurs, wheeling the truck left to circle the block.

When we pull up again, I see Mother's station wagon parked at Voight's across the street. She's sitting behind the steering wheel, but none of us wave. On the opposite corner, Luther stands talking to Miz Lillian, looking at the half-dozen citrus trees in front of her beauty parlor as if they're discussing a pruning job.

Daddy's timed it perfectly. Two of the men have left the coffee shop and are driving away. Emmett Casselton, moving slower, stands beside his truck. The gold lettering of Casbash Groves on the door glitters in the sun.

Daddy pulls in crosswise behind him. As Mr. Casselton looks up, Daddy says evenly, "Good morning, Emmett. Might I have a word?"

Emmett Casselton's eyes rake over Daddy, then Ren, then me last. His weathered face is expressionless but his pale, lashless eyes show a hint of surprise. He plants his feet, folds his arms across his chest, then he nods.

Daddy opens the door and gets out. Emmett Casselton's alligator eyes take in the shotgun pointing out, across Ren's lap and mine. He doesn't blink. *He's not a monster, he's a man, same as me*, Daddy had told us.

"Had a visit from your friends the other night," Daddy tells Mr. Casselton. "Unfortunately, their stay was cut a little short."

Emmett Casselton doesn't move, except for the tiniest squint.

"The way I see it, Emmett," Daddy says, "your men started this thing when they fired on my son. Take a look at his head and you'll see he was about two hairs shy of losing an eye."

As the older man shifts his pale stare to Ren, my brother stares back. His summer-buzzed head shows the trail of red welts from his eye to his ear.

"You can't tell me you wouldn't have done the same as I did, or worse, if someone took a shot at your flesh and blood."

Daddy waits to let his argument sink in. I watch the old man for some sign of agreement. Without changing his expression, Emmett Casselton drops his chin, a definite nod for Daddy to *go on.*

"At that point, I would've called us even, but clearly you didn't agree. You sent those Klavaliers after me. Which unfortunately, Emmett, makes it *my* turn."

Daddy takes a step closer and drops his tone. "I know a few things, Emmett. For instance, I know for a fact that the F.B.I. took all your dynamite. But they didn't take mine. I've got *plenty*, more than enough to blow one, maybe two buildings sky-high. There's your fishing camp, of course. And there's the building you own in downtown Opalakee. And I know you have a warehouse over on Votah Road. What I *thought*, Emmett, is since you went and made it my turn . . . you might help me decide."

Emmett Casselton's eyes drill into Daddy, who doesn't flinch a bit. "You threatenin' me, McMahon?"

"Oh, no, not at all. But you're the Exalted Cyklops, aren't you? The big decision-maker, right? Who better to help decide where we go from here?" Daddy asks.

"Where would you like us to go?"

"Well, that depends on you . . . Emmett. Other people seek your counsel, so do I."

"You askin' me to pick?"

"I'm asking your opinion, looking for advice. You could say here or there. Or, you could suggest something else entirely."

"Entirely what?"

"Well, you could surprise me by suggesting we declare this thing over, right here, right now. We could make an agreement that it's ended. Of course, I'd want your word on it, as a gentleman. You give me yours, I'll give you mine. Then we'd both be done with this."

Old Emmett Casselton stares at Daddy for forever. I realize I'm holding my breath, and when I let it out in a loud hiss, Ren glares at me. Daddy stands steady, ready for anything.

"What guarantee do I have that you'll keep yours?" Emmett Casselton asks.

"I figured you might have a problem with the word of a Yankee. I could arrange to deliver you a guarantee in . . . well, let's say fifteen minutes? If you'd wait right here, I could do that."

"What kind of guarantee?"

"You have to trust me on that, Emmett. Do we have a deal or not?" Daddy asks.

Emmett Casselton's eyes troll over the parking lot. They flicker to Ren and me and the shotgun. They slide back to Daddy standing firmly, legs wide apart. I try to breathe slow and stay calm, like Daddy told me. But inside I'm churning like Mother's Maytag.

A lifetime later, Emmett Casselton slowly, deliberately,

extends a bony hand with enormous black freckles. My head spins as the two men clasp and shake each other's hand.

Without another word, Daddy turns to the truck. He gets in beside Ren, closes the door and starts the engine. As he leans with his right hand to shift into first, he lifts his left wrist out the window, indicating his watch. "Fifteen minutes," he nods to the man standing by his truck.

We exit the parking lot, glancing at Mother in her car across the street, then turn off the Trail toward the Old Dixie Highway and home. Passing Luther and Miz Lillian, Daddy lifts just the first two fingers of his right hand up off the steering wheel, in Marvin's "V-for-Victory" sign. At the house, we head down the driveway, past the car barn, onto the dirt road that leads to the lower grove. Luther's old Dodge appears behind us.

Together we walk into the clearing that surrounds the old sinkhole. Doto and Mitchell stand in the deep, dry center, beside Mitchell's red Christmas wagon.

"So far, so good," Daddy says as he and Luther unload the dynamite onto the dirt. "Wait a minute, Doto, we're missing some. Where are they?"

"We left them in the car barn," Mitchell says proudly.

"Just in case," Doto adds, with a defiant look.

"In case of what?" Daddy asks, carefully stacking the sticks.

"In case your Southern gentleman turns out to be a scalawag," she shoots back.

"Doto," Daddy eyes her, "I had no idea you could be so suspicious." He and Luther twist the fuse strings into two separate cords. "How's our time, Roo?"

"Four minutes," I say, checking the watch he'd handed me in the truck.

"Okay, grab the wagon and head for the hills," Daddy

tells us, pulling a lighter out of his pocket. "Way over there, sit down behind the truck."

"Is that far enough?" Doto asks. "Are you sure the children will be safe?"

"They'll be fine, Miz Doto," Luther tells her. His lighter is out too.

"Sit down, on the ground," Daddy calls as we run across the clearing. He waits until we disappear behind the truck.

"All set over there?" Daddy yells.

"Okay," Doto hollers back.

We duck and watch between the wheels as Daddy and Luther light the extended fuse cords, then run our way. They squat down beside us; Daddy quickly, quietly counting seconds. I hold up the watch and one finger, for one minute remaining. It's been fourteen minutes since we left the coffee shop. Daddy keeps counting: seven-one thousand, six. We cover our ears and join him, mouthing five . . . four . . . three . . . two . . .

The blast of the dynamite rocks Daddy's truck like the floor of a fun house. The noise is loud beyond anything I've ever heard. Dirt clods fly above us, raining dust and dirt and small stones onto the truck, the trees. Later, we learn they heard it in Wellwood three miles north, and five miles south in downtown Opalakee. It rattled the shopping carts in Mr. Voight's grocery store and rang the church bell at St. John's A.M.E. But now we wait and watch for Mother.

We hear her wagon and at last I see her, stumbling through the dust.

"What'd he do?" Luther asks her anxiously.

"He *waited*," she answers. "Stood there, staring at his boots, and once in a while checked his watch. It was fifteen minutes *exactly* when we heard it. People came running out of everywhere, Voight's, Carney's, Lillian's, yelling 'What was that?' "

"And Emmett?" Daddy asks her.

"Stood there for a second or two," Mother says, "then threw back his head and laughed."

"He laughed?" Luther says, smiling.

"Yes, he did." Mother's grinning back at him.

"Laughing's good?" Doto asks, still shaken by the blast.

"Believe it or not, Doto, it's *great*," Daddy says, tracing a smile onto Mitchell's dirty face.

"Warren?" Mother's eyeing the thick fog of dust on the other side of the truck. "Is there anything left of our grove?"

"I think it's safe to take a look," he replies.

We stand up and peer over the truck bed into the mist where the clearing should be. That's when I hear it. Over the sound of dust softly sifting down through the trees, there's a sudden upward rush of . . .

"Warren?" Mother says, uncertainly.

But Daddy doesn't answer. He grabs her hand, pulling her around the truck and through the trees that rim the old sinkhole. The rest of us plunge after them into the dust-clouded clearing.

We hear it first. Then, pressing closer, we see it. In the center of a sinkhole that's been dead dry for thirty years, where minutes before Daddy and Luther stacked and lit our sticks of dynamite, a fountain of fresh water gushes up and onto the earth.

Water glitters and sparkles and splashes onto us. I reach out my hands to catch it, icy cold against my palms. I form a cup to drink it, surprised by the sharp taste of rocks and leaves and the roots of old trees. I stand in wonder as the underground river somewhere deep beneath my feet, released, rushes up to greet the treetops. High above my head, all the colors, Genesis through Jude, arc across the blue, blue sky.

# Revelations

The seven local Klansmen who were indicted by the Grand Jury found a friend in
Federal Judge George W. Whitehurst. In
December 1953, the judge granted their
motion to quash the indictments because,
he said, "the Federal Grand Jury has no
jurisdiction to investigate the acts about
which the suspects allegedly lied." The
Klansmen walked free.

But long before the men returned quietly to Opalakee, it was clear, in the days,
weeks, and months that followed the blast
in our back grove, that Emmett Casselton
was a man of his word. The Opalakee Klan
not only left my family alone, it left the
rest of the community, black and white,
alone as well.

Some people said the Klan disbanded
because of Emmett Casselton's say-so. "The
old man got tired of it," they claimed, and after all, he was the Exalted Cyklops *and* the
area's largest and most powerful employer.

I liked the version Armetta came up with better, that it was the *wives* and *mothers* of the Klansmen who decided they'd had enough of the Invisible Empire. "No more late-night meetings at the fishing camp," "no more political rallies down-town," "no more white robes in and out of the dry cleaners," the women told their men, eager to shore up what little social equity remained in the fine old names that had been "dragged through the mud." Somebody heard one ex-Klansmen joke "the Gran' Jury was nothin' compared to my wife."

Years later, I heard a third version. I was in law school then and had driven home for Miss Maybelle Mason's funeral service. Old Miz Sooky Turnbull, the ancient gardener, her face powdery and pocked like a huge potato, told me, "Y'know, Marie Louise, after that big boom behind your house, Maybelle marched right over to Casbah Groves ware-house, told Ol' Emmett she'd got *wind* of his shenanigans. Told him if the Klan harmed so much as another *hair* on your brother's head, or anyone else's for that matter, she'd report certain rather *large* discrepancies in Casbah Groves' Railway Express waybills to the I.R.S.! Y'know, Maybelle moon-lighted as bookkeeper for the R.E.A. station for *years*. She told Emmett if he didn't think she'd do it, he had another *think* comin'. For some reason, Maybelle thought *the world* of your brother and you," Miz Sooky said.

"Imagine that," I said, sorting my memories of Miss Maybelle and Miz Sooky like suits in a Bridge hand, hearts from spades, diamonds from clubs.

Not long after Daddy and Emmett Casselton's gentle-men's agreement, the fishing camp in the middle of the lake became just that.

The children of The Quarters returned to the communal

fun of "hide-and-whoop," "chick-mah-chick," and other favorite out-in-the-street games. After nearly sixteen months of having to hover near their houses since Marvin's death, they relished their restored freedoms.

My brothers and I and the Samson boys dove in, literally, to new games of our own made possible by the disappearance of Dry Sink beneath the surface of the resurrected Little Lake Annie. Once again, as Miss Maybelle had claimed happened so long ago, kids leaped from the big limbs of the giant live oak and swung from ropes into the clear, ice-cold, spring-fed swimming hole.

One day, I invited Miss Maybelle to come see for herself the little lake. And she did, too, walking stiffly through the grove after work, in her sensible shoes and crisp gray-blue postmistress uniform. She stood outside the range of our wild splashes, arms folded over her chest, shaking her head from time to time.

When I swam over to her and got out of the water to ask what she thought, I noticed two things:

The first was that sometime over that summer, either I'd grown or she'd shrunk, but now we stood eye-to-eye and I wondered at the reasons I'd spent so many years *aggravated* by this little old lady.

The second thing I saw was that, instead of looking at the lake and the boys' high jinks, her attention had drifted to the giant live oak. I followed her gaze up the huge trunk, then I turned to her and said, "It's still up there, Miss Maybelle." She looked at me sharply, but I didn't cower under her gaze as I might have.

"What's still there, Reesa?" she asked.

"The heart carved into the trunk. It's still there, about two-thirds of the way up."

Miss Maybelle's eyes slipped away from mine and lingered on the old tree. Her face gave up a shy smile. "Imagine that," she said.

In the years that followed 1952, before I left Florida for good, a number of curious things happened on a nearly regular basis:

People came to our house. The hesitant tap, never a knock, after supper or before breakfast, announced their need. And, for quite some time, their location, front or back, told us their color. I know Daddy never directed anyone to our front or back door. They sorted themselves, according to their custom.

He wasn't a minister, a lawyer or a psychologist, yet somehow my father became chief counselor to Mayflower's downtrodden. Sometimes it was a letter in need of reading or writing, or a legal form, or a government notice. A man from church in shock over the receipt of "divorce papers," a young woman from The Quarters heading north to Detroit, or a couple having difficulty collecting on a relative's insurance.

The people at both doors trusted my father to help them sort things out, decide what to do. No money was ever offered or expected, nor would it have been accepted. He simply gave them a few minutes of careful listening, some logical, intuitive counsel and an occasional investigative phone call to the proper authority.

And they thanked him in ways they felt appropriate. To those same porches, front or back, they delivered a crate of just-picked white corn, a fresh-baked peach pie, a half-dozen jars of homemade rhubarb jam, and, once, a lactating nanny goat for the child (my little brother Mitchell) who developed an allergy to cow's milk. We were no longer strangers in the strange land we called home.

Another curious thing involved the ladies of Luther's "C.I.A.," our guardian angels who, for their own various reasons, we never came to know. There were many, many black women who worked in the homes of white people in Opalakee, Mayflower and Wellwood. I'd see them all over in their white, pink or pale gray uniforms walking down a road, sitting on a park bench, or waiting patiently for the bus.

Privately, I'd wonder, "Was *she* one of them?" "How about *her?*"

"I wish I knew," Daddy would say, "I'd like to thank each and every one for their help."

One day, Daddy and I were out riding in his pickup truck, the name of our family business brightly emblazoned on both sides. An older maid in a white uniform and thick-soled shoes sat alone on the green wood bench that was her bus stop, both hands resting on top of the big black purse in her lap.

Daddy and I saw *her*, and obviously, she saw *us*. The question ("Could *she* be one of them?") so prominent in our minds must have shown up on our faces. She looked at us squarely, crinkled her eyes, and ever so slowly raised two fingers of her right hand off her purse top, into the "V-for-Victory" that was Marvin's special sign.

Daddy smiled the wide ear-to-ear grin he was known for and nodded his acknowledgment. She did the same, in a secret, silent ritual that was to be repeated by so many other hardworking black women, again and again, for many years.

I will never forget that first exchange of signs and smiles. It was, for me, an homage to the exceptional dignity and grace of my heart's first and unforgettable best friend. Although Marvin Cully died horribly years ago, he will live forever, for me, in the hope-beyond-hope of his parents and others turned luminous by "time in the fire," in the free flight of a honeybee and the whippoorwill's insistent first call to spring.

It was Marvin, I remember whenever I smell orange blossoms, who showed me my stripes and gave me his wings.

## Epilogue

The murder of "Marvin Cully" in March 1951
was never officially investigated. His killers have
never been named.

The assassination of Harry and Harriette
Moore in Florida, four years before the Mont-
gomery bus boycott, twelve years before Medgar
Evers' murder in Mississippi and seventeen
years before the killing of Martin Luther King
in Memphis, made them America's first Civil
Rights leaders to fall in the contemporary fight
for equality. Their death, explored by the Miami Grand Jury in 1952, by Geraldo Rivera
in 1991 and again by the Florida Department
of Law Enforcement in 1992, remains an un-
solved mystery.

Upon its completion, the 3,000-page record
of the Grand Jury's deliberations in Miami,
along with twenty boxes of F.B.I. support files,
were shipped to the State Attorney's Office and,
by court order, sealed for forty years. When re-
opened in 1991, they revealed that Agent "Jim
Jameson" was also a man of his word.

*Although the files clearly reference the Ku Klux Klan materials which Daddy, teenaged "Robert" and clever old "Luther" liberated from the fishing camp, and which eagle-eyed "Armetta" helped identify, there is no mention of their names or of the secret circle of maids who, in a mutual, miraculous leap of faith, brought the walls of the "Opalakee" Klan tumbling down. Our celebrations of these things were small and quiet.*

*There were, however, loud Hallelujahs all around when, in October 1952, 1953 and 1955, Jackie Robinson and the Brooklyn Dodgers made it to the World Series. And, in 1955, finally brought home a victory, for all of us.*

## Author's Note

Every family has its stories. This one was my father's to tell. Anyone who knew my father and mother, or my paternal grandmother, will recognize the inspiration for Warren, Lizbeth and Doto. And anyone who lived through the period, or takes the time to research it, will note my efforts to render historical events and figures as real as I could.

However, this *is* a work of fiction. For two very important reasons, many of the principal and secondary characters—especially Reed Garnet, his wife and daughter, J. D. Bowman and his twin sons—are pure fiction with no resemblance or relation to anyone who ever lived. In the first place, I wasn't even born when bombs lit up the skies above Miami. In the second, the real Klansmen who roamed the back roads and groves of our area, including those who were indicted by the federal grand jury, have their own families and stories. Which are, of course, theirs to tell.

# Acknowledgments

When I was in my mid-twenties, visiting relatives outside Chicago, my paternal grandmother overheard me tell someone, "I grew up in central Florida." Not long afterward, she pulled me aside. "Wild plants and animals—and some unfortunate children—simply grow up, Susan. *You* were *raised!* A whole lot of people invested a whole lot of time and effort in your upbringing. Don't deny them the credit they deserve for the way you turned out."

I turned out to be a writer. And credit for that is long overdue to a handful of teachers who, early on, insisted I take my writing and myself seriously. Thank you to Gladys Wilson, Aronelle Lofton, Sara Harvey, Janet Connelly and Myrtle Hubbard. Belated thanks also to the fistful of professionals who, later on, challenged me to write hard and fast (and paid me for the privilege of doing so): W. R. "Mac" McGuffin, publisher of my hometown newspaper; Wilson Flohr in Orlando, Alan Goldsmith in Atlanta, John VanderZee in San Francisco and Tom Sharrit in San Diego.

Of course, I might never have moved from point A (writing Advertising) to point B (attempting a Book) without the inspiration of Diane Dunaway and the San Diego Writers' Conference. And, I might not have finished the manuscript properly without the help of Elizabeth George and my fellow writers in her Masters' Class at the Maui Writers' Retreat.

From beginning to end, the reference departments of the local libraries in Carlsbad and Oceanside were a huge and constant help to me. The archivists at *The Miami Herald* and *The Orlando Sentinel* could not have been more patient or accommodating. Mr. Frank Meech, retired F.B.I. and one of the lead agents on the Moore murder case, was a generous and enjoyable source.

My book club read the early draft with insight and enthusiasm. And, afterward, became the best cheerleaders any writer could hope for. Bless you, Kathleen Bernard, Mary Blaskovich, Jan Brownell, Lindsey Cohn, Francie Droll, Rosemary Eshelman, Valerie Gilbert, Peggy Martinez, Kitty Meek, Debbie Moyer, Audrey Piper, Tricia Rowe, Monika Stout and Cris Weatherby. Also, Blye Phillips, my favorite contrarian who demanded, "Tension! I need more tension!"

Eternal gratitude to Lane Zachary for becoming my agent and my friend. Lane reads with an editor's eye and an artist's heart. She also, according to Bantam's Kate Miciak, "writes one of the best cover letters in the business." Kate is my editor. Everyone says Kate is brilliant and, in my experience, everyone's right. She's also fun, funny, and a writer's dream to work with. Kate connected me to the big, boisterous Bantam family who, sight unseen, embraced me as one of their own. Heartfelt thanks to attorney Matthew Martin, managing editor Anna Forgione, copyeditor Pat Crais, art director Jim Plumeri, and book designer Laurie Jewell, for your time and efforts on my behalf.

Thanks, above all . . . to my sister-friend Joanne who lent me her passion for baseball and the most patient ear possible. To my husband Paul and our sons, Travis and Connor, who made time and space in our lives "so Mom can write" and let no good news go uncelebrated. To my mother who provided liberal amounts of horticultural detail and maternal encouragement. And to my father. This project began as a present for Dad's seventy-fifth birthday. In the six months of almost daily long distance phone calls, discoveries, and heart-to-heart discussions before he died, it became, clearly, his gift to me. Thanks, Dad. You, more than anyone, get the credit for the way things turned out.

*Susan Carol McCarthy*
*January 2001*